ALSO BY CAROLINE STAFFORD

The House by Exmoor

MOIRA

CAROLINE STAFFORD

SIMON AND SCHUSTER
NEW YORK

Library of Congress Cataloging in Publication Data

Stafford, Caroline.
    Moira.

    I. Title.
PZ4.S7779Mo   [PS3569.T165]   813'.5'4   76–25220

ISBN 0-671-22373-9

FOR MY MOTHER
AND HER CLAN
WITH LOVE

1

There was a heavy mist in from the sea when I awoke on the morning of my twenty-first birthday. Old Morag would have said it foreshadowed the day and the terrible events that were to spring from it, for in all the years of my life my birthdays had dawned fair and remained so until the last light faded from the evening sky. In our small corner of the world, where superstition was a way of life, I had heard it said that the crofters saved their haying for this day, it was so certain to be clear. But I had laughed at such beliefs, thinking the fair weather was simply luck, and luck was bound to change. It was only because I lived in the castle and was heiress to the lands and the tenants that people took any note of me and my affairs—had I been a crofter's daughter, there would have been no cause to remember anything about me or my birthday.

And so I lay in my bed and heard the muffled sea pound the rocks below and felt no surprise or alarm. Instead, my mind was occupied with the coming of the solicitor from Edinburgh. Now that I had come of age, he would make official what had been fact since my father's death so many years before. But nothing would be changed. The house and lands had always been mine, and I would continue to rely on the advice of the steward and the firm of solicitors that had always seen to Lindsay affairs. I felt no driving urge to take the reins of management into my own hands. I had been consulted about and agreed with all that had been done on the estates since I was sixteen, and had the good sense to realize that my meddling further was both unnecessary and unwise. Perhaps I would go to Edinburgh for a month or so, as a present to myself, I thought. But even as I dreamed of shopping and seeing the sights, broadening my horizons—and my circle of acquaintances—I knew that neither the glories of the city nor the possibility of finding a husband there would draw me from my home, even for a little while.

Local girls married long before twenty-one, and usually had a child or two by then. I saw them in their croft doorways, proud and smiling until the years of hard work and childbearing and worry made them old before their time. But I was satisfied with my life and in no hurry to wish away my independence and pleasure, though many might think me an old maid and well upon the shelf by now, heiress or no. And there were no local young men from whom I might choose a husband—we were too isolated here on the cliffs, with the sea loch cutting into the hills to the north and an absentee lord holding the lands to the south of mine. Come to that, the only young man I knew was the steward, Angus, but he had grown up on the estate and was so much a part of its ordinary life that I never thought of him as anything more than an old friend and childhood mentor. Angus had taught me to ride, to use a gun with more than fair accuracy (though none knew of that but he and I), to follow the tracks to every corner of my lands and know them intimately and lovingly as he did, to leave behind for an hour or so the restrictions and encircling care of girlhood. For even in this remote corner of western Scotland the pervasive morality of the young Queen had made itself felt, reinforcing the staunch Presbyterianism of my governess.

I wondered, and not for the first time, that I had been allowed to roam so freely with Angus. Though he was ten years older than I, he was even then of uncertain temper and looked on askance by those who knew him. Perhaps Anna Fraser, my beloved governess and later my friend, had been a very good judge of character, knowing that I was as safe in Angus' care as in her own. He never in any way proved unworthy of that trust, and having grown up a lonely child with only adults about me, I had come to look on Angus as one might an older brother or young uncle—a friend with whom one might be comfortable and happy, though never presumptuous. Mrs. Fraser had recognized the qualities of leadership and the good mind behind Angus' gruff exterior, and had seen to it that he received schooling, finally to become an assistant to the aging MacLeod, our steward, and just short of my sixteenth birthday, steward in his own right, following MacLeod's death.

Turning over, I looked toward the drawn curtains where the pale light left no imprint on the patterned fabric. Dear Fraser! I missed her deeply still. She had been all the family I had, as well as being my governess. The wife of the minister in the village that lay to the east of the castle and a friend of my mother's, she had been widowed near the time of my first birthday and brought here to take over the care of the motherless baby who was fast outgrowing her nurse. It was an agreeable arrangement all around. Fraser did not have to leave the place where she had known the most happiness and the deepest sorrow, where the graves of her husband and two bairns grew moss green beneath the ancient rowan tree in the kirkyard. And my father found someone to love and care for his daughter without having to face either remarriage or a stranger in his house.

I had no memory of my mother. She had died of fever following my birth and my father had never cared to set another in her place. There was no portrait of her, either, for she had gone too soon for the London painter to be summoned to take her likeness.

But I remembered the deep voice of my father, which rang in the corridors like the waves that constantly roared against the great rocks below the castle's western wall. These were the earliest memories I possessed.

Since my father had died when I was three, I could not recall his face. But the portrait in the Long Gallery fit the voice I remembered—a tall, strongly built man whose amused, dark eyes belied the proud set of his finely molded lips. I had often stood staring into his face and thinking about what sort of father he might have been if he had lived. I made up little tales of his care and love for me, the games and good times and laughter we could have shared. It had always seemed somehow unfair that he had missed my mother so much that he had not cared to live on, even for me, that he would have chosen to leave me alone in the world while she had the company of God and the angels to occupy her in heaven.

And so I had poured out all my love to Fraser, dear Fraser, with her comfortable plumpness and her gentle ways that lent femininity to the capable mind behind them. Then, in her own turn, she had left me, scarcely a year ago, and her greatest sorrow was the fact that she had seen me safely to the threshold of womanhood but not completely across it. She had fretted over this in her last hours, and nothing I could say had brought her any peace. It was to Angus she had turned, in the end, sending me from the room while they spoke together. Angus, whom the kitchen maids considered the devil incarnate, from his black scowls and limping walk. And I was left alone once more in *Tigh-nan-Sian*, the House of Storms.

In my earliest childhood I had considered myself mistress of the sea also, for the castle hung at the cliff's edge and my bedroom overlooked the sheltered summer garden on one side and the wild expanse of water on the other. On stormy nights I could smell the spray flung high above the rocky shore and feel the very foundations shake with the sea's fury. In winter the mists coated the walls with a trickling damp in spite of the roaring fire on the hearth, and in summer the westering sun slanted across the floor in long golden spikes, turning the windows to molten fire as it set into the Sound of Mull. I loved this room.

As I lay in drowsy peace, full of memories, the chamber door opened and Elspeth came quietly in carrying a can of hot water. She set about clearing away the night's ashes and laying a fresh fire in the hearth. Then she rose stiffly and crossed the room to open the long drapes. As I watched her from half-shut eyes, I suddenly realized that her face was more lined, her hair perhaps more white than black now, the back less ramrod straight than it once was. But the no-nonsense manner was the same, and because of it she had convinced the solicitors that I needed no other guardian in this last year of my minority.

"There's no call to be laying about in bed, just because of a birthday," she said briskly. "It's chill. I'll set out the gingham and put by the silk gown for now."

"I can't receive Mr. MacEwen in a gingham gown!" I protested. "What will he think of us here, accustomed as he is to the finery of Edinburgh?"

"He'll think the better of you, for being a sensible girl," she said firmly. "What's more, he won't be arriving until noon or after." She opened the door of the clothes press, sending the fragrance of lavender floating into the room as she brought out the gingham gown. I flung back the bedclothes and thrust my feet into the waiting slippers, and then took the wrapper she brought to me. "The dampness has made your hair curl," she added resignedly. "It'll not lay straight and smooth for all my brushing."

I looked into my mirror to see the tendrils of curl that had escaped the night ribbon clustering about my face. Experience had taught me that there was no cure for such unfashionable tendencies. The oval face with its large hazel eyes and long golden-brown ringlets stared back at me, still flushed with sleep. I made a comic grimace at my reflection.

Elspeth's lips tightened in disapproval. "Give over, Miss Moira! Your breakfast will be stone cold while you dawdle here, and Cook already in a temper from the spilling of

11

the egg basket." She poured hot water into the china bowl and stood aside to let me wash my face.

Relenting, I set about my toilet and was soon dressed. As I pinned a simple gold brooch at the high collar of my gown, I said quietly, "I was thinking of Fraser this morning."

"Aye, poor woman," Elspeth replied, taking a brush to my unruly hair. "I mind how she wanted to live for this day, and knowing full well the end had come. 'Twas the only time I knew her to cry. But the Lord's ways are His own, and not ours to question."

"It seems so unfair, all the same. Well, I hope for her sake that this solicitor will find me a credit to her upbringing."

"Aye, and she'd be proud of you herself. Though mind, your temper and your contrariness are nought to boast of yet."

I laughed. "So Fraser herself told me often enough."

Elspeth put down the brush and began twisting my hair into a neat knot as I watched in the glass. " 'Twas enough to try the devil himself when you were a wee bairn," she said severely. "Mrs. Fraser had the Lord's own patience. I never knew a woman to love a child as she loved you. Like her own, you were, after her poor wee daughter died. I remember when I came here wondering if it was a good thing or a bad one for her to be so wrapped up in you. For all that, she never spoiled you as many might."

The only child in a house full of doting servants, I had discovered early enough that competition for my favor could be used to my own advantage. Fraser had soon put a stop to such behavior and made it clear that, heiress or not, I was to be treated as an ordinary child. "Character outlasts money," she had reminded me often. "If you lose everything, you still have yourself." And so I had learned to cook and mend and polish the silver as well as attend to my studies and my responsibilities about the estate.

"Aye, she always put her duty first," Elspeth said, "and there was no harm in filling the emptiness in her life with a wee bit of pretending. I'd not be one to grudge her the comfort of that."

"No one could," I said, rising to follow her downstairs to the breakfast room. In some inexplicable way, talking of Fraser had seemed to bring her nearer, as if she shared in my happiness today as she had always done. Even the gray morning seemed brighter.

The castle had been built by my ancestors to guard the coast and the entrance of the sea loch that led deep into the cleft between the hills, and so it stood foursquare to permit maximum surveillance on every side and maximum strength in defense. I had heard the tales of marauders and invaders and sea battles in which the Lindsays held their own against any who came to dispute their sovereignty here. They had carved this land out for themselves in the turbulent days of Mary, Queen of Scots, and had never lost an acre since except to the ever-encroaching sea. Therefore, its great stone walls, towering high on the cliff's edge, had none of the softness and beauty of the English castles I had seen in prints, but its very strength and massiveness gave it grace. On the south side a ditch had once served as a dry moat, but now this was a summer garden and flowers grew well in the sheltered protection of the ancient earthworks. On the east and north approaches, the ditch had long since been filled in and close-cropped lawns reached to the foot of the wall. Fraser and I had played croquet on the smooth turf, in the shadow of the ramparts. It was from the western side that the castle was most spectacular, rising above the cliff face like a man-made extension of the rough gray stone, while the sea lashed at the tumbled rock at its edge. It was a famous view as well as a landmark for fishermen along the coast.

Inside the walls, the ancient keep had been built against the western rampart. Despite its forbidding outward appearance, generations of Lindsay wives had transformed the interior into a pleasant family dwelling. Now, as it must have when my mother came as a bride, it

13

looked well-furnished and tastefully decorated with heirlooms that suited the great chambers and wide passages. As we walked down the broad stairs and crossed the hall to the small room we used for meals when there was no one to share the echoing dining room with me, I felt a sudden glow of proprietary pride—all this was mine, as it had been my ancestors' before me.

Breakfast was waiting on the sideboard, and I served myself from the covered dishes while Elspeth poured tea into a cup and set it at my place. I brought over my plate and then caught sight of a large thin box tied in gold ribbon occupying my chair. I looked up quickly and Elspeth nodded.

"From the servants," she said. "For today."

Excitedly, I set down the plate of food and picked up the box. The ribbon slipped through my fingers to the floor and I lifted the lid carefully. Inside were layers of tissue paper and beneath them was a shawl of the finest Ayr wool, like silk in my hands, dyed in the Lindsay tartan. The deep red, the rich green and blue, were muted by the soft curling strands into the glowing colors of ancient stained glass. It was very beautiful as well as very expensive, and I felt my throat tighten as I thought of the loving care that had gone into the choosing of this gift for me. There were tears in my eyes as I raised them to meet Elspeth's.

"Aye," she said nodding. "You'd best wear it for all to see."

"Tell them—tell them I shall treasure it always," I said, settling the soft folds about my shoulders. "It is a lovely gift, both for itself and for those who gave it."

The tenants came later in the morning, and I stood in the swirling mist by the front gates to accept their greetings and good wishes. I knew each by name, thanks to Angus, who had seen to it that I continued the visitations that Fraser had always made to the crofts and outlying farms, keeping an eye on every family's welfare and needs.

It was Elspeth and the minister's wife who nursed the sick and cared for the aged, listened to the family troubles and sorted out the problems, for it was not thought fit for a girl to take on such responsibilities. But I had sense enough to guess, in many cases, where help was needed and oftentimes why. And so I managed to respond to everyone personally and felt no shyness of my own. I smiled to myself as each addressed me now as Young Mistress, rather than Young Miss, as if in the brief span of the night I had matured from girl to woman. And perhaps I had, in their eyes, for now the final say in their lives rested with me rather than with an Edinburgh lawyer who had not set foot on these lands since my father's day.

No one spoke of the weather, though the topic must have been uppermost in every mind, until Old Morag hobbled toward me, the last in the long line. She was very old, her back bent into a half-circle and her face lined beyond telling what she might have looked like half a century or more before. Oddly enough, her hair was not white, but streaked gray and black like Elspeth's. Morag lived in a small croft on the hill beyond the loch. The stewards of the House of Storms had always seen to it that her roof never leaked and that her wood was cut for the hearth, and if not, those who lived on the estate would have done so. And while to my knowledge Old Morag had no legal claim to her home, none cared to dispute her possession of it or question her standing here. She was something of an herbalist, more trusted than any doctor would have been, and this brought her chickens and pigs and garden produce in return for her medicines. But above all, Morag had the Sight, and that in itself set her apart and raised her status far above that of a lonely and eccentric old woman.

I waited patiently while Old Morag made her way to me, leaning heavily on her twisted black stick, her cloak clutched tight against the damp. She stopped before me and lifted her head, turning it a little to one side as if to see me better.

15

"Good day to you, Young Mistress," she said formally.

"You have walked far, Morag," I said, honoring the effort it must have been for her to come. Ordinarily she never left her cottage, but then this was no ordinary occasion. She would not have wished to be left out, whatever the cost to herself.

"Aye. There's mist today, Young Mistress. There will be no sun to warm your joy." There was a stir among the tenants a little way off, but she paid them no heed. "Beware the mist that comes again—there will be sorrow in it for you, Young Mistress. *Beware the mist.*" She stared at me for a moment with her faded gray eyes. "A man comes."

"Yes," I said. "Mr. MacEwen, from Edinburgh."

"A man comes," she repeated insistently, disregarding my words. There was a pause as she grasped the gnarled stick more firmly, and I waited patiently for her to continue. "In time to come, be not deceived, Young Mistress, by the mask of evil, for the shadow of death is there, and no mercy. Look not for trust where wanting twists the spirit."

I felt a chill as the slow, thin voice stopped. There was absolute silence in the group of tenants, and no movement. They believed her, every word, and because of the strange spell she wove with her voice and her eyes that seemed to see beyond and into matters outside our ken, I found myself nearly believing her prophecy as well. I might laugh and shrug it off later in my room, but here, now, I was drawn into the mood that surrounded me, like the silent folds of the mist.

"I shall remember, Morag," I said, my voice faltering in spite of myself.

She nodded. "Aye, you will remember. Though you have not believed, even so, you will remember." There was the pause again, and her eyes searched my face, as if seeing it clearly for the first time. "You are your mother's daughter, Young Mistress, though you know it not. I see her goodness in you." Her eyes wandered to the stone

16

mass of the keep beyond the gates, and lost a little of their clarity once more. *"Tigh-nan-Sian.* The House of Storms. It is well-named," she murmured, almost to herself. Then, as if recalling the occasion, she gave me the traditional words of well-wishing and afterward turned back the way she had come.

The tenants stood unmoving until she was well out of hearing, and then with almost shamefaced suddenness began to speak, as if they would not have me know how seriously they took Old Morag's words. But what she had said would stay in their minds and be talked of by the fireside this night and for many more to come.

When the ceremony was finished, I was glad to escape inside to think over what had happened. But before I had walked ten steps inside the door, Elspeth spoke.

"The steward is waiting in the office." She rarely referred to Angus by his name, only by his title.

"Thank you," I replied and turned toward the corner room where the household accounts and estate records had been kept for two hundred years.

As I opened the door, Angus rose from his chair by the window and stood deferentially. "The tenants have gone?" he asked.

I nodded. "Old Morag came," I said.

His dark brows rose in surprise. "Did she! What did she have to say to you?"

I told him, and he stared thoughtfully at the clutter of papers on the desk. He filled the small room, a tall, broad-shouldered man with dark hair and darker eyes. It was said that he was stronger than Dugald, the blacksmith in the village, and I readily believed that. The desk, two chairs, and shelves of ledgers and boxes jostled to make space for him and yet—barring his painful limp—he was the least clumsy man I knew. His roughly hewn features would have been handsome in their way, had he not scowled so blackly at everyone and everything.

"She has never been known to speak other than the truth," he said pensively.

17

"But it makes no sense, and of course everyone knows that Mr. MacEwen is coming today. Perhaps half of her 'Sight' is nothing more than being well-informed."

"Well, if there's truth to it, we'll soon find out." He looked up at me. "I wish you happiness, Mistress, this day and all the others to come."

"Thank you, Angus. Shall I take over the management of the estate?" It was teasingly said, and he knew it.

"By all means. I must see to the mending of two sheep pens this afternoon, and will gladly send you in my place."

As I laughed, for it was an old joke between us, he reached into his pocket and brought out a small blue velvet case. "For you," he said, and placed it in my hand.

I pressed the pearl-shaped spring and the lid came open. Inside, lying in a nest of white satin, was a heavy silver pin set with a cairngorm and bearing the Lindsay badge in its border. I knew from the ornate silverwork that it was very old and had undoubtedly been worn in the plaid of a chieftain long before the last Stewart uprising. Angus must have sent to Edinburgh to find this special gift.

He laughed at my surprise. "You are more of a lass than a laird, but it will do no harm to have the trappings of power."

"It's—*beautiful*," I said, deeply moved by his choice, and then I smiled up at him. "Angus, thank you very, *very* much." I thought fleetingly how often I had taken those who served me for granted, accepting their work as the daily, familiar service that it was, making my life more pleasant, more comfortable without any commotion or, often, sign of their presence. And yet this day, from tenants, from servants, and now from the steward, I had been given gifts of love and thoughtfulness that went beyond my gracious expressions of thanks, however heartfelt they might be.

He brushed aside my words and gestured to the desk. "I've set the books in order. MacEwen will no doubt want to see them before he goes. If I'm still at the sheep pens,

18

you know where I keep all the records. I'll be back before he leaves, tell him that."

"What should we do about the old tower? Shall I ask him if it is worth the repair?" Tall, slim, falling into decay, the ancient peel tower near the sea loch was more than two centuries older than the castle. It was built to guard against invasion by water as well as from the hills it overlooked. Angus and I had debated the wisdom of tearing it down rather than going to the expense and effort of restoring it to usefulness. Grain had been kept there in my father's time, before the roof had collapsed.

"Yes. Tell him, we have the workmen here, it's just a question of paying them for the time taken from their own crofts."

I nodded. Angus came around the desk to the door, then stopped with his hand on the knob. "I'd not worry overly about the mist today. The weather was bound to change, one year."

"No. I don't mind it. Though the crofters do, and the servants. And now Old Morag has made a point of it."

"Well, she was bound to. I'll be back as soon as I can."

I watched his tall figure, clad for this special day in the Lindsay kilt and a dark coat, walk out the door and close it behind him. Then I turned to the window. I could barely see across the courtyard now, and thought of the Edinburgh solicitor making his uncomfortable and slow way up the glen, the carriage horses picking their footing along the rough track that passed for a road in these parts. He would not be in the best of moods, surely, when he arrived at last. There must be few such inconveniences in the life of a man whose efforts usually took him no farther than the outskirts of town, and it was a measure of the respect in which he held my father that he had written that he would make the long journey himself.

The time for luncheon came, and was set back an hour, but still Mr. MacEwen had not arrived. Several callers came from the village to wish me well, but none of them lingered for long, wishing to be at home before darkness fell. I had not worn the blue silk after all, for the chill in the air belied the calendar and felt more like October than August. Instead I had changed from the gingham to a light wool and wore with it the shawl I had been given. The tartan glowed against the dove gray of the gown, and I often saw the servants pause to glance admiringly at their gift as they went about their duties.

I was tempted, after the waiting, to go out for a time and exercise as was my wont by walking across the hills toward the loch or down the glen. But it would have been ill-mannered to be away when Mr. MacEwen arrived, so I tried to possess my soul in patience for a little longer.

Finally there was the clatter of carriage wheels and the commotion of doors and voices that told me he was here. I was already in the drawing room, a finely paneled room with a plaster ceiling bearing the arms of James the Sixth in a border of thistles. I rose from my chair and stood waiting.

The door opened and he came in, followed by Elspeth bearing his case. Mr. MacEwen, of MacEwen, Galbraith and MacEwen, was a small, portly man, partially balding and all of sixty. From his sober black clothes and the formal expression he wore, it might have been the reading of a will rather than an affirmation of majority he had come to oversee.

I stepped forward and greeted him, commenting on the uncomfortable journey he must have had on my account. He made the usual formal replies, and while Elspeth fetched wine and cakes for refreshment, Mr. MacEwen commented in his turn about the appearance of the estate—such that he could see in the mists—and the house. His eyes roved about the room as he spoke, taking in each item as if accounting for it and judging its care over the years. I gathered that all met with his approval.

It was not until the wine was finished and he had had time to warm himself by the hearth that he spoke of his purpose in coming. And as he did so, his manner thawed a little as if he felt more at home in the specifics of the law than he did in the generalities of social conversation.

"Your father considered the matter of legal age very carefully, Miss Lindsay, wishing to set your majority at an age of discretion while at the same time allowing you flexibility in choice without the restrictions that might arise under guardianship circumstances. We talked at some length, corresponded, and at last determined that twenty-one was most appropriate to his purpose. Do you understand this?"

"Yes," I said, grateful to my father for not adhering to the more usual twenty-five or even thirty.

"Very well. Do you wish to make any changes in the staff?"

"No," I said after a pause. Most of them had been with me for years. We were accustomed to one another and had no complaints.

"Very wise of you. Now to details." He took up his case and began to sort through the papers it contained. "Ah. As you are aware, your mother's money, held in trust these many years, becomes yours outright. I would advise leaving it invested as it now is, until such time as you would wish to use it. We will continue, naturally, to supervise this matter for you, but you have complete access to income and capital."

I agreed and signed the necessary papers. He delved into his case once more and came out with a large black box which he unlocked with a gold key on the chain of his watch. His motions were those of a meticulous man, and it was not until the box was unlocked to reveal an assortment of jewelry cases that he spoke again.

"These were your mother's jewels and are now yours outright. They are heirlooms from your Ogilvie grandmother, an heiress in her own right, and were settled on her eldest daughter at the time of your grandmother's marriage, thence to you, since that daughter was your own mother." He opened the boxes and set them before me.

"They have been in our vaults and I have here the deposition of the jeweler who cleaned them last week that they are the same jewels deposited with us at the time of your mother's death."

I signed several more papers and then was instructed on the safe care of my new possessions before I was permitted an opportunity to look closely. I had already been given the pearls and the garnets held to be suitable for a girl, but my feminine soul was delighted with the assortment of necklaces, bracelets, hair clips and spray pins in sapphires, diamonds, and yes, one ruby pendant that caught the fire's brightness in its heart as I lifted it from the case. I would have liked to try on at least one of the pieces, but Mr. MacEwen was not a man to waste time on frivolity. To him the jewels represented sound investment rather than trinkets to wear. He closed the cases and put them aside in a neat stack.

We went on, handling my mother's estate in minute detail, first with an explanation of each matter, then with the proper papers to be signed, until at last my mother's affairs were completed. These papers vanished into his case, carefully filed in their proper order, and a fresh set was withdrawn.

"Now to your father's estate," he began, and I resigned myself to attending to another dry flood of words followed by signatures. But instead, he looked up at me, his light blue eyes staring nearsightedly, and asked, "Did Mrs. Fraser, before her untimely death, explain your father's will to you?"

"Yes. There was little to explain, actually, but we discussed it," I replied.

He nodded. "I am very glad of that. We urged her to do so, of course, but had to leave the timing to her discretion. I am reluctant to interfere when a guardian knows the child more intimately. It never proves satisfactory."

I smiled. "There was never any doubt about my future."

"I am happy to hear that," he said, sounding relieved.

"It isn't as if I had relatives who were close to me," I went on. "I am, quite literally, alone in the world, so it was natural, even as a child, to be aware of my position." Alone as I was in this great rambling house with acres of land about me, it did not require great imagination or intelligence on my part to realize who owned it all. Even if Fraser had been unwise enough to try to keep the matter from me, the attitudes of servants, villagers, and tenants would have betrayed the truth. It was better to grow up with the fact and learn early to cope with it than to have everything dumped in one's lap at once when one came of age, I thought.

"Then you are prepared for the idea. Have you considered a date for the wedding?"

My wandering mind jerked sharply back to him. "What did you say?" I asked abruptly.

"I asked if you have considered a date for the wedding?"

"Whose?" I was bewildered. "Whose wedding?"

He stared at me as if I had suddenly lost my senses. "We were discussing your marriage. Have you set a date for the wedding?"

"Surely," I said, frowning in confusion, "surely that ought to wait until I have accepted a proposal!"

His face cleared. "Ah! Yes, yes. Young ladies do prefer the formal framework, that's quite so. And, I may say, it is in keeping with their modesty." He almost smiled, but in embarrassment rather than humor. "You will forgive me for overlooking the social conventions. Most improper!"

He began to sift through his papers, but I stopped him. "I must confess I still don't understand you at all," I said. "Are you saying that, in spite of the fact that I am now of age, I must ask your permission—or at least your approval—before I marry?"

"Not at all! The marriage may take place any time you wish."

"*The* marriage? Mr. MacEwen, I suspect we have been talking at cross purposes. *What* marriage?" I rose to face him.

23

He set down his papers and stared at me for an instant in dawning comprehension. "Then you have misunderstood me all along. Mrs. Fraser did not tell you that shortly before his death your father had arranged a marriage for you?"

"No," I replied in growing shock. "No, she never said a word."

He clicked his tongue in disgust. "How ill-advised! Then *I* must tell you, Miss Lindsay. Aware that he would have no son, your father wished to hold the estate within the family and provided for this by arranging for you to marry your cousin within a year of your twenty-first birthday."

2

Mr. MacEwen's voice reached me from a distance and for an instant I feared I was about to faint. But then, with a deep breath I got control of myself. As the meaning of the words penetrated the shock, my pulse steadied.

"My *cousin?*" Relief flooded through me as he replied in the affirmative. "But there is no problem! Surely you know he was at Balaclava with the Light Brigade, and he died in the charge against the Russian artillery." I smiled at him in spite of myself.

But the solicitor shook his head. "So we were informed at first. Fortunately, he did survive."

"Survive?" I asked blankly. "But how—"

"There were so many dead," he replied patiently, "and a captain in the 93rd Highlanders thought he recognized Duncan Lindsay from the uniform. However, the French had found him and managed to save his life. It was six months before word reached London and another three before Major Lindsay could be moved. He still bears the scars, of course, but he has quite recovered and is, I assure you, still bound by the terms of the will, just as you are."

I sat down suddenly. "I think you had better review those terms. Mrs. Fraser never told me—only that I had a distant cousin, and later, that he had died in battle. Start from the beginning."

And he did. My father had had no desire to remarry, and yet he had not been happy with the thought of the family heritage passing to someone else when I married. His pride in his name ran deep, it was as much a part of him as his life's blood; and yet his love for my mother ran deeper still. As long as the Lindsay name could be perpetuated in the House of Storms, my father was satisfied—he felt no further tie of blood was necessary, never wished for a son to carry on his line.

And so, in compromise, he had turned to a cousin, the only grandson—in truth, the only grandchild—of my own grandfather's younger brother. Investigation showed that Duncan Lindsay was a healthy, intelligent boy of eleven, living with his widowed mother in Northumberland—in Alnwick, Mr. MacEwen added precisely.

My father invited him to come here, liked what he saw, and arranged with the boy's mother to oversee his education and future in return for a promise of marriage when I came of age. And then in his will, my father specified that if this child lived to fulfill his early promise, and, in the eyes of my guardians, was a fit match for me, the marriage would take place. If the boy failed to grow into a suitable match, I was released from the agreement and a small legacy was settled on Duncan. If I refused to accept the match, the house and lands went to my cousin, while I received the major portion of my father's personal wealth.

"I don't believe it!" I cried. "It's horrible! My father wouldn't have treated me so—"

"The terms are quite specific, Miss Lindsay, I do assure you. There is no possibility of having mistaken them. And your father saw the situation differently. He was providing for you materially, should you refuse to accept this young man, but he had already taken every precaution to ascertain Major Lindsay's suitability as a husband for you

26

and indeed insure it—the best schools, travel abroad, and so on. I must say, I deplored the choice of the military as a career, but it seems that the boy's father had also been a soldier and he had his heart set on it."

"It would have been better if he had indeed died at Balaclava! Mr. MacEwen, you cannot possibly expect me to agree to marry a complete stranger, cousin or no! This is not the Middle Ages, after all!"

He frowned in disapproval of my emotional outburst, but I didn't care. I was fighting for my heritage, and he was merely defending a sheet of paper. I wouldn't let myself think about my father's betrayal of his daughter, not now.

"Miss Lindsay, this has been a dreadful shock to you and quite explains why you are not your usual sensible self. Let me assure you, I have no intentions of enforcing this match if it does not meet with your approval—"

"Approval! Mr. MacEwen, do you realize I lose my *home* if I do refuse?" I broke in angrily. "This isn't a simple matter of yes or no, another paper for me to sign or a velvet case to be locked away in a drawer. This is my very life, and either I agree to spend it with a stranger or I must go away from the house where I was born!"

He sighed. "Miss Lindsay, that is a very melodramatic way of putting the matter, is it not? I have taken the liberty of bringing Major Lindsay with me today, and I am sure that this whole misunderstanding can be cleared up quite easily. Once you have seen the young man, you will realize that neither your father nor I have betrayed you."

"Brought him—!"

"I had assumed that Mrs. Fraser had, as she had promised, informed you at some point that such arrangements for your future had been made. It is unfortunate that she did not do so."

"It is unfortunate, Mr. MacEwen," I said coldly in Fraser's defense, "that someone didn't have the good sense

27

to inform her that the Major had survived after all. And that, Mr. MacEwen, is your fault!"

He had the grace to look perturbed, but not for the reasons I had supposed. "Mrs. Fraser was informed, I assure you. I wrote to her myself and received a reply dated some three weeks before her death." There was no doubting the conviction in his voice. "She was an excellent woman and meticulous in her dealings with us. It is difficult to understand why she failed to do her duty in this particular matter."

"She told me nothing," I said, bewildered now. "Nothing whatsoever. Not even as she lay dying—" I broke off as I recalled how troubled she had been, distressed that she would not live to see my coming of age and restless even as I tried to soothe her fears. Had she sought for words to explain my father's plans for me and failed to find them? She must have found the will as distasteful as I now did—even so, why had she not warned me? It was so unlike Fraser that I was at a loss to understand. I could only assume that her reasons for silence were good ones, that she had left me in ignorance for my own sake, for my happiness and well-being. Her sense of duty had been strong, but her love for me was stronger still.

There was a lengthening silence and then Mr. MacEwen said heavily, "May I at least invite the Major inside? Perhaps when you have met him you will be agreeable to a period of consideration."

I was on the verge of refusing point-blank, and then my anger cooled sufficiently for me to see reason. If the will said I must marry this stranger, then I must have time to find a way out. There were other solicitors in Edinburgh besides MacEwen, Galbraith and MacEwen. If necessary I would contact one of them and set about breaking the will. In the meantime, there was nothing to be gained by refusing to permit the Major to cross the threshold. And I did not want accidentally to prejudice my case.

Reluctantly, I agreed. Obviously relieved, Mr. MacEwen crossed to the door and spoke to Elspeth, who had been hovering in the hall. Then we waited in silence while she went in search of my cousin.

The door opened and he stood there, nearly as tall as the lintel, matching me stare for stare. Raindrops glistened on his cloak and in the fair hair that fell forward over his forehead on one side. In a poorer light, or at a great distance, he might have been taken for a handsome man, but I was close enough to see the terrible scar that marked his face from temple to jaw, the slash of a saber that had nearly killed him at Balaclava. I tried not to look away and it was then I saw the empty sleeve pinned to the breast of his coat. But his arm was not missing, only worn in a sling as if he had recently injured it. The long, tanned fingers were barely visible in the folds of the black cloth that crossed his chest.

His cold gray eyes met mine and his brows twitched together in a frown as if he was no more pleased with his inspection of me than I had been in mine of him.

For an instant my sense of humor rose to the surface as I thought of the picture we must present, glaring at each other in such a fashion. And then the realization of what his presence meant struck me fully, wiping the tentative smile from my lips.

He came forward into the room, closing the door behind him. "Miss Lindsay?" he said in a deep voice that sounded more English than Scots.

"Major Lindsay?" I acknowledged with equal coldness.

The solicitor watched us for an instant longer, and then cleared his throat. "As I recall, you met as children. Thank you for joining us, Major. If we may be seated—" He turned deferentially to me.

I came to myself and said, politely, "Yes, please do. I'll ring for tea—or would you prefer something stronger, Major?"

"No, nothing at all," he said, still staring at me under his frowning brows. He took the chair indicated, negligently tossing his cloak over the back of another.

"I'm afraid I don't recall your earlier visit," I said, unsettled by his steady regard.

"No? It was the summer of your third birthday, as I remember. I stayed through June and July, and much of August. Your father died the following October, I believe. He was already a sick man when I came, but there was every expectation that he would live longer."

There was no awakening memory of the eleven-year-old boy racing about the castle corridors, laughing and chattering as boys do. Or perhaps the Major was even then as quiet as he is now, I thought, and shy in the presence of the toddling infant who one day must be his bride. And was he now prepared to marry me? I felt a chill at the thought, and spoke quickly to cover my repulsion. "I'm afraid I recall nothing about it," I repeated, and then, realizing that it must appear that I doubted his word, I added, "But then, the only memory of my infancy was my father's voice, echoing through the house."

I managed a smile, but his frown only deepened at my words.

"I have explained the terms of the will, Major," the solicitor said hurriedly, as if he sensed the coldness that was growing between us, "and the—expectations contained therein. It is not unusual for a parent to arrange a marriage for his child in such a case as this, where there are no living relatives to assume such a charge when the time comes. However—" He was finding it difficult to maintain a smooth flow of words in the face of the patent hostility confronting him. "However—if neither of you has formed an attachment with another party—and aware of course of the mutual benefit derived from this arrangement—ah—in short, I do not see that there will be any impediment in carrying out the provisions of Angus Lindsay's will. Do either of you wish to discuss any particular point?"

"The marriage must take place within a year of this day?" I asked.

"Yes, exactly."

"And once it has taken place, who then owns this house, these lands?"

"A very good question. If the marriage takes place, the Major will own everything in right of his wife—you—to pass in trust to your son, or lacking a son, your daughter," he explained patiently.

"I see. But if I refuse the match, the house and the estate pass directly to the Major and his heirs?"

"Yes."

I thought of Old Morag and her strange warning, and felt sick. For it had suddenly occurred to me that this was the man whose coming Morag had foretold. And he had more to gain if the marriage were prevented, while I benefited only if it took place as stipulated. I looked across at the cold, saber-marked face. I was not happy with what I saw.

"Does the Major," I asked, as if he were not present, "have the right of refusal, should I agree to the marriage?"

"Yes, certainly. In that case, however, he receives a legacy from your father's estate and is no longer eligible to inherit."

I felt a little better. If all legal attempts to set aside the provisions of the will should fail, I could always try to make him despise me to the point that marriage was unthinkable. It was not a pleasant prospect, but I was fighting for my home, the house where I had lived since my birth, the lands I knew intimately. These had always been mine, I had never prepared myself for the loss of them or dreamed that such a loss could be possible. And now I must plot and scheme and pretend in order to preserve what was—should have been!—mine. I stared at the blaze on the hearth and thought unhappily that the mist had indeed foretold trouble for me for the first time in my life. How had Morag phrased it? "There will be no sun to warm your joy."

I broke the lengthening silence. "The will leaves me no alternative."

Mr. MacEwen glanced uneasily at the Major, as if to

31

apologize for me. "If you care to go over these papers," he said, gathering them up to pass to me, "I shall be happy—"

I interrupted. "I don't doubt that you have read them correctly. I am merely inquiring into the validity—the legal validity—of such provisions!"

"They are completely in order," he told me gravely. "I'd not advise you to spend the money or endure the scandal of taking the case to court."

Swallowing hard, I suppressed my rising anger for the present. Using all the will at my command, I smiled as warmly as I could.

"You have explained the matter very well, Mr. Mac-Ewen, and I'm sure you will understand that the shock and newness of all this has made it necessary for me to ask rather pointed questions. I'm sure you and the Major will forgive my seeming discourtesy. My father had my welfare very much at heart and I must trust to his wisdom. I shall comply with the terms of the will."

A look of pure relief washed over the solicitor's face. He bowed slightly in acknowledgment and said, "But of course, I understand and respect your desire to look at every possible interpretation—very creditable! I prefer our clients to be fully informed." He turned to the Major. "We have discussed this quite fully, but if you now have any further questions—?"

The Major, impassively watching our confrontation, replied quietly, "No. No questions."

Mr. MacEwen began to collect his papers. "Then I shall take the necessary steps to execute the terms." He cleared his throat. "I take it a decision will be forthcoming shortly on the date of marriage?" He glanced uneasily from one expressionless face to another. "Yes," he said hastily, and dropped the subject.

I was wondering how I might begin my plan of turning the Major against the thought of marrying me, when he broke the ensuing silence, speaking directly to me for the first time.

"If you have no objections, Miss Lindsay, I should like to remain here for perhaps a fortnight. It has been a very long time since my last visit, and if I am to assume responsibility for the estate, I'd like to know what is in store for me." He nearly smiled. "Transportation to and from the House of Storms is not the most convenient I have ever known. Brief visits would be very difficult, if not impossible."

I disregarded the attempt at humor. "You wish to remain here?" I couldn't believe my good fortune, and at the same time I felt a wave of anger at his presumption.

"That would scarcely be possible," Mr. MacEwen interceded. "Miss Lindsay has no suitable chaperone for such a visit, and to my knowledge there is no woman in the neighborhood who could serve such a purpose. If you wish, we will find some suitable person in Edinburgh and you may then return."

"I wish to stay here now, if Miss Lindsay will permit it," he said quietly. "As we may be considered engaged, I see no problem."

"But—" the lawyer began to expostulate. He was obviously shocked.

Propriety bothered me not at all. I was thinking of the uses to which his stay could be put. "The Major is in fact my cousin, is he not? And Elspeth is here. No gentlewoman from Edinburgh is half so formidable or so rigid in her standards," I said to the solicitor, and turned to the Major. "You are welcome, sir. With one proviso."

"Yes?"

"That you will not press your suit until I have had time to accustom myself to what I have learned today."

Lindsay's eyebrow quirked, giving his marked face a diabolical expression. "You have my word," he said.

When the solicitor left, he was still grumbling about Lindsay's arrangements to remain, but the prospect of missing the coach at the crossroads shortened his arguments. His impression of the inn on the previous night had not been improved by the sight of the drovers and itinerant haymakers in the taproom. I suspect he had relied on the Major's presence to afford some protection and without that, Mr. MacEwen was in something of a hurry.

Angus had not returned, and when the solicitor had finished his affairs with me, he had cursorily examined the estate books and left his compliments for the steward, assuring me privately that I was fortunate to have found such a dedicated and intelligent factor. When at last the carriage pulled away from the steps, I watched it vanish into the rain and mist with something like relief.

Major Lindsay was waiting in the hall and held the door for me to reenter the drawing room, where Elspeth had ordered the candles to be lit and the draperies drawn. I was thinking how cavernous the room would seem while the two of us tried to make conversation when I realized the Major was not planning to join me.

"I prefer to go to my room, if you will forgive me. I'll disturb you as little—" he was saying, and broke off as the heavy front door crashed open.

Angus stood in the draft of damp air and rain. He was still wearing the Lindsay kilt and there was murder in his eyes.

"They told me it was you," he said. "I had to see for myself." His hands were clenched, the knuckles white under the tanned skin.

Major Lindsay, surprise on his face, said angrily, "What the devil—"

"Aye. The devil. Perhaps that's good enough to describe you."

"Angus—" I said quickly, stepping forward to come between the two men. All I could think of was that Angus had somehow learned the terms of the will.

"What is he doing here?" the steward demanded, his dark eyes turned toward me. "Or perhaps he will tell me himself."

I saw the deep flush spread across the Major's face, but he answered only, "I am visiting my cousin." Whether it

34

was spoken to save me embarrassment, or himself, I couldn't guess.

Angus turned to me once more. "Do you want him here? Say the word, Mistress, and I'll have him in yonder coach within the hour."

"I—no, he is a welcomed guest, Angus," I said stiffly, touched by the man's loyalty.

The steward's angry eyes searched my face, but he found no satisfaction there. After the slightest hesitation, he said, "As you wish, Mistress," and turning abruptly, he left.

Major Lindsay and I stood there, side by side, staring at the closed door. And then he spoke quietly.

"It has been a long journey. If I may go to my room?"

I rang for Elspeth to show him the way, and then sank into a chair by the drawing-room hearth, exhausted by the strain and unhappiness of the day.

I slept poorly that night, tossing about long after the fire's glow faded from the room and the last fingers of warmth retreated into the ashes. Below the western wall the sea broke heavily against the rocks. I wondered if the Major lay awake as well, in the Blue Room that overlooked the hills and the loch beyond. Cousins. And yet he was a stranger. I felt not the remotest call of blood, not the faintest recognition. From his coldness I gathered he had not been drawn to me, either. And yet, because my father had chosen to safeguard the Lindsay name, he had thrust both of us into an intolerable situation. We must marry, or one of us would lose the House of Storms. Since Major Lindsay had joined the Hussars, he must have an income of his own, but that was a far cry from the personal wealth and the house and lands that would come to him at our marriage. I had not thought to ask Mr. Mac-Ewen how large the Major's legacy would be if he refused the match, so I had no way of measuring the difference this marriage would make in his life. Still, it must indeed be impressive. And he was a proud man. I had seen the flush on his face when Angus demanded his business here. As if he did not care to admit that he came to marry an heiress.

My task was a difficult one. How does one make one's self so undesirable to a man that he will forfeit a fortune rather than agree to marriage! It was too late to pretend to madness, and anyway, Mr. MacEwen would have seen through that straightaway. There was no ravishingly beautiful girl in the neighborhood whom I might throw in his way, to sweep him off his feet. And if Shakespeare is right, a man will marry with a shrew with an eye to taming her, so a foul disposition would scarcely answer my purpose. What then? I knew so little about men! I wished I could ask Angus what to do. But from the look on his face, he would have happily murdered the Major and tossed his body over the cliff wall—a solution of sorts, perhaps, if one wished to be hanged.

What had sent Angus into such a rage? Had he possibly discovered the terms of the will? But how, and from whom? Mr. MacEwen had no doubt kept silent on the subject. Still, I could see no other cause for his outburst.

The more I thought, the more confused I became. Finally, as the pale gray of early dawn began to lighten the room, I fell into a heavy sleep, worn out and no closer to the answer. My last coherent thought, as the roar of the sea mixed with the muffled heartbeats in my ear, was that I had completely forgotten my mother's collection of jewelry, which I had planned to try on.

The next morning Angus sent word by one of the grooms that he would be away for the next day or two, making the rounds of the farms and seeing to the haying. So there would be no questions from him, and he would be out of the Major's way.

Oddly enough, the Major stayed out of my way. He rode out early each morning and was often away until late in the afternoon. Consequently we saw each other only at meals, and often only the evening meal. I felt a perverse anger, unwilling to acknowledge his courtesy and sourly supposing that he was taking the opportunity to judge his inheritance.

Elspeth moved about in tight-lipped silence. I had told her very little, but there was always the possibility that she had had an ear to the door. Ordinarily this would have been far beneath her, but I knew that where I was concerned she was capable of anything, guarding me with the same single-minded ferocity that the eagle showed when anyone approached her nest in the hillside above the sea loch.

"I never knew your father, Miss Moira, as well you know, but he was a girt fool to have left matters so! And who's to say that this Major Duncan Lindsay is the same lad who came here so long ago? He was reported dead, and might well be for all I know. With that scar on his face not even his own mother would know him!" she snapped.

"Mr. MacEwen has watched him grow up, Elspeth. Half of Edinburgh knows *him*, and he isn't likely to lie even for the Major's inheritance. Besides, I think Mr. MacEwen truly believes that this is the best thing for me. He's right—if I don't agree to these terms, I lose everything except my father's money. And what good is that, exiled from here!" I replied despondently. "If I could make him —the Major—hate me, or convince him I had the plague or worse, perhaps he would go away."

"Not him!" she snorted. "Poking about the house, asking all manner of questions, wanting to see the family portraits, talking to all the tenants—that doesn't sound to me like a man who would run away from you if you had three heads and no arms."

I laughed in spite of myself. "What do the servants think of him?"

"More fool they, they like him. I'll give him this, he puts on no airs and has sense enough not to open his mouth unless there's something to say. Of course, none of them know what's afoot. He's your cousin and come to visit, that's all they've been told, though I heard that half-wit dairy lass saying he'd make a fair match for the mistress. I boxed her ears and sent her flying."

I sighed. "Do you think the Reverend Mr. Hay would help me?"

"Not likely. He'd tell you that your father knew best, and you wouldn't want to be giving him the whole of the story anyway, so what else could he do but agree?"

I paced the bedroom floor restlessly. If only I could understand why Fraser hadn't warned me!

"If you don't stand still, I'll not have your hair pinned up decent for dinner. And there's no use in pretending to be a drab now, when he has already seen you aren't."

I let her finish the task and then went down to the dining room where the Major, impeccably dressed as usual, awaited me. His arm was still in its black sling, but I noticed that he was now able to put it through the sleeve of his coat. He looked tired, and I thought perhaps the arm pained him from all the hours he had spent in the saddle. I wondered how he had injured it, but since he had made no reference to it, I dared not ask. And Elspeth had said that when she offered to dress it for him or prepare warm water to soak it, he had cut her short. It was none of my concern, anyway.

He greeted me politely and led me into the small dining room. It would have been ludicrous for us to sit at opposite ends of the long table in the formal dining room, though the smaller one made conversation more stilted because of the more intimate atmosphere. Tonight, however, he appeared to be in a better mood, and to my surprise I found myself talking quite comfortably.

He had begun by commenting on the fact that I had had the good fortune to grow up at the House of Storms, and before I quite knew how, he had drawn me on to speak of my childhood, of Fraser and Elspeth and Angus, and the changing of the seasons, the histories of the Lindsays whose likenesses hung in the Long Gallery, all the memories that fill the mind over the years.

He listened quietly, injecting a comment here or there, asking a question, appearing to be deeply interested in what I had to say. I suppose I was flattered by such attention, and I found myself thinking that, under other circumstances, I might have found his company quite pleasant. But I was brought up short by the fact that, after all, it was to his advantage to charm me. As a man of the world talking to a girl who had not been twenty miles beyond the boundaries of her estates, he must have found the task ridiculously simple. This realization hurt me a little and I felt my face flush from injured pride. But the Major didn't notice.

"I suppose you remember very little about your parents?" he was saying.

"Of my mother, nothing at all. She died within a few hours of my birth," I replied, forcing my mind into new channels. "I have no memory of my father, really, except, as I mentioned before, for his voice shouting and laughing down the passages, and his arms as he would swing me high to make me laugh. It was a deep voice, rich and pleasant to the ear, and I connected it with the sound of the sea. The two seem to fit together in my memory. I have always heard the sea beneath the walls—my room is on that side of the house."

"You weren't in the Nursery?"

"If I was, I don't remember it. Perhaps because I was orphaned so young they felt I would be happier in a room of my own. The Nursery can be a dreary place when there is no child but oneself."

"Yes, I was an only child also," he said, and then we began to speak of the horses that my father had bred.

That night as I went up to bed, I walked along the Gallery, which faced the south and overlooked the summer garden. The heavy draperies had been pulled against the darkness and the only light was the candle in my hand.

I went directly to my father's portrait and stood for a

time beneath the ornate gold frame, staring up at the face. The fine dark eyes below the dark brows smiled at me in the flickering candle flame and the strong lines of the face had almost a three-dimensional quality, as if I might have reached up and touched more than paint-covered canvas.

"Why?" I whispered. "Why did you do this to me?" My throat hurt with the tears that wouldn't come, but there was no change in the mocking, arrogant eyes, no answer from the sealed lips. I thought of all the games I had made up about my father, and what we would have shared if he had lived, but they seemed empty to me now. The terms of the will were the greater reality, and childhood dreams were suddenly far behind me.

I heard the Major's steps on the stairs. He had not lingered over his brandy this night, and I had no desire to be caught here with tears in my eyes. Shielding the candle carefully with my hand, I turned away from the portrait and went to my room.

Elspeth told me on the fourth morning that the Major had gone to call upon the minister, and then had been seen walking about the kirkyard. "I can't think why he would do that," she ended.

"Perhaps he is interested in the family graves," I said, looking up from my household accounts. "They are his people as much as mine."

"And well you know, Mistress, that all the Lindsays are buried in the kirk itself. Not even your great-grandfather's wife, the one who ran away and was brought home to die mad in the old peel tower, was buried in the yard. A Catholic custom, that one, but they built the chapel and put the roof on when the storms tore it off and shored up the tower foundations, and not one of the ministers had the courage to say no to the burying inside. So why is the Major walking the kirkyard?"

"I don't know—ask Old Morag," I said irritably, for this was the least of my problems. The Major might climb the cliffs or search for the eagle's nest in the glen or stand on his head in the loch for all I cared, so long as he would refuse to marry me when the time came.

"I just might do that," Elspeth replied, and left the room without another word as I stared after her in complete surprise.

I was to find out what was on the Major's mind the next day. I had had a very trying interview with Angus, who had demanded to know why the Major was staying here when it was obvious that I cared nothing about the man nor he about me. He would not accept my halting evasions.

"It is the will," I said at last. "My father wanted him to marry me when I came of age."

He swore long and feelingly in Gaelic, his face like a thundercloud. "And you will?" he demanded finally.

"I—no—yes—oh, Angus, I don't know! There's more to the story than that, and I don't want to discuss it."

But he gave me no peace and in the end I told him the whole of it, relieved in a way to have it out in the open. "But don't, I beg you, let him know that I have talked about this!" I added.

"That isn't likely! What I have to say to him won't involve you," he told me curtly. "I've a score of my own to settle!"

"What score? Angus, what are you talking about?" I caught his sleeve as he went past me out of the office. "How could you have a score against him?"

He swung around to face me. "I was here the summer he came to visit your father. We were the same age, and as boys will, we played together, though he was the laird's nephew and I a stable lad. And both of us were army mad then. His father had been a soldier, and he said he would be one as well. I was all for running away and going with him, fool that I was. But one day on the peel tower, as we were climbing up and playing at war, he let me fall. By the time they had got me home and found the doctor, it was clear the leg ought to come off. But I begged them to leave it, and in the end they agreed. I kept the leg, but it was never the same, and I have walked with a twisted knee ever since."

"You can't blame that on Duncan Lindsay!" I gasped, horrified. I had never heard the story before, but I could see in Angus' anguished eyes that it was true.

"He let me fall deliberately, because he was angry that I would be a soldier before him, that I could join as a drummer boy while he must go first to school. And so I never left after all! He saw to that."

I released his arm and he strode from the office. Too dazed to think clearly and needing time to myself, I found a shawl for my shoulders, slipped out of the house and walked rapidly toward the loch. And there, at the edge of the water, I came upon Duncan Lindsay skipping stones across the waves. I tried to veer away as if I hadn't seen him, but he lifted his head and then turned to wait for me, standing quietly by the rocky shore almost as if he had been expecting me.

3

When I had joined him, Major Lindsay nodded in greeting and gestured toward the water. "Like the sea, the loch changes its mood with the sky. I haven't seen it the same color twice in the several days I have been here."

"There was an artist who came years ago, when I was a child. I often watched him paint. He couldn't use oils—only watercolors were swift enough to catch the scene before it had shifted again." My eyes went up the loch to the tall ruin of the old tower and I thought of the two boys playing there, and one falling to the tumbled rock at its base. It was difficult to keep my mind on what the Major was saying as I relived Angus' tortured words. And again I heard the echo of Old Morag's voice—"Be not deceived by the mask of evil, for the shadow of death is there, and no mercy. Look not for trust where wanting twists the spirit." Had Angus already learned the pain of trusting this man—as perhaps the old woman had known?

"You pay flattering attention to my conversation," the Major said in wry amusement.

"Oh—!" I said, startled out of my wanderings. "I'm sorry, I—"

"—was thinking of something else. Yes, I am aware of that."

Embarrassed because I couldn't tell him what was on my mind, I kept silent and felt myself blush.

"No matter. I really wished to speak to you about something more important than where the eagle is nesting this season, but the words wouldn't come." We were standing by a flat boulder just above the lapping wavelets of blue water. "I must talk with you, Miss Lindsay. Why don't we sit here and thrash it out."

"I have told you. I don't want to hear anything about marriage—not yet. And you gave me your word," I added stubbornly.

"No, it has nothing to do with us. Only with you," he replied gently as he placed a square of snowy linen handkerchief on the rock's mossy surface. "Sit down. You look rather tired."

I could have told him that I slept ill and that it was his fault, but I kept my unruly tongue in my head and sat down, smoothing my skirts.

He was staring away across the water, blue as the sky above. Where the sea met the mouth of the loch across a rocky bottom I saw gulls flash and dive, their gray bodies white in the sunlight.

"I was debating with myself whether to write to Mac-Ewen first or to come to you, when I saw you cross the hill just now. And of course the honorable thing is to speak to you first," he said quietly.

For an instant my heart soared and my eyes flew to his face. He had been careful to keep the unscarred side toward me, and I noticed for the first time how attractive he had once been. His features were regular, well-cut, and the line of his jaw was firm and strong. He was frowning now, and I thought surely that he was about to say that he had decided after all that he would not care to marry me, that he wished to be released from the terms of the will. I waited in rising excitement for him to continue.

"You knew Mrs. Fraser well, I suppose?" he began, and I was so startled by the unexpected question that I stumbled over my answer.

"Why—naturally—of course I did!"

"And I take it she cared for you deeply."

"Yes. Fraser and I were very close," I said, confused. "Why not? She was the only family I had, in all truth."

"Describe her for me."

"Well—she had fair hair, though darker than yours—more the color of mine. And that lovely complexion which must have come from a Nordic ancestor. Her eyes were hazel, changing color with what she wore. A little taller than I am, perhaps, but not so slender, and a perfectly erect carriage that sometimes awed those who met her. Her features were straight and ordinary, but she had a serenity of expression that few things could ruffle, and a sense of humor that often put a twinkle in her eyes even when she had no intention of laughing." I stopped. "Surely you saw her when you were here as a boy?"

He ignored my question. "You describe her with affection," he said instead.

"I loved her," I replied simply.

He skipped a smooth stone across the surface of the water with his good arm, as skilled at ducks and drakes as any shepherd lad. "Mrs. Fraser would not permit me to return to the House of Storms, though your father had planned for me to spend other summers here. She refused my mother's invitations to bring you to Alnwick and mine when you were sixteen to come to Edinburgh for several weeks. I was never permitted to write to you directly. And yet she must have realized that you would be happier knowing me better, that I would surely need to understand the workings of the estate. I couldn't find a reason for her actions. What possible explanation could there be? She had not been so possessive of you during my first visit, and I had thought she liked me well enough."

"Why didn't you ask her?" I demanded, appalled at his words. Fraser had scarcely mentioned him, and I knew nothing of letters passing between them. Indeed, Fraser must have burned them, for I had found none in her papers.

The Major had flushed at my question. "I had my own life to lead," he replied coldly, and I knew, intuitively, that he had not cared for his role of consort to the heiress, preparing himself while waiting for me to grow up. For a proud man, it was a galling position, and yet the fortune was too vast to cast aside.

"I didn't understand—until I received this letter from her last year. It was waiting for me when I came home." He took from his pocket an envelope addressed in Fraser's familiar hand, and held out the letter to me.

I opened it slowly, apprehensively, glancing at the date —two days before she died. Tears filled my eyes for a moment as I tried to read the single page, for the firmness had gone from her pen and the trembling lines spoke clearly of her illness and distress.

My dear Major Lindsay:
I fear I am dying and will not live to see my dear child's twenty-first birthday. Therefore I must write to you now, for I have done you a grave wrong. In effect, for seventeen years, I have excluded you from your rightful place at the House of Storms, and can offer in excuse of it only a mother's love for her child. I cannot rest until I have confessed my sin, and yet in the same breath I must tell you that I would be guilty of it again, if time could turn backward. I will not say more, for I am sure you must have suspected my duplicity before this. When you have children of your own, perhaps you will understand more clearly why I, a mother and a Christian minister's widow, would live a lie for the sake of a child's peace and security. So far, she has never needed to know that this house is not hers to keep nor that her future is in your hands.

I must beg of you three promises, though I have no right to do so. I ask you not to come here or contact her in any way until she is of age. I ask you not to hold against her what I have done for her sake. And finally, I ask you to remember that the whole of the House of Storms will soon come into your possession, and you can well afford to be generous toward an orphan.

I cannot encourage a marriage between my dear child

and you, even for the sake of Mr. Lindsay's estate. She is not of your wider world and experience, and although I am sure you must have changed greatly from the boy I knew so long ago, I cannot in my heart believe that my poor girl would ever be happy with you. I ask your forgiveness for what I have done, and beg you to remember that by right, even your inheritance should have been Moira Lindsay's.

Respectfully,
Anna Fraser

I folded the letter carefully and gave it back to him. "She was distressed by her deception, wasn't she? Never telling me about you—never allowing you to return to the castle—because she deeply disapproved of the arranged marriage," I said sadly. "It must have weighed heavily on her mind as she lay dying. Fraser was not one to tell lies in the ordinary way. She was scrupulous in all she did." There was rising bitterness in my heart that Fraser had known no peace at the end because of this man. She had not wished me to know him, to marry him. Was it because of what he had done to Angus? Or had she seen him with a woman's intuitive eye, where my father had cared only for the Lindsay in his name? Whatever the reason, she had done everything in her power to keep him away.

The Major was watching my face. "Is that all you read here? Has it never occurred to you that she was your mother?"

I thought surely I had misunderstood him. "My *what*?"

"No, I can see that the idea is entirely new to you," he said quietly. "I must apologize for my bluntness."

"Would you please explain—in plain language—what you are talking about?" I demanded irritably. "I've never cared for guessing games!"

"This isn't a game; I'm sorry. There is every reason to believe that you are not Moira Lindsay at all, but Catriona Fraser, daughter of Anna and Donald Fraser."

"Are you out of your mind?" I was furious. How *dared*

he suggest such a thing! I slid off the rock and stood before him. "You owe me an explanation of your rudeness and, afterwards, an apology. I want you off my property by nightfall. Mr. MacEwen will deal with any further matters between us."

"I don't wish to hurt you, my dear," he said gravely. "But the truth is, you are Catriona Fraser. Moira Lindsay was buried in your place in the Fraser plot beneath the old rowan in the churchyard."

"That's impossible! I don't know who has told you this wild tale. I don't really care, but to suggest to my face—" Words failed me in my anger and I wanted to strike out at him and hurt him in some way, to ease the wound in my heart.

He stood his ground. "It was quite possible! Mrs. Fraser's son and husband were dead when she came to the castle to care for you and your father—that is, Moira and her father, of course. Her own daughter, nearly the same age as the Lindsay child, died soon after Lindsay, in the scarlet fever epidemic that winter. Or so it was said. Both children had it—they often played together when Mrs. Fraser brought Moira to her home near the village—and the Fraser child was taken to the castle to be nursed. Both were quite ill, Moira more so than Catriona. One died and the other had a long, very slow convalescence for fear of heart damage. Oddly enough, the housekeeper, a Mrs. MacNeil, was asked to leave the morning that 'Catriona' died. She and Mrs. Fraser had a violent argument and the woman left at once, without a word to the servants. 'Catriona' was buried and, for a very long time, no one saw Moira except Mrs. Fraser and one of the servants. When at last she was permitted to leave her room, the child was so thin and pale no one thought it strange that she was somewhat different. After all, illness alters people. She couldn't remember the names and faces of the servants, for example, and would let no one but Mrs. Fraser near her. There's more, but it all points to the same conclusion: the child who died was Moira Lindsay, and the

48

one who lived was Catriona Fraser. That's why I was never permitted to return to the House of Storms, and that's what your mother tried to explain in her letter."

"Who has told you such nonsense? I want to know!" I demanded. "There's nothing in that letter about an exchange of children!"

"If you will be honest with yourself, you'll see there is. I've pieced together all I have known and heard, and it fits too well to be coincidence. It was Mrs. MacNeil who nursed Catriona while Mrs. Fraser cared for Moira—what earthly reason do you suppose Mrs. Fraser had for sacking her at such a difficult time, if not to make the switch in children possible?" He shook his head. "You aren't dark like your parents. Your coloring is the same as Mrs. Fraser's. Haven't you noticed?"

I laughed. "You are saying you remember Moira after all these years, while her servants forgot her—me—in a matter of months? I don't believe it!"

"When your father made arrangements with my mother for our future, he gave her a miniature of you. The eyes are unmistakably dark, the hair fairer, without auburn lights. Exactly as I remember you."

"How convenient! I remind you that Henry VIII believed Holbein's miniature of Anne of Cleves, and was furious when he discovered what his Flemish Mare really looked like!" I thought over what he had told me. "Where was the doctor all this time, may I ask? *He* couldn't be misled!"

"There was no doctor. He would have had to come from Oban, or Tobermory on Mull. The women saw to the sick. As they still do."

I remembered Angus and the doctor who had cared for his leg. Angus would know. And come to that, he was as good a witness as Duncan Lindsay, for he had lived and worked at the House of Storms all his life. He would know the truth. "I don't want to discuss this further. I don't believe you," I told him, lifting my chin and meeting his gray eyes with my own. "It would be rather convenient, would it not, Major, for me to be Catriona. You would then have your inheritance without the necessity of marrying me. And I advise you to deal cautiously with Mr. MacEwen on this subject. You may find your legacy in jeopardy as well!"

I turned on my heel and walked swiftly away from him, closing my ears to what he was saying. To my relief, he made no effort to stop me or even to follow me. I made my way up the glen without any thought about where I was going or what I would do. I only knew I had to put distance between the Major and me before his quiet, persuasive voice tore my life to shreds.

I walked for a very long time, but it did me little good. On the wind that blew constantly from the sea I seemed to hear Duncan Lindsay taunting me, and inside myself an insidious voice asked, what if it is true? What then? It didn't bear thinking of! I hurried along the track with unseeing eyes, trying to sort out what had happened, but instead of concentrating on the Major's charges in order to find an answer for them, I could hold nothing in my mind.

If this was true, I thought, I would be penniless. Moira Lindsay's mother's inheritance was not mine, neither the jewels nor the money invested in sound stocks. And I would receive nothing from Angus Lindsay—not castle nor lands, not wealth and position; only—if Mr. MacEwen saw fit—a small pension for my mother's years of service to the family. I stopped aghast. Not even that! For she had stayed at the House of Storms to care for a child who no longer existed, and I had had more than I deserved of education and shelter from a family my mother had deceived. I would find myself looking for a position as a governess instead. I recalled that Fraser had once said her husband left her only a pittance when he died. The man who might have been my father—the minister—had spent all he possessed for his flock and his church, always ready to give of what he had for those less fortunate, without remembering that his wife and family might require his care as well. No, there would be no inheritance, however tiny, to tide me over the days and weeks before someone chose to engage me to teach his children.

And then suddenly furious at my gullibility, I shook off such distressing speculations and let myself consider the facts instead. Why had Fraser written to Duncan Lindsay? *Was* she telling him more than how guilty she felt for keeping him from visiting here? Fraser might have lied to my cousin for my peace and security, but I could not envision her deceiving *everyone* to provide a home for her child.

Or were they one and the same thing? I could also think of dozens of reasons for Mrs. MacNeil's leaving so abruptly. Distraught and bearing the full responsibility for her charge, Fraser might well have lost her temper over what would normally seem a mere trifle. In her heartbreak over her daughter's death, she might even have accused the housekeeper of negligence.

Above all, I must not let myself fall prey to doubts. It was very likely that Duncan Lindsay had decided to use this interpretation to oust me from any share in my father's estate. All I had to do was prove him wrong and then even Mr. MacEwen would admit that he had forfeited his right to any part of the Lindsay heritage. But how did one prove one's identity?

Too exhausted to go farther and not ready to turn back, I sat down on the ground amongst the bracken and heather. Where in God's name should I begin?

I heard someone calling and whirled around, ready to pour out my torment on Duncan Lindsay if he had had the audacity to follow me.

Coming over the hillside above was a complete stranger. He waved and came pelting down the slope toward me. Uncertain and a little uneasy, I rose to wait for him. But as he drew closer I saw that he was dressed respectably in tweeds and carried a gnarled walking stick in one hand. He was of medium height, slender, and dark-haired, with a nice face creased now with a grin of relief.

"I say," he got out breathlessly, "I'm happy to find someone out here besides the sheep!"

I smiled at him. "Are you lost?"

The grin widened engagingly. "Not lost—misplaced. I know I am in western Scotland, on the fringes of Argyllshire, and within smell of the sea. Beyond that, I'm slightly confused about my bearings."

Laughter rose in my throat, and I realized that it was an emotion I hadn't felt since before the day of my birthday.

He bowed. "Bruce Cameron, Miss. I've been on a walking tour of Argyllshire this summer and am currently headquartered at the MacDonald croft, somewhere—" he gestured in a half-circle with his hand "—somewhere in the neighborhood, surely."

The MacDonalds were a poor but proud family on the fringes of my land. They would not admit to it, I knew, but they had lived on the border of poverty since the father had been ill two years before. It was not a very lovely house, though it was spotlessly clean and well-situated for anyone who wished to explore the area. Now there would be money for them without injuring their pride.

"You are off the track by over a mile," I told him. "At this rate, you'll be hours getting back. Fortunate for you that I was here, or you might have gotten thoroughly lost."

"Misplaced!" he insisted in mock gravity.

"You ought to have a compass," I suggested.

He put his hand into his pocket and brought out a brass compass with a shattered crystal. "I had one," he told me ruefully, "until I forgot to watch my feet two days ago. I'm afraid the rocks are rather hard in this part of the country."

"Go back to the top of the hill. There's a track near the foot of the other side. Follow it until it branches, take the left fork there and then left again at the next. By that time you ought to recognize your surroundings."

"Thank you very much!" He paused and then asked

hopefully, "Would you be going in my direction, Miss—"

"Lindsay. Moira Lindsay," I told him, hoping my voice didn't falter noticeably over the words.

"Miss Lindsay!" he repeated in surprise. "Then it is your land I've been trespassing upon. Mrs. MacDonald had suggested that I call and ask permission to wander around here, but I pictured a dragon-faced old spinster, and kept putting off my visit. *Surely* you aren't the mistress here— I mean to say, you are scarcely more than a girl!"

"I was orphaned as a child," I told him coolly, and he let the subject drop as if he sensed my discomfort.

"I shall call tomorrow," he replied. "If I don't lose myself along the way."

I thought of going home to the castle. Angus was furious and the Major thought me an impostor. I didn't care to face either of them or have any further problems thrust upon me today. On impulse, I said, "You are closer to the castle than you are to the MacDonalds. Would you care to come to tea? Afterwards, one of the grooms will guide you back."

"Miss Lindsay, that is very kind of you—I wouldn't dream of encroaching, believe me!" he stammered boyishly. "An imposition—"

"It is no imposition, I assure you. In fact, I should be pleased to have the company going home. I have been alone with my thoughts long enough," I said lightly but honestly.

His dark eyes scanned my face. "You look tired. Would you prefer to have me go along and bring back a horse for you?"

"Good heavens, no! I've walked these hills all my life." I turned back the way I had come, and he fell in by my side. As we went along I pointed out the various landmarks and places of interest, and he made pleasant, intelligent conversation in his turn. By the time we had passed the eagle's nest and reached the head of the loch and the old peel tower, clouds were building up over the Sound and the wind blew gustily.

"I'm glad I accepted your invitation," Mr. Cameron said. "That storm is moving this way rapidly."

"There will be squalls most of the evening," I agreed. "The sunshine rarely lasts along the coast. Do you mind walking in the rain? Many people dislike it."

"I've gotten used to it, of course. But I've never cared for the way water swishes in my boots after a while."

We laughed and were in good spirits as we approached the rising ground to the headland. He stopped to look at the castle, framed now in the massive gray storm clouds, the formidable walls silhouetted against the darkening sky.

"I understand why it is called the House of Storms," he said quietly. "The name is apt."

I looked at my home through his eyes, and knew how striking it must seem. A pang of terror spread through me at the very thought of losing it.

"You are very fortunate to have such a lovely home," he said, as if he had read my mind. "Very fortunate." And I knew he was sincere, not merely offering flattery to his hostess.

"You haven't come this far before in your rambles?" I asked.

"No. I told you—I thought there was a resident dragon. And so I walked mainly east and north of here."

"There is a resident dragon," I said softly as I caught sight of the Major through the gates.

"What did you say?" Cameron asked apologetically.

"I said there is a guest with us now, a Major Lindsay from England. Though I doubt he'll be joining us at tea."

"Major Duncan Lindsay?" he asked abruptly.

My heart sank. A friend of the Major's was not welcome now. But as I glanced quickly at Cameron's face I saw no pleasure, only speculation written there.

"Do you know the Major?" I asked.

"Only by reputation." His manner was almost evasive, as if he didn't wish to criticize a fellow guest to his hostess. "Are you related, or is the common name coincidence?"

"We are—distant cousins," I replied, evasive in my turn.

We crossed the lawns in silence and when we entered the gates, the conversation turned to architecture and the history of the castle.

To my surprise, Major Lindsay joined us in the drawing room for tea. I performed the introductions and the two men eyed each other with cold interest. Bruce Cameron, however, made an effort to appear friendly and I thought it was to his credit, for the Major was quietly formal.

Elspeth brought our tea and let it be known by her grim expression as she set the tray on the table before me that she did not approve of entertaining gentlemen to tea when I had not changed from the dress I had worn most of the day. She examined Mr. Cameron carefully as she finished her duties, and because the lines did not deepen about her mouth I was under the impression that she was not opposed to what she saw. That he was a gentleman was obvious from his speech and his manner. His hands, strongly and bluntly shaped, were well cared for and his tweeds were impeccably tailored. I liked his casual charm that met the world as if he always expected to find a friend and felt myself relax a little under the easy flow of talk.

The Major sat on my right, his face expressionless as he watched Cameron. The sling was missing from his arm now, and yet I would have sworn he was wearing it when I saw him in the courtyard as we arrived. He held the arm carefully, but otherwise there was no indication he had suffered injury to it. I did not understand, but then it was his own choice and none of my affair.

I was glad when Cameron and the Major discovered a mutual interest in Cumberland fell climbing and went off on a discussion of guides and the most rugged tracks. In my turn, I observed the two men and found myself comparing and contrasting what I saw. I had received few men as guests at the House of Storms who were not at least old enough to be my father or even my grandfather.

And neither of these guests was beyond thirty, each attractive in his own way, both active and clearly intelligent. One was dark, the other fair, one was medium in build, the other tall and with the broad shoulders and excellent carriage of a cavalryman, one was warm and the other ice cold. Anyone watching us through the window would have thought me fortunate to have such eligible company at my tea table and perhaps expected me to play one against the other while they vied for my notice. But anyone in the room would have realized at once that these two were measuring each other and were scarcely aware of me at the moment.

And one of these men had called me an impostor.

I found myself watching the Major again, for he was leading Mr. Cameron on to talk as he had led me one night at dinner, though I could see no reason behind his sudden interest in climbing in Cumberland. It could matter nothing at all to him that Bruce Cameron preferred Scale Force near Buttermere to Dalegarth Force, or that he had not climbed Scafell Pike at all. And yet I had the feeling that there was indeed some purpose behind it. The Major did few things without a very good reason, as I had myself learned.

Cameron laughed suddenly and turned to me. "How inconsiderate we are!" he said. "Major Lindsay and I can speak of this passion of ours at any time. You walk often, yourself. Can you suggest any places I might especially enjoy?"

"You have seen the glen and the loch," I told him, "and the castle and even the eagle's nest. The tower as well. That's all we boast in the way of sights."

He seemed to be disappointed, as if he had expected more. And then he said, "I'd like to explore the tower, if I may? Please say no if you'd prefer I didn't."

I caught the look of disapproval on Duncan Lindsay's face and took perverse delight in agreeing with my guest. "By all means. It has been locked since the roof fell. But if you would like the key, come here first and I'll have it for you."

He thanked me and took his leave soon after. With a feeling of regret, I watched him go. He had brightened the world a little for me and prevented the Major from voicing the thoughts uppermost in both our minds. As I turned from the door, I said quickly, before the subject could be broached between us, "I'm rather tired. If you will excuse me?" and fled to my room.

Later, I had Elspeth bring a dinner tray there, leaving the Major to the lonely elegance of the dining room and the companionship of his own thoughts.

Elspeth came to me after the Major had settled down with his brandy. I knew from the way she closed the door to my room that she had questions of her own to ask, and my heart sank.

"I'm tired," I told her irritably. "The walk this afternoon was too much, I think."

But she was not to be put off. With the freedom of an old servant, she placed herself before me and said, "There's Angus as wild as a bear with a sore paw, and the Major sulking over his glass, and now you say you are tired from a junket that two days back would have made you no more than sharp set for your tea. I'll have the truth, Mistress! There's no hiding the fact that all's not well, so I'll thank you not to try."

I was sitting in the blue winged chair by the hearth, but I rose to pace the Turkey carpet, following the intricate pattern with my eyes as I explained. "Angus dislikes the Major. They knew each other as boys, and there is an old injury between them."

"Hmmmpf! Dislike, is it? I'd say pure hatred, and not on the one side, either!"

I had no intention of discussing the steward's story with her. "Do they deal together at all?" I asked instead.

"Only so far as needful. It's 'Would you be so kind' this,

57

and 'If you permit' that, and all the while murdering each other with their eyes. You'll have no peace in this house until that trouble is done."

"Yes," I said with a sigh. "Yes, I'm afraid that's so."

"And what's between you and the Major? Don't tell me it's the will, because I'd not believe a word of it. There's more now."

I told her. There was nothing else I could do, and I needed to go over the story with someone. She listened grimly to all of it, and when I was done, she spoke.

"So he's found a way to the whole, has he? Not enough to have this house, the crofts and the herds, the land itself. There's the money, too. Greed, Miss Moira, that's what it is, and you know what the Bible has to say about that. He'll get what is coming to him, never fear!"

"Well," I said dryly, "I can only hope it is in time to help me."

"What will you do? Write to yon solicitor in Edinburgh?"

"I shall have to. But Elspeth, I'm worried. He has the letter, and there are so many details that I can't begin to check! It's true Fraser treated me as she might have a daughter, everyone knows that she did. She had lost her children and I had lost my parents—it was only natural—" I grasped the chair's curved back and faced her. "Wasn't it?"

"Mrs. Fraser was an honest woman, and well you know it," Elspeth said firmly, her arms folded across her dark gown. "Aye, she loved you, and there was a time when I thought it unwise to give so much of her heart to one wee bairn; idolatrous it seemed. For all that, she never once put her feelings before your good or her duty. And that, Miss Moira, is forever to her credit, whatever yon blethering Major may say of the poor lady!"

"Yes, but Elspeth, in the letter she speaks of me as her dear child—"

"And did she not call you so all these long years? Have done, Miss Moira! She was half-demented when Catriona died, and no time to mourn, for you were slipping away

58

before her eyes. She put away her grief for your sake, and gave you Catriona's place in her heart. Aye, she pretended sometimes, but there was no harm in her ways, and no deceit, either. Do you not think I'd have guessed long since if she had had such a secret?"

"And yet Fraser said nothing to you about this man, or why she had written so to him?" I was pacing again, too restless to stand still.

"She never spoke of him. And the mailbag was her care, not mine."

"Then don't you see, if she could keep one secret, why not another?" It was that question which haunted me more than any other.

"It is not the same thing at all. A deception over the children would be dishonest. To say nothing about the Major was her judgment for your sake. And rightly so. She'd not be wanting you to marry such a one, not Mrs. Fraser. And you may tell yon solicitor as much."

"Opinions won't help. I need facts. The Major has already made certain of his information, and I must do the same." I stopped my pacing. "If only Fraser had spoken to me—*told* me her reasons for distrusting the Major and why she had written him. My only hope now is to find a witness. What of the servants, besides Angus, who were here in my father's day?"

Elspeth thought carefully. "There's Calum, the old shepherd. But he'd not have seen the child. And Mrs. MacBane, Cook's mother, but she has been blind these ten years, and her mind wanders. I'd not say she was reliable. Your father's coachman died last winter, and MacGregor, the gardener in your father's day, is so far gone in whisky he'd swear to both sides and never know it." She shook her head. "There's not been a large staff, as well you know, no more than needed to keep the house. As for the servants who left before my time, I'd have no way of knowing their names or where they are now."

"What of the village?" I asked desperately. "If the child Moira was taken to play with Catriona, surely someone saw her. And what of our housekeeper, Mrs. MacNeil, who nursed Fraser's daughter? Where did she go when Fraser dismissed her?"

Elspeth frowned into the fire. "I know nought of her. Dead most likely, for she'd served your father long before he married your mother. And I'd not know about the Fraser house—being before my day. There's those that might. But as to the villagers, or the crofters for that matter, they have not had cause to question you, and haven't! That ought to satisfy even an Edinburgh lawyer!"

"It isn't enough," I told her wearily. "Because of that letter, the burden of proof will be mine, and I shall have to find someone who remembers both children." I sank into the chair. "*I* haven't known the solicitor all these many years. How can I convince him that I am really Moira Lindsay? Because if I don't, there will be no inheritance for me. I shall have to leave here and find a way to earn my own living, while I grow used to being called Catriona Fraser!"

Elspeth faced me squarely. "It'll not come to that, Mistress! Over my dead body—or his!"

I sought out Angus early the next morning and asked him to meet me in the garden. I had no desire to be overheard in the house.

The rain squalls the night before still dewed the grass, and the mignonette smelled of summer in its sheltered place beneath the wallflowers. The Michaelmas daisies raised lavender heads on dark green stalks and there were raindrops still in the bells of foxglove. I waited, drawing my shawl more closely about me in the brisk wind from the sea and watched the eagle soar high above the glen— smooth, effortless flight far removed from the earthbound cares that beset me. I envied him.

Angus came along the path, limping like some outsized Vulcan beside the dainty profusion of plants. I smiled at the thought.

60

"If it's laughter you feel, there can't be much wrong," he growled. "Why did you drag me all the way out here?"

"I don't feel like laughing, God knows! Angus—do you remember me as a child—before my father's death?"

"Do you realize MacDonald is waiting for me, and one of his ewes down sick with God knows what? And here you want to ask me about your childhood! What *is* the matter?"

"It is important, Angus. I want you to tell me what you remember. And then I'll explain," I promised.

"Oh, aye, very well. I saw you sometimes about the garden, dressed in bonnets and long coats and the like. Your father didn't want me near the house, and you were too wee to wander about on your own—the nursemaid and then Mrs. Fraser were always at your heels. It was not till your father died and you were recovering from the sickness that Mrs. Fraser sent for me and asked me to find a pony and teach you the way of riding it. You remember Tam for yourself."

It was not a promising beginning. "But what did I look like?" I asked. "Do you remember that?"

"Long skirts, dirty face and set on having your own way. Mistress, no boy of thirteen is interested in an infant who cries at the least thing and can't speak a half-dozen words!"

"*Did* I cry often?" I asked, dismayed at his picture of me.

"Well, no, not as much as some bairns. You weren't a watering pot. Still, I took no chances—I'd not care to be whipped for upsetting you." He searched my face. "Now in heaven's name, what is the matter?"

"One more question. When you—injured your leg, who was the doctor?"

"The doctor?" He stared at me in surprise. "It was Mac-Kenzie. Your father sent to Oban for him, when it was seen that the leg ought to come off."

"Oban. Then there was no doctor in the village?"

"No. He'd have starved to death while the silly fools went to Old Morag for her cures," he told me. "That's why none ever settled here."

"Then who cared for me when I had the fever?" One more hope gone!

"Mrs. Fraser. She'd let no one in the room. Several of the maids quit to flee the epidemic, moving away to Oban, it was said. There was a rumor that it was a good place to take service, so the scarlet fever might have been only an excuse. The elderly housekeeper left, too."

"Did you know Mrs. Fraser's family—her husband and children?"

"That's an extra question, but yes, I knew the Reverend. He'd a voice like thunder in the pulpit, for all he was a mild man."

"And her children?"

"They died young. I seldom saw them."

I nodded and launched into the story that Duncan Lindsay had told me beside the loch. Angus was aghast, but at the end of it he laughed grimly.

"He'll be wanting the whole of it," he said, echoing Elspeth unknowingly. "It fits the man. I'd not worry overly if I were you. As for your coloring, the Major himself is fair-haired, is he not? And with gray eyes to boot. But he calls himself a Lindsay." He reached out, and in a rare gesture, touched my shoulder. "Let it rest," he said gently. "He'll make a fool of himself, no more."

I hoped Angus was right. But I couldn't let it rest. Instead of waiting for Bruce Cameron to come, I left the key to the tower, and an apology for not presenting it in person, with Elspeth, and walked to the village.

It was not large—a scattering of houses, an old stone church surrounded by its overgrown churchyard, the Manse—nothing more than a stone house fifty yards away —the forge, and what passed as an inn.

I approached the churchyard from the rear, climbing gracelessly over the tumbled-down wall that ran along the border of MacDonald graves, and made my way to the old rowan tree where the Frasers were buried.

The earth was sunken with time, mossy and ringed with ivy that I had helped Fraser plant. Only her stone had not grown the heavy coat of lichen that eventually etched its way across the names and dates. I thought of that day so long ago, and wondered if she had asked me to come with her because these were my people also. With a finger I traced the indented letters spelling out "Catriona Fraser. 1835–1838."

Catriona Fraser. I sounded the name on my tongue, but it was no more familiar than any other name I had known all my life. It called forth no response, and I had no feeling of kinship with these people lying here, except for the love and gratitude I held in my heart for Fraser. Or was that a child's love for her mother? Mine had never known me, nor I her. There was no way to tell what I should feel.

I heard a step along the walk behind me and thought it was the old sexton. Perhaps he could add something to my meager store of knowledge. I turned to meet him, but instead I came face to face with Bruce Cameron.

"I thought you were climbing the peel tower," I said lightly.

"To be honest," he said dryly, "I got such a cold welcome at the castle that I thought I ought to ask you again if it is really all right if I explore there. Please, don't be polite—I'd speak out quickly enough if someone wanted to trespass on my lands and I didn't care for it!"

He looked rather like a small boy denied a much wanted treat. "By all means, explore. And I'll walk back part of the way with you."

He hesitated. "Before we go, I'd like to presume on our acquaintance and speak what's on my mind. I don't like to interfere or to mind business that isn't my own, but I have a feeling that no one else has told you. How well do you know the Major? Aside from the fact that you are distant cousins?"

"Not well at all," I replied, my curiosity aroused. "I saw him only once before he came a week ago, but I was a child of three then."

As if arguing with himself he turned to look up at the church tower, and the windflowers that nestled in cracks and crevices of the stone. At last he said, "It is gossip, mind you, nothing more. I oughtn't to repeat it, but you have no family to look out for you. The Major has a rather wild reputation in London. I don't know that he has ever done anything that might be—well, illegal or criminal. But he has made a name for himself at cards and with the ladies—more often, other men's wives. The latest story is that he was injured in an encounter with an irate husband." He dropped his eyes to his boots. "Not a very pleasant tale to pass on to a young lady. I'm sorry."

"Do you mean he was shot in a duel? But duels are illegal!" It would explain why the Major was so determined to keep the nature of his injury to himself. And the sling was missing last night, when we had a guest.

"I don't know the details of how it happened." The dark eyes came up to meet mine. "There's one thing more," he said.

"What is it?" I asked, hoping for the worst and unprepared for his next words.

"They say he is deeply in debt and outrunning his creditors by the narrowest of margins—and that he plans to marry a rich heiress as soon as possible to save himself from prison."

I knew then why the house and the lands were not enough. The Major must have my father's fortune as well if he would stave off the disaster that surely awaited him. I wondered what Mr. MacEwen would say about that.

4

We were leaving the churchyard and turning into the village street when we heard the commotion at the far end. A farm cart was ambling into sight, drawn by an old horse I recognized as belonging to a family whose lands bordered mine. I paused, curious, and soon realized that there was someone on the seat with Mr. Campbell. Beside me, Bruce Cameron swore sharply under his breath.

The passenger was a woman heavily wrapped in blankets, her lovely face contorted with pain and streaked with tears. I hurried forward and Mr. Campbell doffed his bonnet to me.

"Guid morning, Mistress Lindsay."

"Good morning, Mr. Campbell—what has happened?"

"The lass has had an accident in her carriage. The wheel came off and she was thrown. 'Tis a miracle, nae less, she didna break her neck. The horse had to be shot, and I left the groom to that and brought the lady in for Mrs. Hay." He jerked his head the way he had come. "What with the bairns and my wife's mither, we didna ha' room!"

I smiled at the woman beside him. The "beauty" I had wanted so desperately to attract Duncan Lindsay and make him forget both me and the will had arrived too late. She was perhaps twenty-eight, and she *was* beautiful—burnished red hair that set off the soft cream of her skin and added luster to the wide green eyes. I wondered if Mrs. Campbell had sent the woman to Mrs. Hay because of lack of room—or too great beauty.

"I'm Moira Lindsay, ma'am," I said to her. "How uncomfortable you must be! We'll soon set that right. Could you manage to travel a little farther? My house is out along the cliffs and we should be very happy to have you as our guest."

She returned my smile and said huskily, "You are very kind, Miss Lindsay! I'm Fiona Douglas, from Inverness. Yes, I can manage. It's my ankle—I think I may have broken it."

I turned to Bruce Cameron, who was still staring at her with open mouth. "Do you want to go back with us? Or shall we plan our tour of the tower another day? Either way, you already have the key."

"Tomorrow will be best. I'm sure you will be occupied by Miss Douglas. May I call later to see how she does?"

"By all means," I said, as he lifted me into the body of the wagon, and stepped back.

Campbell gave the signal to his horse and we moved off again at the same slow pace. We left Bruce Cameron by the side of the village street, frowning thoughtfully after us.

We got Fiona Douglas to the castle and into bed with a minimum of pain and effort. Elspeth examined her ankle and pronounced it badly strained but fortunately not broken. The foot was soaked in cold water to reduce the swelling and prevent discoloration, then bound in strips of linen. When I came into the room later, Miss Douglas was propped up against the pillows of her bed and wearing one of my nightgowns until her groom could bring in her cases from the carriage.

"You are looking much better," I said, smiling.

"You have been very kind, Miss Lindsay. I feel such a fool! I had decided to drive—it was an empty track, after all, and I enjoy trying my hand once in a while. I don't know what happened, perhaps it was the sheep. The horse bolted, and I couldn't hold him. We lost a wheel and overturned. I've never been so frightened in my life!"

"You were very fortunate—you might have been killed."

She shuddered. "No, don't say so. It is too terrible to think of."

"If you would care to have dinner in your room tonight, tell Elspeth or one of the maids. I'll leave you now, to rest."

She smiled up at me. "How dreadful to impose in this way!" she said. "No, I shall not make matters worse for your staff. If someone could carry me—?"

"Yes, certainly," I said, and left her then. It didn't occur to me until I was in the corridor that I had not thought to ask her what she was doing in this remote part of Argyllshire.

It was Graham, her taciturn groom, who carried Fiona down to dinner later. The Major had been away all day and I was looking forward to his reaction when they met. She was pale, but otherwise there was no outward sign of her injury. The red hair was brushed to copper and piled in a very fashionable way that emphasized her heart-shaped face to perfection. I had never seen anyone so lovely. She wore a soft green gown that darkened the color of her eyes, and when she smiled at the Major as I performed the introductions, the grim expression of his face relaxed. I was not as pleased as I ought to have been.

Dinner was a lively affair. Miss Douglas knew the same world of fashion and people in which the Major moved, and they found no difficulty with conversation, only with including me in it. I felt the small mousy country lass that I was, and wished that I had worn some of the Lindsay jewels to brighten me, even if I had no true right to them.

And so, for a time, Fiona Douglas became a part of our household.

•

I was on the stairs, on my way to bed that night when Duncan Lindsay called me back.

"I want to talk to you," he said.

"Can't it wait? I'm tired—"

"No. Come into the library." He held the door for me as if already he were master of the house. I had no choice but to follow.

The smell of leather and books came to me as we walked toward the chairs by the hearth. It was a part of this room, with its row upon row of volumes ranging upward toward the old banners in the dark cavern of the ceiling. I sat down and forced myself to meet his eyes.

"I know this is distasteful to you, Miss Lindsay. But we must talk about it, nevertheless."

"Have you written to Mr. MacEwen?" I asked coldly.

"No—not yet. Have you found any shred of proof that you are Moira Lindsay? Or for that matter, Catriona Fraser?"

"I have told you, I don't believe a word of this," I said. But in spite of myself, I was afraid. "I suspect your purpose is to cut me out of the will entirely."

"No," he said quietly, "I'd not do that."

"And how shall you prevent it, Major?" I asked angrily. "If I am indeed Catriona, what possible claim do I have to the Lindsay inheritance! At least be honest, Major!"

He stood by the hearth, leaning against the mantel, his arms folded. "I have no desire to punish you for what is none of your doing—believe me, I'm not vindictive! The day I came, I thought you were aware of the switch in children. I'm satisfied now that you weren't. It all fits, my dear! There is no escaping the fact."

"It may appear to fit in your eyes, but not in mine!"

"Then how do you explain Mrs. Fraser's letter? She calls you her child quite openly."

"Affectionately so, of course she did! We had both lost our families. It was natural for us to be close," I pointed out angrily.

"Why did she prevent my coming here, year after year,

refuse to allow me to see you or correspond with you? She was well aware of your father's wish for me to visit often and learn my duties here."

"You should know why, if you will but face the truth. You crippled Angus when you were here and I suspect Fraser wanted no part of such a monster!" I knew the words would hurt and had meant them to.

He flushed a deep red. "That was not to my credit—nor his. I have no excuse to offer you."

"So we are at an impasse, it would appear." I changed the subject, unable to probe as I would have liked.

"Let me stay beyond the fortnight. We'll explore this situation together and make a decision ourselves before we contact MacEwen."

It went against the grain to make even this small a pact with him, but I nodded agreement and rose to go. "Stay as long as necessary," I said, slightly emphasizing the last word. "I'll prove my identity even to your satisfaction."

"I hope you may," he replied gravely.

There was no peace for me. Angus was waiting by the office door and called to me as I left the library. I followed him into the chill of the little room and sat down.

"He is going to stay here until we solve the riddle," I said with a sigh of weariness.

"He still believes you are a *sibhreach*—a changeling?" His mouth tightened grimly as I nodded. "He'll learn his lesson, that one." There was a pause as Angus stared out the window into the darkness. Then, as if he had just remembered me, he turned and said briskly, "We don't know what is wrong with the ewe. MacDonald is all for shooting her now, but I've penned her up away from the others. I want to see what she has before we destroy her."

"Not anthrax!" I asked quickly.

"I can't tell. She is trembling and stands about with her head hanging down, but no staggers, no bloody flux, and no convulsions."

Anthrax could spread through a flock like wildfire, wiping it out and even affecting people. Where sheep meant livelihood to a household, anthrax was devastating. Men could die merely from handling infected wool. "Is it wise to wait?"

"No. But if it isn't anthrax we have nothing to fear. In the meantime, we're checking all the beasts."

"Well, you know best, Angus. I trust your judgment." I rose to leave. "Is there anything else?"

"No. Don't be worrying about yon Major, Mistress. He'll not be doing you any harm."

"We'll see—I hope you are right." At the door I stopped. "Has Miss Douglas' groom been settled in?"

"Aye. The Major came out and spoke to him, then had the lads put him in the wee room above the stables."

"Oh. Well enough, I suppose." I said good night and went to my room and the waiting Elspeth. She had not a little to say, most of it against Fiona Douglas.

As the candles were pinched out, she was quoting the Old Testament, an indication of strong dislike. And Fiona had been in the house for less than twenty-four hours.

I came out of a deep sleep to sounds that didn't fit the usual pattern of night noises. I lay listening, thinking perhaps Miss Douglas had summoned Elspeth because of pain in her ankle. But the direction was wrong—there were voices in the stairwell.

I reached for my dressing gown and found my slippers as I wrapped the woolen folds about me and tied the sash. Without bothering to light my candle, I felt my way to the door and opened it quietly.

There was light in the direction of the stairs, and I moved toward it. The curving stone steps projected the voices clearly.

Elspeth was talking to the Major. "—say what you will, there's no proof you didn't fall yourself!"

"And if I had been unconscious then, would I have rolled over the end of the cliff and on to the rocks below? A convenient 'accident'!"

70

I was able to see now, shrouded from their eyes by the candles' glow and the darkness at the top of the steps.

The Major was dressed in shirt and trousers, as if he had hurried into his clothes. There was a stain along one sleeve as if he had smeared it with earth, and blood trickling from a cut over his eye and dripping onto his chest. Elspeth wore a plain woolen wrapper. As I watched, Angus came up to them, his nightshirt shoved into his trousers and his hair still tousled from sleep.

"There is no one about," he said shortly. "I searched for myself."

"Of course not," the Major said grimly. "Did you expect them to wait your coming?"

"I say he was half-asleep and fell over the shrubbery," Elspeth maintained.

I spoke, and the three faces turned swiftly toward me, startled. "What has happened?"

"Mistress!" Elspeth cried, shocked that I should appear in a dressing gown, my hair hanging down my back.

"I'm sorry our noise woke you," the Major added.

"What has happened?" I repeated.

The Major replied slowly, "I heard something outside— a voice calling my name. There was nothing to be seen from the windows, so I went down to investigate. By the corner of the shrubbery, someone was waiting. I sensed the movement too late to do more than jerk around and caught the rock on my forehead instead of the back of my skull. Whoever it was ran before I could shake off the effect of the blow. If he had succeeded in knocking me unconscious, the edge of the cliff was not two feet away. I daresay I'd have gone over."

"But who would wish to do such a thing?" I demanded, shocked. It was clear, as he faced me, that something had indeed struck him and hard.

He laughed, a deep, natural laugh of pure amusement. "You ask me that?"

"You are suggesting—" I began, but he cut me off.

"—that you did it? Certainly not! You don't have the

71

strength. Whoever it was—man or woman—put considerable force into the blow. He hadn't counted on the fact that campaigning in the Crimea and elsewhere teaches a man to be wary. I never saw my attacker, but I sensed him even as he moved. Quite possibly this saved my life."

I glanced uneasily from Elspeth's grim face to Angus' expressionless one. Would they have gone so far in my behalf? "You are making too much of this, surely," I said. "No one would deliberately harm you here."

"Miss Lindsay," he said forcefully, "I am not given to dramatics. After my years of military service, I damned well know when someone wants to kill me! Let us now say I am—forewarned." He turned to go.

"Elspeth will bring warm water and bandages," I said. "You must let someone attend to that cut!"

"No need," he said shortly. "I'll see to it myself. We have lost enough sleep over this—incident. Good night."

The three of us stared at one another for an instant. Angus' eyes met mine squarely, and there was no hint of evasion in Elspeth's face, either. I could not imagine either one of them attempting murder. And yet I knew that Angus hated the Major with angry passion, that Elspeth would place my need even before her concern for her soul.

"He'll be trying to drive a wedge between us, I'm thinking," Elspeth said into the silence. "Turn us against one another and you against us. Well, 'twas not I out in yon shrubbery with a rock, but whoever it was, he has my blessing!" She turned to Angus. "Lock up as you go. I'll be seeing the Mistress back to her bed."

He nodded and turned on his heel. Elspeth came up the stairs to me, her candle shielded in her hand. I waited for her and silently followed her to my room.

Except for an ugly bruise, the Major was none the worse for his experience of the night. I saw him at breakfast but he made no reference to the incident and neither did I. He told me he was riding out with Angus to look at the sick ewe and suggested that I join them. As a buffer? I wondered, but did not say so.

"Thank you, but I plan to go to the old tower with Mr. Cameron this morning," I replied.

He frowned. "I don't care for him," he said. "The man is very likely a fortune-hunter."

I laughed. "Come now! The pot calling the kettle black!"

He scowled, giving his marred face a satanic expression. "If you are in the mood for proverbs, I'll give you one of your own. 'The de'il's no ay the ill chiel he's ca'd.' " With a nod, he turned on his heel and left the small dining room.

The devil is not always the bad child he is called. His arrogance infuriated me. I caught up my cloak to ward off the tower's chill and went out to meet Bruce Cameron.

He was standing in the gates, talking idly to Fiona Douglas' man, Graham, but as soon as he saw me, he broke off and came forward, smiling. "Good morning! Do you suppose it will last?"

I looked up at the clear skies and shook my head. "Rain before eleven," I said lightly, and we started across the courtyard.

"How is your guest this morning?"

"Still sleeping. It will do her good. There is swelling, Elspeth said, and considerable bruising. She won't be walking yet a while."

We walked to the tower in comfortable silence broken only by his comment on the bracken, permanently bent by the wind that sweeps down the Sound all year long. We skirted the edge of the loch, where the wind had already kicked up choppy waves on the blue surface. On the far horizon now were the piling clouds of rain, as I had foretold.

The tower stood tall and stark against the blue sky, the base swallowed by purple heather, which gave life to the ancient stone. As we approached, Mr. Cameron said, "I thought the peel tower was a border style."

"So it was. My ancestors were not above borrowing the idea, though, because it had its uses. The tower has four stories. The base is vaulted and the beasts were herded there in time of danger. The entrance is that small door on the next floor—and the ladder could be drawn up. Both you and your livestock would have been well-protected. Fire was the greatest danger, if the enemy got near enough to pile bracken and dried grass against the base."

"Where is the ladder now?"

"Below. Since the roof fell, we have discouraged lads from the crofts exploring inside. It is tempting to them, and someone might be hurt." I thought again of Angus falling to the tumbled rocks below the place where Duncan kept his foothold in the crevices of the square-cut stones. Windflowers and lichen and moss spilled from the mortar now, softening the harsh outline.

We unlocked the heavy door at the base, withdrew the ladder, and clambered carefully about the dim interior for an hour or more. Built into the thick walls, the now crumbling stone stairs were designed so that the defenders, retreating up two stories from the main floor to the battlemented roof, still held an advantage, even when the tower entrance had been forced. The width of the steps increased to the right, leaving the attacker a solid wall of stone not inches from his sword arm while the defender had the whole sweep of the curved stairwell in which to wield his blade. With the roof fallen in, there was no way to enjoy the magnificent view that had served lookouts in ancient times and impressed visitors in more recent centuries. Yet from the top one could have seen down the loch and across the Sound to the mountains of Mull or command the length of the Sound itself, from the castle perched above the gray-brown cliffs on the left to the hills on the right. Behind the tower, cutting into the land for several miles beyond, stretched the glen.

When he had finished, we climbed down the ladder, and restored it to its proper place. After locking the door, Bruce Cameron returned the key to me, and then we sat in the waning sunshine to watch the clouds and gulls along the Sound.

I don't know what we talked of—I found myself relaxing and enjoying his conversation, responding to it naturally and without the fears of the past week or more. Bruce Cameron was a pleasant companion, making me feel like an intelligent and interesting person in my own right, and I resolved to invite him to join us one evening. If he fell prey to Fiona Douglas' charms, Mr. Cameron would never be obvious in his attentions or neglect his hostess.

We parted at the tower for he had a long walk back to the MacDonald shieling before the rain fell. However, he had accepted my invitation for tomorrow's dinner and I returned to the castle in lighter spirits.

Fiona Douglas spent the afternoon downstairs, her foot resting on a cushioned stool. I would have found some excuse to leave the pleasant yellow sitting room and go outside but rain beat against the windows. She spoke of Inverness and Edinburgh, of London and friends who lived a life I barely understood and made me feel as provincial and unworldly as I undoubtedly was.

Trying to stem the tide, I cast about for some new topic of conversation and recalled that I had not yet asked her how she came to be in this godforsaken corner of Scotland.

She laughed. "It was a wager, my dear Moira. And I'm afraid I lost it."

"A wager?" I repeated, intrigued.

"Yes. I was visiting in Edinburgh and it was late in the evening—and a charming man said I must always be surrounded by excitement or perish. Naturally I took exception to his unkind words and told him I was quite as content in solitude as in the midst of friends. Well, the upshot was, he challenged me to spend a month in solitude and I accepted. Someone present knew of the house next to your land and got permission for me to spend a month there. This sounded ideal—a gentleman's home and

75

therefore adequate, but at the same time in the middle of nowhere, so to speak. I was on my way when the carriage overturned."

"And so you lose the wager," I said.

She sighed. "Yes, I sent Graham over with a note of regret yesterday."

I was glad when Elspeth brought in our tea.

Try as I would, there was no way I could break the barrier of the past and locate a clue to my possible identity. I could not question too openly for fear of putting doubt where none had existed before. The tenants and villagers accepted my questions with friendly indulgence. And so I heard about the little girl who came to kirk with her governess, who ate scones and heather honey at a croft door, and who tagged at the heels of gangling Angus or trotted along the tracks on a fat pony. Endless tales, some of which I remembered having heard before, others new to me, but all from those who had watched the laird's daughter with the interest set side for important people— yet who never really saw *me*. The Frasers' servant was long since dead, and undoubtedly Mrs. MacNeil, the housekeeper before Elspeth, was as well, for she had been in her fifties eighteen years before. One old woman recalled I had been ill in the scarlet fever epidemic because her granddaughter had it at the same time, but the length of my stay in the sickroom escaped her.

"We were worrit, Mistress, you were the laird's ain daughter. Poor Mrs. Fraser lost her ain bairn nursing you night and day for fear of the heart ailment from it."

But she couldn't recall what Catriona looked like. "Why did no one send for the doctor?" I asked then.

"Och, and what would he be doing here? He had his hands full and could na' spare the time for us sae far fra' his regular patients."

And so it went. It was interesting, even enlightening to see myself through others' eyes, but scarcely proof to offer against Duncan Lindsay's charges.

While I was making my inquiries in the rain the Major was entertaining Miss Douglas. Although it was my duty, I found it increasingly difficult to sit and talk with her, and instead made excuses of having to attend to household affairs or call upon my tenants. He seemed to enjoy her company.

I loved this world which they must find so boring. I had seen the sea rise up in anger like an avenging God, sending spray like imprecations against the cliff walls. And the loch so still that wildfowl floated in their own reflections as if painted upon the surface. Sunset gilding the castle's plain stone to warm gold, and moonlight etching the stark contrast of battlement against sky. I had watched dawn burst over the glen on midsummer's morn, filtering through the lingering mists and catching dewdrops on the turf like lost diamonds. Winter nights when the stars hung so low that they seemed caught on the rim of the sea and danced on the hilltops. These were the moods of the House of Storms, and had no place in the busy life Fiona Douglas and the Major loved.

Yet she made me feel—oh, inadequate, I suppose—like an awkward girl, a country girl, for all that I was (as far as she knew) a great heiress in my own right.

And so, my face as dour as the day, I came back to the castle in anything but the proper spirits for an intimate dinner party.

I wore my blue silk, for it was the most becoming of my dresses, and cursed the dampness that once more curled my rebellious hair in every direction but that of the brush.

While Elspeth watched in grim disapproval, I brought out the cases containing my mother's jewelry and tried each piece. But diamonds and rubies are designed to sparkle against the pure white of skin and looked only tawdry against the blue of the gown. I bit my lip in dissatisfaction as I tilted my head to view myself in the mirror. No, they would not do. Even the brooches, worn at the high lace collar, were too much, as if I had the money

77

to buy such trinkets but not the taste with which to wear them.

"Blast!" I said, and heard Elspeth cluck her tongue. "Put them away! If I were certain that I was Moira Lindsay, I would order a dozen new gowns tomorrow—cut low as the Queen wears them, and without sleeves."

"And die of pneumonia," she said, coming forward to take the cases and lock them away. "Virtue is the only ornament of a good woman."

"Yes, well, it stands up poorly beside copper hair and creamy skin!" I retorted. I looked at myself once more. Too plain. And then I remembered my lovely new shawl in the Lindsay tartan. I searched it out and arranged it over my shoulder, as a woman wears the colors of her clan, and into the heavy folds I pinned the badge that Angus had given me.

The effect was splendidly Scottish, though not quite what one might wear to such a dinner as this. I smiled at my reflection and the long-lashed hazel eyes smiled back. "I'm ready," I told Elspeth finally. She opened the door for me and stepped back.

"You are looking fine, Miss Moira, though well I know why!" She shook her head. "That woman should have broken her neck, not her ankle!"

"It isn't broken, thank God!" I replied, and turned from my mirror to go down the stairs.

Though Cook had grumbled about the extra work involved in preparing meals for guests and then in concocting a menu for a dinner party that would not shame us in the eyes of our visitors, she clearly enjoyed the challenge. There were three courses and four removes, ending with a chantilly torte that quite took me by surprise. I had never been so indulged in my life—perhaps because, reared as I had been on good but plain fare, I had never thought to request such delicacies.

The wines had been laid down in my father's day, and I left to the Major the choice of what was most suitable.

Fortunately, my father had known what he was about, and my cousin informed me that the cellar was excellent. Elspeth eyed the array of dusty bottles with dislike, thinking no doubt that half the number would have been sufficient, but she set about washing up the antique crystal goblets without a word.

I had chosen to use the formal dining room, even though there were only four of us. The long expanse of polished refectory table was covered with damask and set with the Sèvres service and the heavy crested silver. Tall, ornately wrought candlesticks, undoubtedly from some devastated abbey, marched in sentinel splendor down the cloth, and the massive epergne was replaced with a silver bowl of flowers, which I arranged in a low, flowing style that would not block conversation.

In all truth, I had enjoyed these preparations, my first attempt at entertaining on the grand scale, and wished that we were not so remote from civilization, after all. It would have been thought ostentatious had I invited the Hays or any of the other local families to such a display of grandeur, and therefore I had never seen the room so lovely. The heavy crimson drapes, drawn over the windows in the lingering twilight, caught the candle glow, and the gilt frames of the Highland landscapes enhanced the polished paneling of the walls. So it must have looked in my father's day, when houseguests laughed and chatted about the table, or lingered over their port while the ladies retired to the brightness—and warmth—of the drawing room. A new world to me, but one I knew how to appreciate for having lacked it all these years.

When we gathered in the drawing room for sherry, I found myself alone with the Major, in elegant black, and Bruce Cameron, apologetic for not having brought evening clothes with him. Fiona Douglas had not come down. The three of us kept conversation to generalities and were making headway toward a relaxed and pleasant relationship when Elspeth opened the door and Graham walked in with Fiona Douglas in his arms.

I could not imagine a more dramatic entrance. Graham paused as Duncan Lindsay brought forward a chair and Bruce Cameron hastened to help the groom settle Fiona upon it. And all the while, Fiona Douglas said nothing, merely smiled and received their courtesies as if these were her due.

I must admit she might have been mute entirely and no one would have noticed. Dressed in black, with a fall of lace that cupped her shoulders and frothed about the low-cut neck of her gown, her burnished copper hair piled high and set with a diamond clip before spilling in two long curls down her creamy throat, the wide green eyes sparkling with mischief, she presented quite a picture. Even I stood in awe of such beauty, and what effect must it have had on the two men!

I made the introductions in case Fiona Douglas did not remember meeting Mr. Cameron in the village. But she claimed she remembered, and he was soon drawn into her circle, almost, it seemed, against his will.

As I sipped my sherry and watched the interplay before me, I must confess that I was guilty of a very unladylike wish that she had been at least sixty before she had ventured into this corner of Argyllshire. Her wardrobe was ravishing for one who had accepted a wager to remain in solitude for a month. Was she the sort of woman who traveled even into the antipodes with a full complement of fashionable clothes, or had she hoped to find, even in so isolated a spot, just such sport as this? She could not have known that two such attractive men were in the neighborhood to help her while away the time with gay flirtations.

Or had she? It was an interesting thought. I tended to forget that the Major would inherit a sizable estate and the wealth to maintain it, even without my father's personal fortune. He was a very eligible bachelor by any definition, and not every woman had my reasons to dislike him so thoroughly.

5

Thanks to Bruce Cameron, my dinner party was a success. He kept the conversation moving smoothly, never allowing it to slip beyond my reach and recapturing somehow the early pleasantness in the drawing room. While he was clearly attracted to Fiona—I saw his eyes flicker in her direction from time to time—he left her to the Major. She seemed to prefer it that way.

It was difficult not to picture her in my place, the lovely and charming hostess of the House of Storms and the perfect wife for Duncan Lindsay. But I did not let my thoughts roam too far in that direction, for as long as I could fight, the House of Storms was mine.

To give credit where it was due, that night Fiona Douglas gave me the will to fight. I suppose one does not stand to lose one's lifelong identity without some crisis of the nerves, and in spite of my best resolves, I had felt myself sinking into the belief that I was more likely Catriona Fraser than Moira Lindsay. But seated at the head of the table this evening, facing the Major down the row of candlesticks, I felt every inch a Lindsay. Perhaps Fiona Douglas had unknowingly tapped the strange feminine streak of contrariness that springs up in every woman who is challenged by another of her sex. The Lindsay shawl lay warm about my shoulders and the laird's crest caught the colors of candlelight deep within its smoky depths. And while I knew beyond doubt that I could never compete with the Fionas of this world, I was content.

I laughed at some remark that Mr. Cameron had made, a genuine laugh from the heart that reflected my new-found peace. And Duncan Lindsay lifted his head to give me a long, considering look. Fiona had to speak to him twice before he heard her—surely a new experience for her. But he made up for his discourtesy by concentrating his attention on her in a most flattering way.

It is strange how a topic will begin at a party, someone else picks it up and changes the direction ever so slightly, and suddenly the excitement of it catches up all the guests. I don't really know how this one began, but it was Bruce Cameron who shifted it from unusual traveling experiences to the oddities to be found in Scotland. He began a list with the kilt—"women in long skirts and men in short ones"—and then the Major added the Highland cattle, those shaggy, gracefully horned beasts that are so unlike the usual concept of the friendly cow. Miss Douglas said that her grandfather's father had seen the great monster of Loch Ness. I suggested our whisky, at which the gentlemen laughed.

"The Sight," continued Fiona, not to be outdone. "Coinneach Odhar—Kenneth the Sallow—and Thomas of Ercildoune."

"It isn't distinctly Scottish," the Major objected. "The Irish, among others, claim to have the Sight."

"They claim whisky as well!" she pouted prettily.

"Ah, but there we can prove them wrong!" Cameron put in. He turned to me. "Did you know that there was a seer of sorts on your land? I have heard the MacDonalds speak of her—and with respect."

"Who is she?" Fiona Douglas asked, delighted to find a new interest. "Do you know her?"

"Old Morag," I said reluctantly. "But she is more involved with cures than magic, though some of the crofters like to associate the two."

In spite of my efforts to dissuade her, Fiona was much taken with the idea. I suppose it was the boredom of her convalescence that made her snatch at trifles to amuse her. At first she insisted I send for Old Morag to have our fortunes told. I refused point-blank. I would not have the old woman walk such a distance for the sake of a mere whim.

"She is old, and not well," I said. "I can't ask such a thing of her."

"If I could be driven there, perhaps she would cure me!"

There was no track into the area where Old Morag lived, and I told her so. In the end, it was decided that we would go on horseback and after Fiona had consulted Old Morag about her ankle, she would cajole her into telling our fortunes as well. To do him justice, the Major was not especially taken with her suggestion, but he politely agreed to the plan.

And so the dinner party came to an amicable and pleasant conclusion with an engagement to meet on the morrow for our excursion to Old Morag's wee croft. I resolved to send a groom ahead with the news of our coming, so that the old woman could be out if she had no desire to deal with us. With that decided, I felt better. I might smile at her prophecies myself, but I would not have her ridiculed for Fiona's pleasure.

Bruce Cameron made his farewells and left, shortly after which Fiona herself retired. I suspected her ankle was troubling her more than she admitted, but better the pain in company than comfort in solitude. I still could not picture her choosing to spend a month alone in any isolated spot, whatever the wager. Companionship, laughter, excitement—these were in her blood.

After Graham had come to take her away, I excused myself as well. The evening had been tiring. The Major followed me to the foot of the stairs to hand me my candle.

"You don't care for the expedition tomorrow?" he asked.

"I—it is just that I am afraid that Morag will be hurt by their amusement. I would not have it so."

"Then we shall not go."

I frowned. "No, you have promised," I said, and then to chase away the shadows I smiled. "If she is indeed a seer, Morag knows we are coming, and why."

He gave the candle to me. "It was a successful evening. For your sake I am glad."

I murmured a disjointed reply and turned away. His sudden kindness had caught me unaware. Or—perhaps he thought I was enjoying Bruce Cameron's company more than I ought. Until Mr. MacEwen pronounced me otherwise, I was still an heiress. If the Major *was* badly in debt, he might close his eyes to even such beauty as Fiona possessed, if the choice came between that and my money.

"Wait," he said, and touched the Lindsay crest on my shoulder. "Where did you come by this?"

"It was a gift on my coming of age," I replied, holding the candle so that he might see the badge more clearly.

"From whom?" he asked.

"From Angus, the steward."

His face changed subtly. "So," he said softly. "It was true after all."

"What was?" I asked quickly.

"Nothing of importance. Sleep well." His eyes met mine and then he turned on his heel and was gone.

I went slowly up the stairs, listening to his steps echo down the corridor and vanish into the Turkey carpet of the library.

There was rain in the early morning, but the weather cleared sufficiently for our excursion and we set out at ten-thirty.

Angus, his face giving every indication of displeasure, was to accompany us. Since the early hour at which I had sent the groom on his errand to Old Morag's croft he had known of our plans and had presented himself in the role of faithful gilly along to carry the lunch basket. This last Elspeth had arranged for the Major, who had suggested that Miss Douglas should break the trip to spare her ankle as much as possible. Angus would give me no reason for his decision to ride with us other than his general distrust of my companions.

He was one of the few men, surely, who was immune to Fiona Douglas. After the briefest of nods at my introduction, he dropped back to his place at the rear of the group and spoke to no one.

We set a leisurely pace, stopping from time to time to admire a particularly fine view or, once, to watch an old and wise sheep dog round up his charges and take them back to the shepherd standing on a far hill. Guided by the sharp whistles of the man, the dog made his task seem graceful and effortless, though I knew how hardworking he actually was. We passed several crofts, the tenants stepping to the door to nod to us, or if we were too far away, to watch curiously as we passed.

As we cut through the narrow glen where the Mac-Donald croft was built, one of the little girls shyly waved to Bruce Cameron and he responded with a smile and a word of greeting. One of the older boys stood with his hands behind his back before a younger brother and was chanting the old rhyme:

> "Nieve-nievie nick nack,
> Whit haun wull ye tak?
> Tak the richt, tak the wrang,
> I'll beguile ye gin I can."

I caught sight of half a scone hidden in his palm while the younger child danced gleefully and debated which choice of hands to make.

Morag's croft was high on a windswept hillside, remote and lonely. A small vegetable patch grew on the sheltered southern side and herbs rambled in the gardens along the walls. There were flowers as well, but only those such as marigold and foxglove, which had medicinal purposes. Bunches of herbs lay in the sun to dry, and I knew that more hung in the smoke-blackened rafters above the hearth. Morag herself was sitting before the open door blending sachets from the collection of small sacks at her feet.

As we drew rein, she glanced at us, her gray, penetrating eyes moving from one face to another. As she looked at Bruce Cameron, her hands stilled at their task and she smiled, as if she recognized someone she had been expecting for a very long time. Then her eyes clouded, in the way of the old, and the fleeting impression was lost. Cameron, busy helping Fiona from her saddle, had not seen it, but Angus had and I saw his black brows twitch together thoughtfully.

I greeted Morag formally, as was her due, and presented my guests to her. She responded with the courtesy of old Highland tradition and bade them welcome.

After helping Fiona into the house to have her ankle examined, Bruce Cameron returned to wait with us.

"Does she live here completely alone?" he asked.

"Yes, except for an old sheep dog whose leg she mended a long time ago. He is probably lying across the hearth or under the bed."

"I thought cats or hares were the proper familiars," Cameron said with a smile that robbed his words of offense.

"Only the dog. I've never known him to leave the croft."

"Where did she come by her herbs?" the Major asked, walking about the neat gardens. "I didn't know that Scotland grew such variety."

"When she came here she brought them with her. The crofters say she can grow anything, cure any animal, or person, for that matter. Which reminds me—" I said, turning to Angus, "have you thought to have her look at the ewe?"

"She says 'tis nought but something it ate," he replied. "We still have it penned." He gathered up the reins. "I'll be leading the horses down to the burn, Mistress." Without waiting for me to answer, he took them away, favoring his bad knee as he made his way down the slope.

"He's a dour Scot," Bruce Cameron said. "I suppose, though, he is an old retainer."

"Angus?" I said, and laughed at the description. But I wouldn't give him away—whatever his reasons, I trusted Angus' judgment implicitly. "We are accustomed to his gruffness. But yes, he has served us well."

The Major gave no indication that he had heard the exchange and I adroitly shifted the subject.

Fiona called to us from the cottage as Morag opened the door. She was smiling broadly. "Your turn! I've had my ankle seen to and my palm read." She tilted her head to glance at the Major out of the corners of her eyes. "A handsome man is to be my downfall," she said. "Shall I trust you to carry me back to my horse?"

Whatever Morag had said to her, Fiona was in excellent spirits and greatly pleased. With a smiling rejoinder, the Major brought her to sit upon a rock in the paling sunlight. Bruce Cameron gallantly suggested that I go next, but Morag motioned to the Major. He followed her indoors.

After a time the Major returned, frowning thoughtfully. Even Fiona couldn't persuade him to tell what he had heard.

"But that is half the fun," she cried.

"She tells me it won't come true, if I speak of it," he replied, smiling. "Would you have me spoil my future for your sake?"

My turn came at last, and I passed Bruce Cameron, who was shaking his head in mock wonder. "I shall come by my just reward," he said. "All that I deserve is waiting for me."

"There is nothing left for me!" I chided, and crossed the threshold.

Morag was waiting for me in the gloomy shadows by the hearth. "I thank you for your messenger, Mistress," she said as I closed the door behind me.

"They are bored, Morag. I'm sorry."

"I have spoken your future, Mistress. There is no more

to tell—save one final thing. The devil has two horns to his head and death has two hands—I see this clearly, Mistress. Remember it."

"I shall," I replied, uncertainly, once more caught up in her spell. "Is there still danger in the mist for me?"

"Aye, Mistress," she replied gravely. "There is nought to be done to spare you grief. I have warned you, and I can do no more. Remember." She smiled gently, her worn face softening. "My time is nigh at an end. Death waits for me outside, but I am old and have no regrets."

I was stirred by the simple poetry of her words, the ancient imagery that was recaptured by this old Highland woman whose eyes saw beyond the limits of her stone croft and whose world was bordered by her spirit, not her body. I felt the tears well up as the soft voice went on.

"If you please, Mistress, I'd be buried in the glen by yon big stone above the croft, not in the kirkyard. I'd be wanting to know the heather was in bloom and feel the hoof of the deer. I'd not be happy in the kirkyard with so many folk about me."

"It shall be so, Morag. I promise."

She nodded, accepting my word. An ancient grace spoke in this wise woman of the glen.

I walked to the door and then, with my hand upon the latch, I turned. She had said something to me on the day of my coming of age when she walked to the castle to greet me. She had called me my mother's daughter. It had had no special significance to me then, other than a gracious gesture on her part. Now I realized what this could mean to me. In all my questionings, I had not thought to come to Morag.

"Do you remember my mother?" I asked slowly, afraid to hear her answer. "Were you here when I was born?"

"Aye, Mistress. I helped with the birthing." Her eyes clouded as if they looked into the past.

"And when I was ill—with scarlet fever—were you there also?"

"Aye, Mistress. I was there."

I took a deep breath to steady my voice. "Whose child am I, Morag?" I asked. "Can you tell me that?" Hope rose wildly within me.

She lifted her head and looked into my face. "You are your mother's daughter, Mistress. The daughter of Ealasaid Moira Ogilvie Lindsay, wife of the laird of the House of Storms. And no other."

"Are you sure, Morag? Are you very sure?" I whispered.

"Aye, Mistress. There is no changeling in the House of Storms."

I nodded gratefully and turned back to the door, feeling the relief flood through me like a warmth in my blood.

Her voice reached me from a distance. "She was a very good woman, and her heart was as pure as her face was lovely. In my time of need she listened to me and did for me what few women do willingly, grudging none of herself or her pride. I have served her, and you in her place, ever since. I am hers, in the grave or out of it, and all that are mine will be the same."

"What did you ask of her, Morag?"

"It is not the time to tell you this, Mistress. One day, perhaps. Not now." There was a firmness in her voice, and I pressed no further. "Be silent, Mistress, till the time for truth comes. It will be enough."

"Yes. I will. Thank you, Morag. If there was ever a debt, you have paid it now, in full."

"Not yet, Mistress. Not completely," she said with finality.

I nodded and lifted the latch, schooling my face to show none of the emotion I felt raging through me. I had my proof and against that Duncan Lindsay could do what he liked. I was safe. I was Moira, not Catriona Fraser. There was no doubting Morag's words—she had known me all my life, from the very first breath of it, and had stood watch in my sickroom. There had been no substitution of children. Anna Fraser had not betrayed her trust and I had not lived my life as a pensioner of a dead child. Morag knew that.

I smiled at her over my shoulder and stepped out into the sunlight.

I found it easy to mask my feelings for the sheer joy of misleading the Major. As I closed the door of Morag's croft, I looked at the ring of faces waiting for my first words. Fiona Douglas appeared to be curious, there was open interest in Bruce Cameron's eyes, and the Major was scanning my expression as if he could read beneath the flesh and into the mind. Angus, standing a little apart, watched me warily.

"You were gone a very long time," Fiona said, speaking first. "I must say, I hope you have no desire to keep your fortune to yourself."

"No, I can't possibly do that," I replied, laughing. "She tells me I am to travel far into unknown lands, looking for my happiness. There is a man waiting for me there, a handsome mysterious stranger who will be known by his dark red hair and his foreign manner. We shall meet with all sorts of difficulties, but if I persevere, he shall be mine. We shall live by the sea and have six sons."

There was an undercurrent of relief as I embroidered my tale, and an outburst of laughter as I finished. The Major was watching me still, but without the same intensity of interest.

"You have by far the best reading," Bruce Cameron said. "Did you slip her an extra coin?"

"No," I replied lightly. "I own the croft." Angus brought up the horses and we mounted. "Shall we picnic on the hill above the loch? The view is fine there, and the heather thick."

There was general agreement and the Major led the procession. I stared at his flat, straight back and the superb cavalryman's seat in the saddle. Had I misled him with my silly banter? If I was to play the game of wits with Duncan Lindsay, I must be on my guard every moment. He was too intelligent, too much a man of the world to be led astray by an inexperienced girl. If I would give him enough rope to hang himself, I must be careful not to entangle myself in the process. If he had come to Scotland to pay his debts at my expense, even the firm of MacEwen, Galbraith and MacEwen would be forced to admit that Duncan Lindsay was not fit to be master of my estates, or my husband. Morag was right—silence was to my advantage for the present while I sent for the solicitor. In the meantime, I must be wary of betraying myself before I was ready.

We rode with gaiety, for Fiona was in high spirits and used her finely honed wit to strike a spark of response from Bruce Cameron and the Major. I kept silent, for fear of seeming too suddenly released from the depression of the past week. Angus, bringing up the rear with the picnic basket, was watching us covertly as if he sifted each word, measured every glance. I felt that he had no intention of leaving me alone with three strangers, and was in turn irked and then grateful for his care. His attitude had subtly changed since leaving Morag's croft, though he maintained his dour expression—he had not cared for our visit to the old woman, that much was clear.

For our luncheon we chose the hillside above the loch on the western side. While Angus took the horses down to the loch to drink and graze, the Major volunteered to carry Fiona anywhere she selected. With much laughter and indecision, she sent the Major to investigate the terrain within twenty yards, vowing she could not bear to find herself seated on an ant's nest or any other crawling beastie. Impatient, I wondered how the Major could lift her at all with his injured arm. Finally he carried her to a good flat stone and she settled herself gracefully, taking care to let her trimly booted foot extend full length.

Bruce Cameron, who had been guarding the basket all this while, brought it forward and said lightly that he hoped its weight indicated a prodigal spread.

Elspeth had provided just that. There were meat pies and smoked salmon, pastries and honey, cheese and thick slices of roast mutton from the spring crop of lambs. It was Highland fare, but I saw Fiona eat as well as the men without a thought for the missing dainties she must have preferred. She insisted that the Major try the first slice of salmon to judge if its taste was too strong, but once reassured, she accepted his serving her plate. Cameron declined, as I did, and concentrated on the mutton.

"You are fortunate in your cook," he said. "Having walked a good deal and taken my meals where I found them, I've seen every variety of Highland cooking. To be honest, I was hungry enough to eat whatever was set before me—saving haggis—but the cook at the House of Storms puts them all to shame."

"I like the name. Storm Castle. Very picturesque," Fiona said.

We could see it, high on its cliff, from where we sat. Distance softened the walls' massive strength and smoothed the turf that spread before them. It was still mine—I had all the rights of blood and heritage that made it so. And God willing, I would keep it! Looking up, I caught the Major's gray eyes and had to force myself to drop my own first. I would have preferred to challenge him, but dared not. It was too soon.

"Will you walk with me?" he asked. Bruce Cameron was talking to Fiona.

"Yes," I said reluctantly, and he gave me a helping hand to rise. We moved off, picking our way through the heather, stopping on the crest of the hill and just out of earshot of the other two.

"You should not encourage Cameron to linger in this neighborhood," he said. "Whatever his reasons for a walking tour in this part of Scotland, he has surely seen all there is to see at the House of Storms and along the Sound."

I stared at him in angry amazement. "Do you dare to tell me what I may do in my own home? For it *is* my home until you have proven otherwise, Major Lindsay!"

"For God's sake, must you call me Major Lindsay as if

the name signified half of hell's imps?" he asked, angry in his turn. "We are distant cousins, after all!"

"So you admit it!" I cried, throwing the words back into his face. "I am *not* Catriona Fraser!"

"You may or may not be—but in the eyes of the law, we are cousins for the present, and I remind you that it is you yourself who insist we are indeed related. And don't change the subject."

"Very well," I said, mastering my fury. "And as long as I am mistress of my house, I shall choose my guests."

He was on the point of retorting in kind, then thought better of it, staring off across the gray–blue waters of the Sound. "I can understand your position," he said slowly. "It had not occurred to me until last night that in proving you to be the governess' child I leave you with no means of supporting yourself. That isn't my intention, I assure you. If you are indeed Catriona, I'll arrange a trust for you—"

I could stand it no longer. "How kind of you, Major! Or is that a new form of bribe? I'd rather earn my livelihood as a governess than accept your charity!"

The scarred face darkened with fury or shame, I couldn't be sure which it was, and his eyes held mine. "I should like the taming of you," he said through clenched teeth, "and may yet have it!"

I wheeled away from him and walked back the way we had come. Bruce Cameron glanced up as I approached and smiled understandingly at my flushed face, but he made no comment. Fiona, busy repacking the remains of the luncheon, hadn't noticed—and I was grateful for that.

The paling sunlight had brought with it the cooler sea winds and we decided to turn homeward. As we came around the loch, Bruce Cameron dropped back to ride beside me and we watched Fiona and the Major, still talking amiably, move out of hearing.

"It is none of my concern," he began slowly, "and I

have no right to intrude, but—I do know the Major rather better than you do. If you want someone to talk to, I'll listen and help, if I can. Remember that."

I nodded. I was not yet ready to confide in anyone, although I appreciated his gesture. He seemed to be a sympathetic listener and a reliable one, able to keep his own counsel and to respect the rights of others. It would be an easy matter to tell him of the worries that beset me. But not yet.

For the rest of the way home we maintained a lightly bantering conversation, avoiding the subject of the Major.

He declined a second invitation to dinner, saying he thought that Fiona was more tired than she cared to admit. It was true—there was a tightness about her mouth. Perhaps she should not have ridden so far, even with the injured ankle in the side saddle, safely out of harm's way. I felt rather guilty that I, as hostess, had let her risk the outing. On the other hand, she had been the one who insisted on visiting Old Morag.

Fiona retired to her room to rest and I busied myself with my duties, leaving the Major to entertain himself. By the time the dinner hour had arrived, my anger had cooled. The Major's offer to set up a trust for me out of my own father's money had rankled deep. I tried to tell myself that he had wished to be generous, not insulting. As he saw the situation, I was indeed Catriona Fraser. Still, I was furious with him and with myself for having permitted him the opportunity to speak of such things. I knew now beyond the shadow of a doubt that I was Moira Lindsay. As soon as possible, I must take Mr. MacEwen to the croft and let him hear for himself how false the Major's contentions were. And then I would be left in peace at the House of Storms.

I was the first to enter the drawing room, and Fiona joined me shortly. She appeared to be feeling refreshed, and tonight she wore a gown of antique gold, a flattering color against her skin. Graham deposited her in a chair by the hearth and then withdrew as silently as he had entered. I found I didn't care for the man—he was so completely the dour, uncommunicative kind. Undoubtedly he made an excellent and devoted servant for Fiona, but I preferred the pleasant-faced, friendly lads who served in my own stables.

Fiona and I talked at random while waiting for the Major to join us. She claimed that the herbs given to her by Morag had been remarkably effective. They had been mixed with warm water and used as a soothing bath, taking away much of the afternoon's discomfort. I found myself wishing for a miraculous cure.

Conversation faltered after a time. The Major was late. I rang for Elspeth and asked her to knock on his door. Dinner would be spoiled if we waited any longer. She nodded grimly and went out, only to return to tell me that he was not in his room.

"The door is locked, Mistress," she added with disapproval. "As if we were savages, or worse still, thieves!"

"I'm sure he meant no such thing, Elspeth," I replied soothingly. "Will you send someone to the stables? And ask Cook to set back dinner for half an hour."

"She'll not be liking that!" Elspeth warned and closed the door ungently as she left.

To ease the awkwardness of the situation, Fiona began a tale about one of her friends whose predilection for gaming made him willing to accept any wager his many acquaintances could think up. But I was not really listening. Instead, I wondered where the Major could be. Perhaps I had made him angry enough to write to MacEwen, Galbraith and MacEwen and he had gone into the village with the letter to post it. Then we would have Mr. MacEwen down upon us with preconceived notions that would surely prejudice *my* case.

I was telling myself that such were the rewards of letting one's temper get the better of one's good judgment and was prepared for the worst when Elspeth returned.

"He's not riding out, Mistress," she said. "The lads say they've not seen him since the afternoon. And he has not gone for a walk, for the gardener was working by the gate and says no one has left here at all. He's up to something, wherever he is! I'll have the maids search the house—"

Suddenly I remembered the attempt on the Major's life in the night, and felt a cold chill down my spine.

"Are you certain he isn't in his room?" I asked sharply, without waiting for her to finish.

"I can't be seeing through doors, Miss Moira, and well you know it! The lock is turned and there is no key on the inside. So much I can say."

I excused myself to Fiona and hurried Elspeth outside. "Where is the master set of keys? Do you have them?" I demanded as soon as the drawing room door swung shut behind me.

"They are in the housekeeper's cupboard where they always are, Miss Moira."

"Fetch them, will you? I'll go upstairs. And hurry!" I said. Lifting my skirts with both hands, I ran up the stairs. It was hard to say what drove me. I was not given to such forebodings, and yet I was uneasily aware that what had happened once might readily happen again. I had to take the chance that he was telling the truth about his first accident and might truly be in trouble now.

Out of breath when I reached the door, I gave my pounding heart the several seconds necessary to calm it and then listened with my ear against the heavy wood.

The room was silent. There was no sound at all, nothing to indicate that the room was occupied, and yet I knew that it was. Emptiness has a quiet of its own, and this was entirely different. Someone was there. I knocked sharply on the panel and called his name but there was no answer from within. After several seconds I repeated this, but still heard nothing. After the third try I waited impatiently for Elspeth to come with the keys.

She arrived in grim silence and passed over the heavy ring. With trembling fingers I fitted the great iron key into the lock and turned it. The well-oiled bolt slid back smoothly and I turned the knob, swinging wide the door.

The room was lighted only by the lingering paleness of the evening sky, but I had no difficulty picking out the figure of Duncan Lindsay sprawled across the bed, face down. The stillness of his body was unnatural, deathlike.

"Good God!" I whispered and ran toward the bed.

"Miss Moira—no!" Elspeth cried out and tried to catch my arm.

I eluded her and reached the Major in two steps. I touched his shoulder with gentle fingers and felt unspeakable relief when I realized that it was warm. At least he was alive.

"Open a window, Elspeth, and then light one of the candles. Quickly," I ordered.

The sound of my voice must have reached him suddenly, for he jerked back from me, then relaxed again as he realized who I was.

"Keep them out of here!" he said with difficulty. "Leave me alone!"

"You are ill—we want to help!" I replied. "You need our help!"

"I'm all right—get out!" He tried to get to his feet.

"You mustn't—please, Major, lie down—why won't you let us help?"

Elspeth brought forward the candle and his face was a ghastly hue.

"I don't trust anyone—I dare not," he whispered, holding on to the shreds of consciousness with all the strength of his will.

"But why?" I asked, and had to bend low to hear the faint words.

"Someone has tried to poison me," he said, and as his hold on himself slipped away, he reached out and caught my hand.

6

I scarcely remember the next hours. They sped by in a confusion of fear and uncertainty and frantic effort as we worked over Duncan Lindsay. Elspeth tried again and again to send me from the room, but I stubbornly remained.

"Not fitting," she had grumbled. "'Tis my work, not for the likes of you. And you'll spoil that gown, mark my words, and it being your best!"

But I remembered the way the Major's fingers had gripped my hand as if I were the bulwark between him and the nightmare he was enduring. No one could have persuaded me to go, for I knew that he would expect to see me there beside him when his mind cleared.

As soon as he had lapsed into unconsciousness, I had sent Elspeth for Angus. Between the two of them they had managed to undress the Major and get him into bed while I opened the windows to air the room and set about putting it into order. When this was done, we forced paregoric into the Major to ease the pain as much as possible and then kept him warm with blankets and heated stones, for he shook like a man in fever and yet fought the constrictions of the bedclothes. He managed to tolerate the second spoonful of paregoric, and then an hour later, one of Elspeth's remedies, but his face was still drawn and white, and his pulse rate erratic.

"Will he die?" I asked Elspeth desperately.

" 'Twas nought but something he ate, Mistress," she said dampingly. " 'Tis like the English to make a to-do over emptying the contents of his stomach. Like enough he'll feel the fool when he knows the uproar he started. I'll have Cook make up a broth."

I had never seen anyone so ill, and could find no comfort in her words. While she was away in the kitchens, I sat by the bed and stared down at the scarred face on the pillows. Against the pale skin the saber's mark was livid, but somehow with the cold gray eyes closed and the muscles of the face relaxed, the Major appeared less sardonic, more human. The shallow, rasping breathing seemed to fill the room and I caught myself listening intently, for fear it would stop.

My life would be happier if this man died, and yet I did not have even the smallest wish for that. Certainly I could never take his life. My people had always fought—and indeed, died—to hold these lands, but even as they did so, they knew the right was theirs as they faced their enemies. There had been no need for murder, no necessity for stealth. They faced their danger and met it squarely, honestly, in open confrontation. I must do the same. Perhaps the Major had realized this, had known what value I placed on my own honor. Perhaps that was why in his extremity he had placed his trust in me. It was odd that he would choose me when I had the most to gain from his death, and I was strangely moved.

Had he been poisoned as he had said? But Elspeth had dismissed it as bad food. Spoilage could not always be tasted. One of the stable lads had once been quite ill after eating fresh eggs beaten in a jug of milk, and was a week or longer in his bed. Cook had said he should have taken the precaution of adding whisky to the jug, as well. Yet the Major had eaten with us at luncheon, and with me at breakfast. Surely any food that had been spoiled would have affected someone else as well!

Elspeth returned with the broth to heat upon the hearth, but we were unable to feed the Major anything more than weak tea. This he tolerated in minor amounts and the frightening convulsions grew less frequent. As the windy dawn broke and the darkness lifted on the hillside to the east, Duncan Lindsay slept at last, a true sleep and not the half-conscious drifting that had troubled the night.

I sat by the bed, weary and drained of every emotion except relief. The low voices of Angus and Elspeth talking by the hearth floated away from my understanding and into some limbo that rose and fell like the sea. I believe that I would have been asleep myself in only a matter of minutes when suddenly I came clearly, startlingly awake.

"Dear God!" I cried, and whirled toward the hearth and the two standing by it, staring now in my direction. "Fiona!" For all I knew, she was sitting in the drawing room, still waiting for her dinner. In my all-consuming worry for the Major, I had not had one thought to spare for my guest.

Elspeth smiled. "In her bed and asleep these many hours. What's more, she ate her dinner, too, which is more than can be said for some I know."

I smiled back. Thank the Lord that Elspeth at least had kept her wits about her. I realized I had missed dinner, but had no desire for food after the night's ordeal. Angus came to stand by the bed.

"Go to your room and sleep. There is no more to be done here," he said quietly. "I'll watch in your stead."

"No," I said stubbornly. "I must stay here until he is awake." With that the concern on the steward's face changed to cold wariness.

"You believe that he was poisoned?" he asked sternly.

I shook my head wearily. "I don't know what to believe, and I don't have any idea why he has been ill. But *he* thought it was poison, Angus. He didn't want you or Elspeth near him, so I stayed—I'd not have either of you blamed for something you had no part in doing! And if he had—died, there might have been doubts. He was depending on me to keep him safe—I want him to know that I did just that. Angus, if he blames you or Elspeth, it is a reflection on me as well. Don't you see?"

The anger in his face was still there, but I knew he had understood and accepted what I must do. "We'd all be better satisfied if he were dead," the steward said after a moment. "But not under this roof. There is truth to that." He walked away to stand by the fire, his shoulder against the mantel as I had seen Duncan Lindsay stand. The two men somehow reminded me of each other— the same fierce pride, the same intensity of living, the same fires of hatred burning deep within. And yet their lives had been vastly different.

Angus had grown up on the estate, and except for his schooling he had lived a solitary life, often out alone on the hills or exploring the glens. When he had taken me about my lands, it was clear that he knew and loved every part of them as deeply as I did. The House of Storms was his world, and he felt no urge to leave it for another, except perhaps for the childhood dream of becoming a soldier.

Duncan Lindsay, on the other hand, was a stranger to the House of Storms except for the summer he had spent here with my father. In place of roaming the estate, he was learning to deal with the position he would one day fill. He had gone to school and then to University, afterwards taking his part in the social life of Edinburgh and London. Then he joined the Hussars—in defiance of my father and Mr. MacEwen—and won distinction in battle. Moreover, he knew the capitals of Europe as well as the backwaters of the Crimea.

But somewhere in the complexity of their makeup the quarrel at the ancient peel tower had become such a part of their beings that it had lasted undiminished in their lives, enough so that the Major readily suspected Angus of murderous intentions and Angus in turn might easily be capable of just that.

Yet I could not see Angus lingering in the dark to strike the Major with a rock before heaving him over the edge of the cliff. Nor was he likely to resort to poison. Any attempt on his part would surely be face-to-face for the full flavor of revenge. But how could I really know what was in Angus' heart?

It was too much for my weary mind to cope with, much less comprehend. And there was no proof that Duncan Lindsay had been poisoned—for all I knew he had made use of a naturally occurring case of food poisoning to suit his own purposes.

I must have fallen asleep even as I tried desperately to stay awake, for the next thing I knew there was the roughness of blanket beneath my cheek. Somehow my head had fallen forward to rest on the side of the bed. How long I slept I had no way of knowing. Feeling guilty, I straightened myself in the chair, aware of the stiffness of my chilled, tired muscles even as I did so. Someone—Elspeth, surely—had thrown a shawl about my shoulders and I was on the point of catching it as it slid to the floor when my eyes met the Major's.

He was awake and himself, for as I looked into the gray depths I found recognition and awareness. I could think of nothing to say to break the silence, and he was too weak for the luxury of words. But a slow smile spread from his lips to his eyes, warming them and changing them in a way that I had never seen. One eyebrow lifted in a questioning quirk as if he would have made a facetious comment if he had had the energy. And then with a sigh he closed his eyes again and slept once more. Tears of relief suddenly burned beneath my lids.

"Come away," said Elspeth, at my side. "He'll sleep for several hours, I've no doubt. And you'll be ill yourself with not eating or resting all night."

Putting aside the disturbing memory of that slow smile,

I nodded and got to my feet. The world spun crazily and for an instant I thought I would be sick. Then I realized that I was only feeling the effects of my vigil and the long strain of worry and effort. Elspeth said something I didn't catch, and the next thing I knew Angus was there and lifting me in his arms. Elspeth went before us with the candle while he carried me to my room and laid me upon the bed.

With Elspeth's help I managed a bath and felt a little better. Then there was a bowl of hot thick soup, a cup of strong sweet tea, and afterwards, oblivion for hours.

Fiona Douglas managed quite well on her own. Bruce Cameron was sent for and they spent the day in the drawing room. When I came down for tea, he rose to set my chair and showed a flattering concern for my welfare. I assured him that I was quite well indeed, merely feeling the effects of a sleepless night.

"And the Major?" he asked. "Fiona tells me he has been quite ill."

"Elspeth feels he must have eaten something that disagreed with him," I replied casually, not wishing to involve him in our problems. "Although he is tired, she tells me he will be himself in a day or two."

"I'm happy to hear it," he said politely, but it was evident that his concern was more for me than for the Major now that the danger had passed. Fiona was clearly bored with the subject already.

I had no desire to spend the evening alone with Fiona and I persuaded Bruce to remain for dinner. With his help it would be possible to maintain the dignity and hospitality of my house while permitting myself a few moments of relaxation here and there. With a handsome man to occupy her thoughts, Fiona was her usual charming self and even tried a few painful steps to show us that her ankle was improving.

And so the evening passed, and I was happy to reach my bed at last.

Though Elspeth had predicted that the Major would not have the strength to leave his bed for several days, I found him in the library shortly after noon the next day. My surprise must have shown on my face for he smiled and spoke lightly of his condition.

"I am not a ghost," he said reassuringly, "though God knows I feel something like one."

"Should you be up?" I asked. "You don't look strong enough!" Indeed, he was still quite pale and I saw that he was gripping the back of the chair to stop the tremor in his hands.

He shook his head. "I'll not regain my strength while lying in my bed. Besides, I'm not used to inactivity—my own company palls after a time." There was a pause, and then he said in a different tone, "I want to thank you for what you did. Elspeth told me you remained in the room all that night."

"Yes—I felt responsible. Major Lindsay—why did you say you had been poisoned?" I asked, trying to bring his suspicions and my own concern out into the open. I had expected to feel shy in his presence but he had managed to set me at my ease.

"Because I was," he said slowly, frowning down at his hands.

"Elspeth felt it was simply a case of food poisoning."

"No," he said gravely. "I have campaigned in the field, lived under incredible conditions where food and water as well were scarce and of questionable quality. I have seen men die of dysentery and from eating rotted horse-flesh. I have been ill myself from water that gave every appearance of purity but was sufficiently contaminated to make my life a misery for days on end. No, this was no simple case of having eaten something that disagreed with me—I daresay that my system can tolerate more than the usual level of oddities. In all my time in the Crimea, in hospital where flies and dust and God knows what were constant trials, I have never been ill as I was day before

104

yesterday. Somewhere, somehow, my food was deliberately poisoned. It was nearly enough to kill me—possibly more than enough if I had not had the sense to act at once."

"Everything you tasted was prepared in my kitchens and was served to both of us—indeed, the picnic luncheon was eaten by *three* other people. How could anyone have planned to poison you without taking the risk that at least one or more others would die as well?"

"I don't know how it was done—yet. But I remind you that Elspeth arranged for the luncheon to be prepared and packed. And that Angus carried the hamper during our ride."

I laughed. "However much either of my people dislike you and might wish to see you dead, do you suppose that they would have taken the chance that I might die as well? Come, Major, you must find more opportunity and better planning than this!"

"It is possible that something was included in a food that you never eat—for example, you refused the salmon as I recall."

"So I did. But Fiona didn't refuse and hasn't had the slightest problem. How do you explain that?"

"I told you—I can't at the moment. But I will," he replied grimly.

"There is the possibility that you have pretended to be poisoned," I told him. "It might suit your purpose to do so."

He laughed shortly. "You were there. Can you seriously believe that I was pretending?" He gestured helplessly. "And will you please sit down, so that I may? Otherwise I shall disgrace myself by fainting at your feet."

I took the chair opposite his and watched him lower himself carefully into the seat. "You ought to be in bed!" I said firmly.

"No. I manage quite well as long as I am not long on my feet. Do you really suppose I was pretending?"

"No, of course not. The illness was genuine—the cause

is something else again. We don't agree on that."

He shrugged. "I don't blame you. Either I have manu-
factured two accidents or one of your people is deliberately trying to do away with me. Either suggestion is
rather difficult to accept." He gave me a long searching
look. "Do you suppose that I would attempt to discredit
you in this way?"

"You have called me a changeling in my own house," I
replied, meeting the look. "What else am I to think? I have
known Angus all my life, and Elspeth for most of it. You
are the stranger in our midst." And the one who Morag
foretold was not to be trusted, I added to myself. "We
are working at cross-purposes, Major Lindsay. My father
has linked our lives in such a way that one of us must
lose a great prize unless we agree to marriage. And marriage is the one thing neither of us wants!"

"Are you so sure?" he asked quietly.

I felt myself blushing and was furious. "I can't speak
for you, Major," I said, rising and making my way to the
door, "but it is the furthest thought from my mind!" Before he could speak again, I had escaped, shutting the
door quickly behind me and hurrying to catch up a cloak
from one of the hooks beneath the stairs. And then I was
outside on my way to the loch where I could sit and
search for an inward peace.

Bruce Cameron found me there later, sitting upon the
tumbled rock below the peel tower.

"Am I disturbing you?" he asked as he came near.
"Please tell me—I'll go away if you like."

"No. I've been sitting here thinking for long enough.
Have you been walking far?"

He laughed and sat down on a nearby rock. "Far
enough. I have been up along the Sound, watching the
seabirds. There was a gannet, I think, though he was too
far out for me to be certain."

"Yes, we see them from time to time."

"You are still rather tired, aren't you?" he asked sympathetically. "Would you like to have me walk you home?"

I sighed. "It isn't really fatigue," I told him.

"Then it must be worry. Look, as I told you before, it is none of my affair and you have every right to send me packing if you like. But something is indeed worrying you —I've sensed it since that first day up the glen. I don't mean to pry, but I suspect it has something to do with the Major."

I said nothing, toying with a spray of heather.

He was staring down the loch, watching the sun dappling the blue surface. "I told you—I knew something of his reputation in London. And I can see that for all he is your cousin and a guest, there is precious little love lost between the two of you. In his place, I'd take the hint that I wasn't wanted and go away. But—if he is fortune-hunting, he may not care to notice your dislike for him."

Suddenly I felt the need to talk to someone, someone who could judge better than I in this tangled situation, someone who knew the Major better than Angus or Elspeth or I. "By the terms of my father's will, I am supposed to marry him," I replied slowly.

"I had gathered that, from something Miss Douglas told me. He had spoken to her, I imagine," Cameron said.

I frowned, not caring for the thought that the Major had discussed my affairs with a third party. But then, I was preparing to do the same.

"He has accused me of being a changeling," I went on. "He claims that my governess substituted her own child when the real Moira Lindsay died in the scarlet fever epidemic."

He turned to face me and said sharply, "There's no truth to that, surely!"

"Of course not. But if there were, you see, the Major would stand to inherit not only the house and lands but my father's private fortune as well, while I would be penniless. It is much to his advantage to prove that the substitution was made and so he has been trying."

Bruce Cameron swore beneath his breath. Then, recollecting my presence, he said, "I told you the man was the worst sort! Miss Lindsay, I strongly advise you to put this matter in the hands of your solicitor! It is unthinkable that you must be bound by the terms of the will under such circumstances. I hesitate to speak ill of a member of your family, but I can't sit idly by and watch you trapped into such a marriage." He reached out and laid his hand over mine where it rested on the rock between us. "I have no right to speak for you, but I would not wish my sister, if I had one, to be left in this way. I'd be grateful to anyone who had the decency to step forward and speak up in her behalf."

While I was grateful for his concern and his approval of my stand, I felt suddenly that I had somehow betrayed the Major and myself. I withdrew my hand from his and said firmly, "I don't intend to be trapped, Mr. Cameron. It was wrong of me to speak of this to you, and I apologize. It was just that I have no one but the servants here, and sometimes the need to talk is more than I can bear."

He smiled. "I understand. I am happy that you felt free to speak to me as a friend. And you have said nothing about Major Lindsay that I had not already known or suspected—his reputation could not possibly suffer more through your words than it has already by his own actions." Then he pointed out the eagle circling high above the glen and gave our conversation a new direction.

I chided myself for being abrupt with him after his kindness, for I liked Bruce Cameron very much and had come to value his quiet friendship and pleasant manner. It was for these reasons that I had found myself talking to him in the first place. Although I had left much of the story untold, I felt guilty for speaking at all. It was the Major's fault for disrupting my life so completely that I could no longer cope with it on my own, as I had learned to do since Fraser's death. How different my coming of age would have been had she lived!

Bruce Cameron refused my invitation to lunch, saying he was promised at the Hays', and so we parted company by the side of the loch. As he turned to go, he hesitated and then came back to me.

"Miss Lindsay, I had planned to cross over to Mull shortly, but I have misgivings now. If you have no objection, I'll postpone my departure for a few days—I dislike leaving you and even Miss Douglas alone in the company of the Major. And I'd like your promise that you will turn to me at any time I can be of assistance to either of you." He spoke gravely and sincerely, and I felt a flood of warmth toward him for such consideration.

"Thank you," I replied, equally gravely. "I shall remember."

He nodded, and then was gone, walking in long strides through the purple blossoms that fringed the track. I went on toward the castle, happier than I had been for some time.

For all that he made every effort to recover as swiftly as possible, it was clear that Duncan Lindsay was far from well. I saw the tense jaw muscles clench to stave off the recurring weakness and the shadow of gray fatigue about his eyes. For one thing he was refusing solid foods, taking only soups and tea laced with whisky until his system was able to tolerate a normal diet. This in itself was enough to cause weakness in a strong and usually active man. For another, he was walking again, sometimes disappearing after breakfast and returning after tea, often drenched to the skin in the frequent showers that occur along these western waters. Elspeth shook her head and predicted that he would fall ill on one of his walks and not be found until too late to help him.

I caught myself watching for his return each day, and a feeling of relief mixed with anger at his persistence would well up to greet the tall figure approaching the walls. Fiona grew restless again with only my company to amuse her, and, to be honest, I tried my very best to lighten her day, but two such different women quickly found themselves at a loss for words. She too began to watch anxiously for the Major, sending for Graham to carry her to a chair by the windows, or, if the weather permitted, outside by the gates. Her ankle was improving, though still swollen and painful enough to make another excursion on horseback impossible. Idleness irritated her and once she lost her temper with Graham, giving him a savage dressing down. When the Major returned, however, she was once again smiling and charming for his benefit. The light vein of flirtation and teasing must have grated his tired nerves, but he gave no sign of it. I avoided him as much as possible.

Bruce Cameron came from time to time, careful never to wear out his welcome but always ready to take Fiona off my hands. Though they got on very well and seemed to find much to talk about together, I was never left out of their conversation or made to feel that it was Fiona and not I that he preferred to meet.

Angus had little time to spare for me. He had commented on the length of Cameron's stay in the neighborhood and the fact that he was usually walking about the lands and talking to tenant families, but he made no objections to this. Still, I had the feeling Angus would have been happy to see the last of all our guests. He made no secret of his dislike of the Major, and Elspeth told me that the two men had had words one morning by the gate. What was said no one knew, but the general atmosphere had reeked of brimstone and my steward was unapproachable for the remainder of the day.

The matter of the sheep came up again on the fifth afternoon after the Major's illness. MacDonald, understandably concerned for his flock, was insisting that the animal be put away, before the disease spread to others. Angus was still holding out for time to see what the problem was.

"It is clearly not anthrax, Mistress," he told me. "The ewe would have been dead long since. But MacDonald is not a patient man, he can see nothing before him but a dead flock, and starvation this winter. There's no reasoning with him."

"Yes, I can see his point," I replied, staring out the office window as the Major left for his day on the hills. "But I prefer to wait, as you do. Could we offer to reimburse him for any dangers to his flock?"

Angus shook his head. "A stiff-necked, prideful man is MacDonald. He won't take chances and he won't take charity."

"Well—we have no choice, do we?"

"None," Angus replied. He took a deep breath. "So be it." He drew out his keys and unlocked the gun case on the far wall while I watched. "The trouble is," he was saying, "if we shoot this one and burn the pen and carcass, we'll never know what was making the poor beast ill, and the next time there might be a dozen down with the same thing. Morag says it is nought but what it ate, and indeed, I've seen the ewe looking better one day and worse again the next, just so." He carefully closed and relocked the case and then broke open the pistol with the ease of long practice, assuring himself that it was empty. "I'll be back before dark—we'll have to stay with the fire until it burns itself out." The pistol snapped closed with a crack that filled the small room. Angus grinned at me. "I mind the time yon gun was too heavy for you to hold, and you balanced it on a stick to hit your target," he said. "Want to try your hand today?"

"No," I laughed. "MacDonald would die of shock."

He nodded, and was off, the pistol in his belt. I finished looking at the household accounts and then braced myself for an afternoon with Fiona.

Mrs. Hay came to call and remained for tea. She was a tall, spare woman with graying hair and the tired blue eyes of one who worries about the problems she can't solve, in this case the problems of her parish. It was small and widely scattered, but she made an effort to visit the crofts and the shielings regularly, involving herself in the lives of her husband's flock. Out here in this far western section of Argyllshire, there was no room for pride of place, and Mrs. Hay felt as much at home in a crofter's kitchen as she did in my drawing room. I think Fiona rather overpowered her, and yet she bravely made conversation.

Fiona was gracious and pleasant to Mrs. Hay and answered her many questions about life in Edinburgh and London with great patience. Wearing an afternoon dress of pale green, Fiona sat by the fire with her foot cushioned on a stool and her beautifully manicured hands busy with a square of cambric she was embroidering. I had had time to accustom myself to Fiona's choice of occupation, but to Mrs. Hay it was completely unexpected. I found her watching in awe as Fiona busied herself with her task. Indeed, her stitches were neater than mine.

Mrs. Hay left shortly after tea, and I had just turned away from the door when it opened abruptly and Duncan Lindsay strode in.

His face was black as a thundercloud, his hands clenched at his side, as he came toward me.

"Where is Angus?" he demanded, his voice deep with rage.

"Angus? He has gone to the MacDonald croft," I replied. "Is something the matter?"

"Is it the ewe?" he asked.

"Yes—Mr. MacDonald insists that it be destroyed. Angus has gone to shoot it and then burn—"

But he had wheeled about and started for the door. I ran forward to catch his arm, but he shook me off.

"What is it?" I demanded. "What is the matter?"

He was out the door and down the steps with me at his heels. We were outside the gates before he would heed my questions, and even then I think he stopped only to be rid of me. Trying to keep up with his long strides, I was caught off guard and nearly ran into him. He set me out of his way as if I were a child and ordered me to return to the house.

"No, I'll not have this! Tell me what has happened!" I pleaded.

At first I thought he was too angry to explain himself, and then he pointed to the shoulder of his coat. "You have accused me of lying, Miss Lindsay, when I told you that someone was trying to kill me. I might easily have hit myself on the head with a rock, I might even have tried to poison myself. But tell me, if you will, how I could shoot myself through the shoulder of my coat at long range!"

Beside the long slender fingers of his right hand, I saw the blackened hole in the fabric of his coat high on the left shoulder.

"Angus did this, and by God when I have finished with him, he'll not be able to lift a pistol or anything else for a very long time! We have long had a score to settle and added to it is attempted murder. You won't believe me, but by God, you'll hear him admit to what he has done before I send him to the authorities in Oban!"

"Angus?" I cried, stunned by what he was saying.

"Your precious Angus! All I needed was your word that he had indeed taken out one of the pistols. Now get back to the castle where you belong!"

"No, you are mistaken!" I said.

He was so furious that for a moment I thought that he would turn on me. "Mistaken, am I? Who in God's name shot at me if not Angus!"

"I don't know," I cried desperately, "but it couldn't have been Angus! I have seen him use a gun. I know that if Angus had tried to kill you today, you would be lying in the heather dead, not standing here showing me a hole in the cloth of your coat!"

"At that distance even he could have missed," the Major replied shortly and started toward the MacDonald croft.

I tried to match my stride to his, gave up and ran at

113

his side. "When you find him, what will you do?" I asked, hoping to find a way to cool his anger sufficiently to allow him to listen to reason.

"Half kill him," he said savagely, "and then hand him over to the authorities."

"You can't possibly fight Angus after your illness—" I said breathlessly.

He ignored me, setting a pace that matched his temper.

"Why do you hate each other so much? What is there that has been between you since you were boys at the peel tower?" I asked. "Please tell me!"

"No!"

"Is it because of the past that Angus has—to your way of seeing it—tried to kill you?" I asked.

"I don't know and I don't care! Go home, Moira Lindsay, or I'll take you back myself!"

"Then take me back—it is the only way you will stop me. I'll not have you fighting Angus until I know what this is all about!" It was difficult to speak and stay in step with him, but I had to make the effort.

His answer was to walk faster. I could feel my heart pounding, half from fear, half from exertion, and my lungs burned. I had come out without a cloak, but hurrying as I was, I was warm. It would be later that the chill of the dusk would come and make me cold.

We crossed the hillside, took the track along the burn and then angled across the heather toward the pastures where the MacDonald flock fed. Say what I would, he gave me no answer, concentrating instead on his own effort.

The fires of fury were burning themselves out and leaving the Major without the enormous reserves of energy they had provided. The lines were tight about his mouth now, and a nerve twitched sporadically in his jaw. I was beginning to hope that before we could find Angus he would see how impossible it was for him to go on in this way.

I saw Angus approaching the top of the hill just beyond the MacDonald boundaries, the pistol still in his hand. He stopped as he saw us, then with something like excitement in his step, he strode forward to meet us, only the twisted knee preventing him from breaking into a run. Sick at heart, I fell back, knowing that nothing short of death itself could prevent the long-delayed explosion of pent-up wrath when the two men came face to face.

7

While he was still several yards from the Major, Angus lifted his hand to gesture in my direction. "Why did you bring her with you?"

"I didn't," the Major replied shortly and added. "I want to settle what is between us. Now."

Angus grinned, but there was no humor in his face. "I am at your disposal, Duncan Lindsay." He stooped to place the pistol on the ground and then stepped away from it.

"Wait," I said desperately. "Wait until the Major is well enough. This won't settle anything!"

"Keep out of it!" the Major said harshly. "If you must stay, be silent." He did not look in my direction as he spoke, his eyes resting instead on the steward's face.

"Go home," Angus said to me. "Take the pistol and go home."

I moved closer, so that I stood between the two men, but to one side. "Listen to me. You may take pleasure in hurting each other, but what answers will you find?" I began earnestly, but they paid no heed.

"Three times you have tried to kill me. Three times to my once. I am tired of watching my back for a knife wielded by a coward. You'd have made a damned poor soldier, skulking in the dark and tampering with the food, afraid to stand face to face with your enemy. Well, I am here, within arm's reach. Do you have the courage to kill me now?"

Angus' face had flamed scarlet, and he swore viciously in Gaelic. The Major laughed, a grimly bitter sound that subtly altered the relationship between the two men. It had been Duncan Lindsay who walked here in a white heat of anger that had burned out into coldly calculating fury. Now it was Angus whose temper flared high and seared his judgment. Before I could speak or move, he threw himself on the Major and they went down in a wildly thrashing heap. I watched in horror, for I knew Angus must have outweighed the Major by several stone, and felt that I was a witness to certain murder.

The pistol was behind me, and I whirled to pick it up. The Major must have seen me, for he yelled a warning to me. Angus turned quickly to look.

"She knows how to handle it," he replied curtly.

I broke open the pistol and found that it was empty, the smell of recent firing wafting gently upward. A cold shiver of suspicion crossed my mind and was instantly repressed. Angus had gone to shoot the ewe and he never missed his targets. But then he had not shot at a man before.

Feeling helpless and increasingly frightened, still clutching the weapon, I watched the two men. I had seen the stable lads engage in friendly bouts of fisticuffs, and even occasionally settle their private arguments in such a fashion. But this was different. Angus and the Major fought with an intensity that I had never before witnessed, accepting whatever punishment was meted out in exchange for an opening to strike home. The thud of fists against flesh and clothing sickened me, and there was blood now on the Major's face. But I had begun to realize that he had deliberately angered Angus to the point of madness to equalize the battle. There was a precision in what the Major was doing and a devilish savagery about Angus' movements. Whatever pent-up emotions had burned within the steward these many years poured out now in violence. Oddly enough the Major was making every effort to punish Angus viciously, but murder was no longer in his heart. But then, I reminded myself, the Major had more to lose—if he killed the steward he would forfeit not only the House of Storms but his own life as well.

The first wild explosion had given way to a close-quarters fight that flattened the bracken for ten feet in either direction. I moved out of range of their thrashing legs, desperately trying to think of a way to stop them but holding my tongue for fear of distracting one or the other at a critical moment. Even as I watched the pace slowed, for they were both gasping for breath now and feeling the brunt of their efforts and the punishment that had been dealt them. And then with almost superhuman effort, Duncan Lindsay unleashed a hidden reserve of strength. With a twist of his left leg against Angus' bad knee, he threw the steward off him and followed up his advantage even as Angus fell. In seconds the steward lay still, and the Major slowly got to his feet.

His face was so white that the bloody smudges stood out garishly. I watched him stumble and then, with only his iron will to sustain him, stand erect to stare at me defiantly. I could find nothing to say, and his cold gray eyes moved on to Angus who was stirring. Their clothes were stained and torn, their faces streaked with dirt and blood. Angus got clumsily to his feet, ignoring the Major's outstretched hand.

I waited breathlessly to see if he would try to continue the fight, but to my infinite relief he merely stood, swaying slightly, his dark eyes holding the Major's gray ones. And then without a word, the two men turned and began the slow, painful journey home, leaving me standing there still holding the useless pistol.

I had walked the acres of my land in many moods, but never in such a one as I felt now. I straggled behind the two men, watching their silent progress, but my thoughts were elsewhere. Whatever had happened on the old peel tower in their youth had left deep scars on both of them. The question was, had it been settled now, or was this only the beginning, with neither of them satisfied until the other lay dead? I had no way of knowing what they harbored in their hearts. Even now, scarcely five yards from each other, were they measuring their chances in the next encounter?

I might question them until doomsday without a single word of explanation. But Elspeth might know. She had not been here at the time of Angus' accident, but she had been close enough to Fraser to hear the story, surely. It must have come out at some point in those long years when Fraser had found one excuse after another to put off Duncan Lindsay's return to the house. Once I knew the source of the trouble, perhaps I could prevent a recurrence of today's horror. I wanted no murder in my house, neither that of my lifelong friend and mentor nor, to my surprise, that of the hateful Major.

The first words were spoken in the hall. Elspeth and Fiona Douglas were waiting anxiously, shocked to see the small procession that filed in the door. Angus had followed us into the house to take the pistol from me and replace it in its case. At the foot of the stairs, the Major turned to face Angus, and the steward halted. The Major's words were clear, though he spoke to Angus alone.

"I am sending a message to MacEwen tonight. Before he comes, before I am master of this house, I intend to settle my own affairs. One way or another."

"Aye," Angus replied briefly. "I know where to find you."

And they were gone, leaving me to explain as best I could what had happened on the hillside.

Fiona was excited and full of curiosity. As she talked, I began to realize that she had developed a well-hidden liking for the Major, for she gave short shrift to the steward's role. What had been a flirtation born of boredom appeared to have come to more. I refused to speak of the matter that lay between the Major and Angus and instead implied that the fight had grown out of the Major's intention of displacing me at the House of Storms—for in a sense it had—and made light of it. But she had seen the two combatants herself and was no fool.

"The Major must have good cause to think he can do this," she said.

"He has a miniature of Moira Lindsay as a child," I replied lightly, and made no mention of Fraser's letter or of Morag, my own witness. "People change as they grow older. I hardly think it is sufficient proof."

"But surely someone knew you as a child; you have lived here all your life," she said, sifting the possibilities.

I smiled. "Ask the Major. I'm told he has interviewed nearly everyone on the estate."

"I hadn't known," she said. And yet, hadn't Bruce Cameron told me that the Major had already discussed the subject with Fiona? Suddenly she asked, "What about the old seer in the glen? Have you heard her speak of this? If she indeed has any strange powers, this is the time to use them."

I was not to be drawn on that question. "She has already told us that I will leave the estate and travel far," I answered, laughing. "Something about a handsome man with red hair."

"Yes," she said slowly. "Not very comforting, is it? From the sound of her prediction the Major will displace you after all."

I felt a sudden chill even though the silly prediction had come from my own imagination and was glad when she abruptly changed the subject.

It was not until much later that I could speak to Elspeth privately. I found her in the linen room where she was fuming that neither the Major nor the steward would allow her to wash and dress their hurts.

"For their sins, they'll both likely die of the blood

poisoning, and good riddance I say! Carrying on like small boys in a back alley of Glasgow, they are!"

"It was scarcely a fight between small boys," I answered. "Can you tell me, Elspeth, what precipitated that first quarrel so many years ago?"

"Ask Angus," she said, evading my question. "Or the Major."

"That does precious little good and you know it," I said shortly. "All Angus has ever told me was that the Major was responsible for the fall that injured his knee. Very well, I accept that. But *what* was behind that incident? Surely Fraser told you something about it."

"Aye," Elspeth replied grimly, "and it's not a tale for young ladies, so no more of your questions."

"I won't be able to stop them from killing each other if I don't know what this is about! It isn't finished yet and I'm helpless unless you give me the information I need."

"Let them fight and beat each other into their graves. I'd not lift a finger."

"Please, Elspeth, I've got to know," I pleaded, but it was a half hour more before I could break down her silence. And only then because I threatened to ask the Reverend Hay's wife.

"For she'll not be knowing, but you'll have her asking more questions than you'll care to answer!" she predicted. And then she plunged into the story.

"I've no doubt you know as well as the next girl what men can be like in their youth. God knows, we have sent enough baskets to yon croft down by the sea for that dim-witted Ailis and her bairns—and no two having the same father, likely enough."

I knew the place, and the buxom, light-minded woman who accepted her misfortunes with a shrug and never seemed to bother with the brawling, raucous family she had produced, except to laugh with them and out-yell them if necessary. I had been forbidden to go near there, but knew enough from the maids' gossip to draw my own conclusions.

"Yes," I said. "What has that to do with anything?"

"Well, your father went to live in Edinburgh for a time —long before he met your mother—and was not the Christian he might have been, though, mind you, he settled down quick enough when he met her. Have you never thought why Angus was known by only the one name? For if he could not claim Lindsay, he wanted no other, not even his mother's."

I sat down on the pile of sheets she had neatly stacked. "Angus is my father's son?" I asked in disbelief. "My half-brother?"

"Aye. He was with his mother in Edinburgh until she died, leaving the young boy to the workhouse. Proud she was, and never asked for a penny from his father. I've no doubt she loved Lindsay. But someone sent word, so that your father could take him. He wanted no part of the lad —well, to do him justice, your father had just married and likely enough considered the shock it might be to your mother. In the end, it was Mrs. Lindsay herself who brought the lad here, and gave him a place as a groom." She looked up at me. "You'll not be thinking the less of your father for this. Men's ways are different, though the Scriptures tell them what's in store for their sins, clear as print."

I was beginning to understand. Angus, brought here as a small child, loved this place and found a home for himself. And his growing attachment had expressed itself in the excellent work he had done as steward, caring well for the land that might have been his had he been legitimate. It also explained why, though the household called him a devil, Fraser had trusted me implicitly in his care. My respect for Angus had increased, for to my knowledge he had never presumed in any way upon his position, nor asked for more than he had himself been able to earn in his own right.

"But where does the Major fit into this?" I asked after a moment.

"He came here when your father wanted to look him

over as a prospective husband for you. At first he and Angus were inseparable—exploring, fishing and hunting as boys will. The Major had been army mad, as his father before him, but when he had discovered the House of Storms, he wanted nothing more than to stay here forever. He'd not known such freedom living in Alnwick with his widowed mother. But your father told him he'd not have the army *or* the right to stay here. Instead he must go to school and make himself fit to marry you, as well as being laird here afterward. I'd have no way of knowing what happened on yon peel tower, but Angus and the Major had words. The Major was jealous of the boy who could stay at the House of Storms as he willed, or run away and join the army any day he pleased, so he taunted Angus with his bastardy and flung in his face that he himself would one day be laird here. Angus said the Major would be no more than his wife's pensioner, that as the eldest son—legitimate or no—*he* had already been given the ancient crest of the Lindsays. And then Angus fell and Duncan Lindsay brought him back to the castle. Small wonder they hate each other yet."

This was why neither of them would discuss the past. Now I understood why the Major had recognized the crest Angus had given to me on my coming of age and why Angus had been so furious the night that Duncan Lindsay arrived to take up the terms of my father's will. More importantly, I saw the explanation for their need to settle their quarrel physically. Had there been reason enough for Angus to try three times to kill the Major? In his eyes, perhaps.

Elspeth finished folding the neat stacks of linen, sprinkling them with lavender as she worked. I had spent hours embroidering initials and the Lindsay badge on sheets and tea towels, tablecloths and runners. Rue. The herb of repentance. Proud blood ran in Lindsay veins—I was well aware of that—and repentance was foreign to our natures.

I took a deep breath and got to my feet. "I'm glad you told me. It explains so much." And then as an afterthought, "My father was callous about the feelings of others, wasn't he? He must always have his way."

Elspeth shook her head. "Not callous—only proud and willful. You are old enough to see this clearly? I'd not have your father's memory tarnished by words of mine."

"No, I understand. And he did love my mother so deeply that he had no desire to marry again. That is what matters, after all."

"And Angus? You'll not hold his want of a name against him?"

"No, why should I? He has certainly proven himself in every other respect." At the door I stopped and smiled back at her lined and sober face. "In a way, I'm glad the Major has sent for Mr. MacEwen. I'll be happy to have this doubt settled once and for all."

"Can you be so sure?" she asked grimly. "It might not turn out to your liking—there's the saying, Mistress, that the de'il's bairns hae ay the de'il's luck."

"Not this time," I said lightly. "I have my own luck, Elspeth."

But she was shaking her head as I left.

Angus had nothing to say to me about the fight, but he confirmed that he had shot the ewe. "Once it was done, the shepherd's lad admitted he'd let her get at the lupines," he added. "If MacDonald doesn't whip him, I miss my guess."

"So Morag was right—the ewe's problem was what she had eaten."

"Aye. She hadn't been at them long, and the boy thought she'd recover. More fool he. Still, we put the carcass and the pen to the torch to be safe."

"Just as well. Angus—if the Major does inherit the estate, what will you do?" It was a question I had to ask.

He didn't hesitate over his answer, and I suspected that he had already given careful thought to his future. "I know my work well enough. There'll be other landowners looking for a good man." His voice was level, but I saw his eyes stray to the office window where the last rays of the sun picked out shadows in the hillsides. He was the sort of man who would do well wherever he went, but his heart would remain here in spite of the Major or anyone else. "If MacEwen is coming again, I'll have to look over the books," he said, and I knew he was asking me to leave. The scraped and battered knuckles had swollen twice their size, making the holding of a pen a painful and clumsy matter. I left him to his thoughts.

The Major presented himself for dinner, his face defiantly bruised but his manner unchanged. The meal was rather quiet, for only Fiona had any desire to talk and she eventually faltered before his monosyllabic replies. Nor did we linger over the tea tray. As the Major handed us our candles, he waited until Graham and Fiona were halfway up the stairs before saying anything directly to me.

"I have written the letter to MacEwen, and will see that it is posted myself."

"You needn't bother," I replied coldly. "No one will try to prevent you from sending it."

"Please understand," he said, "this is for the best. Ordinarily I'd have worked it out in my own good time, but that isn't possible any longer. Attempted murder is a serious matter."

"You ought to know that better than anyone else," I said, and watched the slow flush rise in his face.

His next words took my breath away. Holding his temper with an effort, he said, "Will you marry me, now, before the issue is decided? As your father wished?"

"Is that an admission of my right?" I asked, and kept my voice from trembling by clenching my teeth.

"No, only an offer of protection for your future," he replied with equally strained detachment.

"Well, I don't need your protection! Didn't you hear Old Morag's prediction, Duncan Lindsay? I'm going to travel far and marry a man with red hair who won't care whether I am Moira Lindsay or Catriona Fraser! I don't need you!" I whirled away and started up the stairs, tears blinding my eyes. But he caught my arm and spun me around to face him, causing the candle's flame to dance wildly.

"What did she say to you?" he demanded.

"I told you!" I lied.

"It is nonsense and you know it as well as I. *What did she say?*"

"I won't tell you! Ask her yourself," I replied, refusing to look into his face.

"I did—and all she said was it wouldn't matter to me who you were, Moira or Catriona. That the pattern of my future in no way depended upon your identity, now or evermore. She knew, but for some reason she appeared to dislike me and in spite of every persuasion I could think of, she wouldn't say more than that. *But she knows!* Is she hiding the truth for your sake?"

"Why should she? She told me once that you were coming, and I mustn't trust you, because you were merciless and evil and death stood in the shadows behind you. Perhaps she can see into your future after all, and reads death there! Perhaps that is why you will never have need to know the truth!" I had lost my temper and in the wake of my tears scarcely knew what I was saying. Wrenching my arm out of his grasp, I started up the stairs once more, half-stumbling in my haste to escape.

He made no move to stop me, but his voice came clearly to my ears. "I doubt it—because she gave me one more part of my future to fit into the puzzle. She said my wife would know the truth if I did not."

I turned at the landing, unable to prevent myself from answering him. "Does that frighten you? Send for Mr. MacEwen, Major Lindsay, and let us see what he has to say about the rightful owner of this house!"

And as I shielded my candle to hurry on my way, I realized that in my blindness to everything but his cutting words, I had forgotten the stone castle steps, which carried every word we had spoken upward in the echoing spiral to the floors above—there were no secrets to be kept on these stairs. Standing in the corridor of the bedroom wing were Elspeth and Graham. From the look on their faces, they had heard the exchange—indeed could not have prevented hearing without interrupting us. I didn't pause to listen to their apologies, instead I went on my way and for the first time in my life locked my door against Elspeth's intrusion.

As I lay in bed listening to the sea pounding on the rocks below, I tried to make sense of the tumult that had torn apart the serenity of my life. I should not have let Duncan Lindsay stay here. That was my mistake. I had hoped to talk him into foregoing the terms of the will, or at least in some way prove that he was not worthy of my father's trust in him. How innocent I had been! How very innocent to think that I might in some fashion turn a man like Duncan Lindsay from his goal! Morag could prove that I was indeed Moira Lindsay, but on that slender thread alone my case rested. He was in a better position to achieve his ends than I had dreamed possible. I couldn't begin to guess why he had offered to marry me, now, before the issue was decided. I only knew that such an offer had hurt me and shattered my peace of mind.

For days now, that tempting question had been shoved far into the corners of my heart and closed away as if it were too dangerous to be allowed into the light of day. Why not marry him and settle the matter once and for all? asked that small voice. Because whether I faced the truth or not, I had felt myself increasingly attracted to my cousin. To such a green girl as I was, a dashing figure would naturally appear quite romantic. Infatuation, I told myself, and listened to the sea echo the word through the foundations. Every girl at some time in her life must surely be attracted to a charming rascal or worldly fortune-hunter. But even as I had convinced myself that this was so, I lay miserably in the darkness waiting for sleep to come.

The next afternoon, Bruce Cameron presented himself to say he had decided to spend several days on Mull, possibly exploring as far as the ancient holy isle of Iona.

"To be frank with you, I believe Mrs. MacDonald would be happy to have me out from under foot for a while," he said with his engaging grin. "I might as well take the opportunity of visiting Iona, since I have come this far. They say MacBeth is buried there."

"Yes." I was finding it hard to hide my disappointment. I had grown accustomed to his pleasant companionship and had been glad of his company to help me entertain Fiona and the Major. "There are Irish and Norwegian kings as well," I added, rousing myself to remember the lessons I had had with Fraser. "And the murdered Duncan."

"If I were more of a hand at sketching, I'd bring you a watercolor of the site," he said ruefully. "I hope a word picture will do."

"It will do nicely," I replied, and then asked if he would dine with us before he left. But he was already committed to the Hays, and could only promise to call as soon as he returned.

"It won't be long," he added. "Mrs. MacDonald assures me that accommodations are regrettably few and I have no liking for sleeping with the sheep on the hillside."

I laughed. "It won't come to that, surely."

He made his farewells to Fiona shortly after and then left to dress for dinner at the Hays.

Mr. MacEwen sent word that he was on his way to Argyllshire. I had no idea how much of the situation the Major had explained in his letter, but whatever he had written, it succeeded in persuading the solicitor to venture into this faraway corner once more. Angus had left on his rounds, Fiona was restless, alternately flirting with the Major and sitting in uncomfortable silence when he was away, and he himself was busy with his own thoughts. I walked, even in the rain, to find escape from the dreary atmosphere of the house, and as I did, planned what I must say to the solicitor. Surely he would not turn a deaf ear to me now! Against the letter, I had Bruce Cameron's evidence of the Major's character and Morag's witness to my survival of the epidemic. Let Duncan Lindsay dare challenge them! And so I formed my phrases and thought out my defense, and hoped that I would not lose my tongue when the moment came.

It was Monday before Mr. MacEwen arrived, complaining of the impossibility of traveling on the Sabbath and the delay it had caused. I made him comfortable in the library and offered him refreshment while one of the stable lads searched for the Major.

As he set his cup upon the tray and stood looking down at me, he asked, "Have you made any decision regarding your marriage?"

I felt myself blushing. "We must discuss this when the Major has returned," I replied lamely. "He will wish to explain for himself."

Mr. MacEwen's eyebrows rose, but he made no comment, instead suggesting that the autumn would prove to be milder this year than last. I answered in kind, and we had already covered the weather, the price of wool, and the state of the country, when the Major strode in at last.

He apologized gracefully for not being present at Mr. MacEwen's arrival, and after the pleasantries were disposed of, he launched into his reasons for summoning the solicitor to the House of Storms.

To do him justice, I must say the Major presented his case with an economy of words and a complete absence of emotion. Mr. MacEwen listened without comment, his face expressionless. I heard again the charges against Fraser, the Major's admission that I was not a party to the deception, the difficulty in finding anyone who had had sufficient contact with Moira Lindsay in her babyhood to say with certainty that I was indeed the same child. Above all, the steady voice carried absolute conviction. I felt waves of doubt assail me once more, and clung to Morag's witness to steady myself when the time came to respond.

Fraser's letter was produced and Mr. MacEwen read through it carefully, twice. I could see his eyes linger at certain points, weighing words and phrases for every inflection of meaning. Finally, he laid it aside and said in his noncommittal way, "It is very clear that Mrs. Fraser was suffering from a deep sense of guilt. Unfortunately, she does not state the source of this guilt, and we are left to infer that it was a matter serious enough to engage her attention as she lay dying."

I began to speak, but he lifted his hand to stop me. As though summing up a case before the bar, he went on in his dry voice, "Major Lindsay feels that Mrs. Fraser was confessing to an exchange of children, and you, Miss Lindsay, interpret the letter to mean that she had been unfair in denying Major Lindsay his proper rights to visit the estate. I did not know Mrs. Fraser *personally*, but in all my contacts with her I was impressed with her calm competence and her understanding of her responsibilities. One therefore asks, why did she fail in her duty to inform Moira Lindsay of her father's wishes in regard to her cousin? It would appear that Mrs. Fraser had no expectation of the marriage taking place. Again, one must ask why this should be so. And one answer, naturally, is that Moira Lindsay no longer exists."

"Or that Mrs. Fraser felt that my cousin was unfit to marry me," I broke in. "She says as much in the letter!" My heart was beating rapidly now, fear edging into my composure, spoiling my self-control.

Mr. MacEwen nodded thoughtfully. "That is another interpretation. Were Mrs. Fraser's last days coherent? Was she responsible for her actions?"

"She was in full possession of her senses," I replied firmly.

"Did this matter weigh on her mind?"

"Something did. She said nothing to me, and I suspect, to no one else." I was sifting each word now. "Fraser— Mrs. Fraser—was a woman of strong principles and abiding Christian conviction. She might have lied to Major Lindsay in order to prevent his coming here—*small* fabrications, surely—but she would not have denied him his lawful inheritance. You needn't take my word in this matter; ask anyone who knew her, they'll speak highly of her character."

"If she would have told small lies for Moira Lindsay— as you yourself agree—contrary to her principles, how much greater lies would she have told for Catriona's sake?" the Major asked. "She herself has indicated that she would gladly do it again—hardly repentance!—and that only a *parent* could understand why she had acted in this way. I cannot believe that a few small lies to put off my visits would have caused her such agitation of mind and such a strongly worded apology."

I lost my temper. "You have the advantage of your London sophistication, where white lies are nothing! Mrs. Fraser was scrupulously honest, and to lie to you, to fly in the face of my father's plans for you, to try desperately to prevent a marriage she felt was wrong for me—these might weigh heavily on the conscience of a dying woman and loom larger in her eyes, because they were her *only* sin! How many sins weigh on *your* conscience, Major Lindsay?"

He was as angry as I. "If you will, explain why she calls you her 'dear child,' when in every other letter I received from her she refers only to 'Moira'?"

"She often called me her dear child. Ask Elspeth or anyone!"

Mr. MacEwen cleared his throat and said judicially, "I must tell you that in a court of law this letter would support the theory that an exchange of children was *pos-*

sible, since the opportunity for it existed." He stared at his peaked fingertips as he finished speaking. I searched his face for some sign of his personal opinion, but there was none. After a thoughtful pause, he added, "It's a pity that so much time has elapsed since the epidemic. If we could question Mrs. Fraser, or Mrs. MacNeil—who *did* leave abruptly, as I recall, after an undisclosed disagreement with your governess—or even the Fraser servant, our difficulties would be at an end."

I held my tongue. There was still the miniature to discuss. Let the Major present his evidence first, show himself for the grasping man he was, and then I would speak out.

"What of this likeness of me as a child?" I asked. "I haven't seen it and cannot say whether there is a resemblance or not. Children do change as they grow, and of course we must assume that the artist was capable of capturing what he actually saw."

"A very good point," Mr. MacEwen commended. "Do you have this miniature, Major Lindsay? I should like to examine it before we go further."

"I believe you have it with you, forwarded from Alnwick," the Major said.

"Just so! There was a package to be delivered to you. If you will permit me?" He left to retrieve it from his luggage.

I smiled at Duncan Lindsay. "A precaution?" I asked coldly. "Did you suppose one of us might steal it from you?"

"Let us say I was concerned about delayed mails." There was a long silence, and then he added gently, "My dear, I do not enjoy subjecting you to this—"

But he was interrupted as Mr. MacEwen came back into the room. The small packet was handed to the Major who opened it carefully and returned the contents to the solicitor.

While I sat in a torment of curiosity, the little man stared from the painting to my face and back again. I kept

132

my gaze levelly on his and held my chin high, but I knew with a sinking heart that he was not especially pleased with the comparison before him. It seemed an eternity before he finally passed the miniature to me.

It was an oval framed in ornate gilt, perhaps three or more inches high. The workmanship was delicate, the fine brush strokes conveying detail, and unquestionably that of a highly competent artist. The child was dressed in a white gown that I'd seen in camphored tissue paper in one of the attic trunks. The likeness was not amateurish, even I must acknowledge that. My eyes traveled to the face.

A fair-haired, dark-eyed child stared back at me, the full round face rosily smiling at the silver-and-blue ball in her hands.

Try as I would, I could find no resemblance to me. My eyes were hazel, my hair a golden brown, my face oval. Hers was more the coloring that I had seen in Angus and in my father's portrait. While I could argue that the Major was also fair, with gray eyes, I could not explain away the changes that had been wrought by the passing years. The child in the miniature *could* be me, for there was no distinguishing feature to prove otherwise—the nose was small and tilted as most children's are, as yet not formed in the shape it would take with maturity. The cheeks were full and dimpled with the plumpness of a young child, the lips were softly curved. And yet I would not have picked this painting out of a hundred and called it mine. I understood why the Major had not expected *me* the night he had arrived with Mr. MacEwen and why he had felt the miniature confirmed Fraser's letter of apology. I could not deny that he had some cause for his suspicions.

"She and I are not similar," I told Mr. MacEwen, looking up from the lovely little painting in my hands. "And yet—can you say that I am *not* this child?"

"There is one other point, I think," the Major put in. "Miss Lindsay has said she recalls her father's voice clearly, booming about the corridors and laughing. When I knew Angus Lindsay, he spoke scarcely above a whisper, and before he died, lost his voice entirely. I suggest she recollects her true father, the Reverend Mr. Fraser, still remembered locally for his impressively thunderous sermons."

"That isn't true!" I cried. "I remember! Ask Angus!"

"I am afraid it is, Miss Lindsay," Mr. MacEwen replied gravely. "Your father died of a throat ailment, and did in fact lose his voice completely a few weeks before his death. I am forced to agree with the Major in this instance." He paused, and then asked, "Have you any evidence of your own to refute these charges, other than your steward's testimony?"

I could see that he was nearly convinced in spite of his attempt to maintain a legal detachment. The time had come to challenge Duncan Lindsay once and for all. Here was my triumph, and I would enjoy it!

"Yes. I have a witness who was in the sickroom with Mrs. Fraser during Moira Lindsay's illness. She can verify that no exchange of children took place. And since she was devoted to my mother she could not have been persuaded to allow such a change, even if Moira had died. Perhaps you will accept her word. Morag has never been known to lie, and she will undoubtedly be able to identify the miniature as well. I suggest that you go to her croft, Mr. MacEwen, and speak to her yourself!"

8

As I finished speaking, I turned defiantly toward the Major. He had suspected that Morag was my defense and now merely nodded, as if confirming his own thoughts. I felt some of my satisfaction drain away, and glanced back to Mr. MacEwen.

"As it happens, I recall the old woman—something of a recluse, I believe, and rather odd in her own way."

I had not anticipated this. If he had heard that Morag was looked upon as a dispenser of herbs and medical advice, he would accept her word readily enough—but would he believe a woman known locally as a reader of the future? Would her reliability crumble in his eyes because she claimed to have the Sight? I could not know how they viewed such matters in Edinburgh.

"She lives in a small croft up the glen," I replied warily. "I am afraid you must go to her—she isn't able to walk far these days."

He frowned, clearly not liking the need to leave the pleasant comfort of the house for the arduous excursion to the glen. And then, resigning himself to the discomforts required by duty, he said, "Very well. We shall visit her."

"I think it would be best if my cousin did not accompany us," the Major added quietly. "After all, the old woman is her pensioner."

"Are you suggesting that she will tell a different version if I am present?" I asked angrily.

"No," he replied, "not precisely. I do feel that it might be easier for her to speak freely if you are not standing by."

"Yes, it is a point well-taken," Mr. MacEwen said. "If there are no objections, Miss Lindsay, we shall leave you behind."

What could I say? If I insisted on accompanying them, it would prejudice my case. And yet I wanted desperately to be present, to hear Morag silence the Major's claims for good. "I understand," I said slowly.

"It is unfortunate that we must carry this matter outside the family, and I quite appreciate your concern," Mr. MacEwen said, missing the point entirely. "I assure you that we shall employ the utmost discretion."

"Thank you. Will you conduct the questioning? If Major Lindsay may be heir to the entire estate, he too should stand apart in the matter."

It was agreed, and I felt that I had gained a point in my favor at last. And then Mr. MacEwen, perhaps recalling that he represented me primarily and the Major secondarily, added a very good question.

"Do I take it that you know this old woman—Morag?"

"I have met her," the Major replied. "She would say nothing specific to me at the time."

"Do you consider her evidence, whatever it may be, to be reliable?"

There was a pause while the Major looked at me. "I see no reason not to believe her," he replied carefully. "Yes, I should say that I am willing to let my own case rest on her testimony."

I stared back at him in surprise, unable to speak. He made a small wry gesture with one hand as if trying to explain away such inexplicable words. By not calling her sanity into doubt or using her claims as a seer to prove that she was an untrustworthy witness, he was practically surrendering his own position—the careful facts he had marshaled, the letter, the miniature, his own memories of the child Moira—and accepting my sole witness! This made no sense to me, and yet in Mr. MacEwen's presence I dared not question Duncan Lindsay's reasons, for in so doing I might also betray a flaw in my own evidence. I could only accept—with private reservations—his seemingly gracious act.

"Very good. If there is no further business I suggest we start on our way," Mr. MacEwen said.

I rose to send word to the stables, for the solicitor was not accustomed to walking as we were in this part of the west, and left the two men to their talk. How was I to possess my soul in patience while they were away deciding my future for me?

The horses were brought around, and Mr. MacEwen proved to be a more capable rider than I had anticipated. He was scarcely experienced, but he knew what he was about and would not fall off halfway to his destination. Nevertheless, I sent one of the grooms along to keep an eye on him. Elspeth stood in the hall watching them go, and, as the door closed, expressed her feelings on my being left behind.

"I've no doubt it was the Major's doing," she said in her best Old Testament voice of doom. "We'll see what we'll see!"

"No, he was right, Elspeth. I might influence Old Morag—after all, she has lived on my lands for many years, and I have never interfered with her in any way. It is only fair."

"Fair, is it?" she said harshly. "Since when is *fair* the question? Yon Major will see you put out in the cold and never think of fair at all. Mark my words!" She jerked her head in the direction of the drawing room. "That one is quiet enough, and asking questions of nobody," she added, referring to Fiona Douglas. "If I didn't know, I'd say she looks like the cat at the mouse hole."

137

I had no interest in Fiona at the moment. "She realizes that this is none of her affair," I replied, my mind on the disappearing riders.

"Does she?" Elspeth asked grimly. "Then why was she hobbling out of the Major's door two nights gone, and him just coming up the stairs?"

I turned to stare at Elspeth. "Fiona? Walking?"

"Aye, walking it was, and in her night dress! She didn't see me along the corridor, or she'd have made more to-do. I'll grant that she was not graceful but she managed the length of the corridor twice, in her own fashion."

I tried to bring my thoughts back from the glen and concentrate on Elspeth, frowning with the effort. "How long was she in the Major's room?"

"Not as much as five minutes," Elspeth replied grudgingly. "As soon as she heard his foot on the stairs, she was gone like a crippled ghost."

"What could she have wanted?"

"I'd not like to say. And the Major has complained of nothing missing." She shook her head. "Take my advice, Mistress, and send her packing. Let MacEwen escort her back to Edinburgh, or wherever it is that she belongs! There's no place for her sort in this house, and well you know I have told you so from the day she was carried in!"

"Yes, all right, I'll ask Mr. MacEwen. Elspeth, I'm going for a walk. I can't stand here waiting, it will drive me mad. Will you fetch my cloak?"

She left the subject and went to do as I asked, though I knew I had not heard the last of it. In five minutes I was out the door and on my way down toward the loch, hoping to find in the exercise a much needed outlet for my restless energies.

The afternoon had turned gray and chill, with a strong wind from the sea promising rain before long. I made my way up the shore of the loch to the ancient tower standing at its head. Gulls were resting on the choppy surface like sheep in a watery meadow. The tower stood stark and lonely against the sky, its formidable emptiness catching and echoing the gusting wind. I found a rock at its foot and sat in the shelter of the high walls, looking out toward the sea. Mull was hazy beyond the Sound, its hills blending into the overcast. I thought of Bruce Cameron and wondered how he had fared in his journey to Iona, whether the grave of MacBeth was worth the occasional hardships he must be enduring. Somehow I could not picture him sleeping on the hillsides as Angus might, or even the Major, accustomed to the rigors of campaigning.

So much depended on Morag now. Even the Major had acknowledged that fact. At best, they would be gone several hours, and who knew how long if she were out gathering herbs—or deliberately avoiding her visitors! Any other tenant would have come willingly at my call, but I had sent my guests to her croft. Granted she was old and unwell, still one had a tendency not to ask more of her than she willingly might give. Such was the respect she had received from the tenants and even from my household. Angus alone greeted her as an equal, but then Angus himself was apart. And on her words now an Edinburgh solicitor would decide who had the right to the House of Storms. She had already given me the assurance that I was no changeling, and I had believed her implicitly. Whatever must become of me, I at least had the satisfaction of knowing myself to be Moira Lindsay, and the reassurance that Fraser had not betrayed her trust.

A light misting rain began to fall, blowing softly across my face. Unwilling to turn homeward yet, I moved closer to the wall's shelter and tried to occupy my thoughts with other subjects. Why had Fiona been in Major Lindsay's room? It made no sense, but I was more and more convinced that Elspeth was right when she told me that Highland hospitality notwithstanding, the time had come to be rid of Fiona. I would ask Mr. MacEwen to escort her back to Edinburgh or wherever else she wished to go.

And in his care, even her difficulties with her ankle—if there were difficulties still—would not prevent her from making the journey safely and comfortably.

I felt relieved, having decided to act on this matter. However, I had the very strong suspicion that Fiona Douglas did not wish to leave my house. Her reasons would be charmingly explained, but the blunt truth was her growing interest in Duncan Lindsay.

There was a movement in the bracken and I jerked around as a cold wetness touched my hand. Behind me, wagging his tail in greeting, was an old sheep dog. Wet and bedraggled, he moved closer to the wall and dropped down with a sigh as if tired from his efforts. At first I thought he was one of the working dogs and wondered what had brought him here, for neither rain, snow or anything else deterred these capable creatures from performing their duties with the flocks, and they never wandered away on their own. I had just decided that he was too old for work and had been permitted to live out his years in honored retirement by a grateful owner, when I recognized him. Wet as he was, and coming upon me so suddenly, I had not known him as Morag's old dog.

He had never been known to leave her cottage except to drink at the burn running below it or lie in the sun near the garden. Why had he come here—and where was Morag? Was she on some errand of her own and unaware that the Major and Mr. MacEwen were waiting for her?

I stepped out of the sheltering overhang of the walls and called out. Though I spoke her name several times, there was no answer and I walked around the tower in case she had been on the far side and had not heard me. There was no one about. I even tried the tower door, but it was locked as usual and there was no way that she could have come by the key. Wrapping my cloak about me against the rain, I walked farther up the hillside, but there was no sign of Morag or anyone else, only the bracken bowed by the sea wind.

I stood there for perhaps a quarter of an hour, expecting

at any moment to see the stooped, frail figure cresting the hill in search of her dog. My hair grew damp beneath my hood and the shoulders of my cloak felt heavy with wet. Still there was no sign of anyone. I turned to search the shore of the loch and the long narrow cleft of the glen. But Morag was not there.

Concerned now, I debated going back to the castle and organizing a search party. In this weather, if she had become ill and lay in the open for long, she would surely die.

I stifled the fright rising in my heart and called to the old sheep dog. If I could retrace his steps, I might be in time. But, worn out by his exertions and unaccustomed to taking commands from me, he merely raised his head to stare mournfully in my direction and then dropped it back to his paws. Try as I would, I could not persuade him to accompany me. By the time I had become aware of his presence he was already by my side and there was no way to judge which direction he'd come from or how long he had been in the vicinity of the tower.

I decided to take the most direct route to the croft first and then try to determine where Morag might have gone from there. There was still the possibility that she had gotten back or even that she had sent the dog out for help. On my way to the croft I might meet someone who could carry word to the castle.

Even though the Major and Mr. MacEwen had gone before me, I couldn't shake the unpleasant feeling that time was against me. My throat felt dry and my heart behaved queerly as I scanned the land about me, afraid, and yet hoping to see some sign of the old woman. The wet bracken and heather hindered my progress and sometimes trapped my feet as I cut away from the track and across the hill behind the tower. But I dared not concentrate on where I was going and chance passing Morag. The rain beat down in earnest now.

I was perhaps three-quarters of a mile from the croft when I saw the horsemen coming. They were in a tight group speaking gravely together and so did not see me out in the open but I easily recognized the Major, Mr. MacEwen, and the groom I had sent with them. I was debating whether or not to let my presence be known when the groom suddenly pointed in my direction.

The Major and Mr. MacEwen broke off abruptly to stare at me, and I lifted an arm in tentative greeting. But there was no response as they turned their horses in my direction, and the Major's first words were scarcely reassuring.

"What are you doing out here? Where are you going?" he called.

Mr. MacEwen said something to him, and as they drew to a halt before me asked gravely, "Have you been here for some time? Your cloak is quite wet."

"I have walked from the old tower. Is there anything wrong at the croft?" I replied, puzzled by their manner.

"Should there be?"

I was tired of their questions. "The old sheep dog came to me by the tower. He has never been known to leave Morag since he came into her care. I was afraid she might be ill or in need of help," I retorted. "So I have come to see."

"I am afraid she is dead," the solicitor said.

"Dead?" I echoed.

"Dead," he replied gravely. "She was seated in the chair by the hearth, and I cannot say with any degree of certainty when she died. It appears that she fell and struck her head by the door and then managed to make her way to her chair."

"Dear God!" I whispered. "Then you didn't speak with her?"

"No, Miss Lindsay, we did not." He paused consideringly. "I must say, this is extremely unfortunate from your point of view. But of course she was very old, and death might have come at any time. Your man Donald tells me that she had no family."

I could see disaster all about me. Trying to steady myself, I made an effort to concentrate on his words and shove my own misery aside until I could be alone. He had spoken of Morag's family—

"Family? I believe there was no one. We knew very little about her life before she came to the House of Storms, and no one ever came to visit her. She was something of a recluse." I gestured in the direction of the croft. "I will go back—" Someone ought to sit with her until the women of the village could be summoned.

But Mr. MacEwen would have no part of it. "It is not fitting for a young woman, Miss Lindsay. No harm will come to her now. I suggest we return to the castle." He added irritably, "It is raining."

I nodded, and felt the drops cascade from my hood in a shower. I was suddenly cold and wet and depressed. Morag had foretold her coming death the day of our excursion to the croft. Perhaps had already been experiencing dizzy spells that would eventually lead to her falling and striking her head at the door. Instead of hugging my secret to me in confident silence, I should have asked the Reverend Hay to take down her deposition the next day, and then I would have had an indisputable record that would not have depended upon the slender thread of an aging woman's life.

"Are you feeling unwell?" Duncan Lindsay asked sharply. I had been standing there in dazed silence.

"No," I answered, lifting my eyes to his face, where I read concern. But one can afford to be concerned for an enemy when he is laid low. Or perhaps he, like most men, dreaded to be burdened with a fainting female. "I was considering what must be done."

He nodded and said no more. Donald dismounted to give me his horse, but with the weight of my drenched skirts it was impossible to ride astride. The Major solved the problem by setting me pillion behind his saddle. I would have much preferred to walk back alone, but they would not leave me and so there was no alternative except a graceless argument while all of us got wetter.

And so I found myself behind the Major, my face

pressed against the damp cloth of his coat and my arms wrapped about his chest. It was uncomfortable and I tried to keep my grasp as impersonal as possible, but I felt him laugh silently as if he understood, which did nothing for my temper. He was a superb horseman and knew how to make my journey as easy as the terrain allowed, for which I should have been grateful, but I wished no taste of the Major's charity.

I would not let my thoughts stray to Morag's death and what it might come to mean for me. All my hopes had been pinned on her testimony, and now these had drained away with her life. Nothing would bar the Major from setting me aside, now. He would pay his debts and perhaps then return to London to waste the remainder of the estate on the frivolities of society. He would not have been the first Scottish laird to have done so, leaving their estates to the management of stewards or—which was infinitely worse—to the rack and ruin of running themselves. Even my own father had been drawn to the exciting life of the city, much as he had loved his lands. True, he had come home after his marriage and found contentment here and an interest in horse breeding and sheep raising. The horses had been sold at his death, but the sheep were in the steward's care and had prospered. We had gone far in improving the strain, and thanks to Angus' watchful eye, our record of loss in the lambing season was impressively low. But such matters could scarcely appeal to Major Lindsay, knowing as he did the capitals of Europe and the pleasures of London. Even if I had listened to his persuasions and married him, I might have found myself alone most of my life as he made one excuse or another to go away.

My clasp tightened involuntarily and Duncan Lindsay turned his head to ask if I were in difficulties, but I ignored him. Mr. MacEwen rode in morose silence, buried either in his thoughts or in the utter misery of the rain, backed now by a chilling wind. The shoulders of his coat were black with water, and the brim of his hat had not been designed to protect his face. His whole posture bespoke his discomfort, and I began to consider the possibility that he might take a chill.

At the fork in the track, where once Bruce Cameron had gotten himself thoroughly lost, Donald left us to ride on to the village and Mrs. Hay, who would see that Morag's last needs were attended to, and arrange for the old women to watch through the night.

I remembered Old Morag's words to me about wishing to lie in the glen, near the rocks above the croft where she could hear the deer and smell the heather. I would see to it that this was done. It was likely that no one would wish to move into that lonely croft now anyway. Highlanders had a fine grasp of economy, but long memories for the past as well. MacBeth and Tam O'Shanter were not the only Scots to have regard for spirits. Morag had possessed the Sight, which set her apart in life as well as in death. She would find her peace as she had asked.

I sent Mr. MacEwen to his bedchamber for a hot bath and a stiff toddy of whisky and sugared water, hoping to counteract the effect of his ride. Duncan Lindsay shut himself into the library as soon as he had changed his wet clothes and made it clear that he wished to enjoy his privacy. Fiona was waiting to hear all the details of Morag's death, and I sat in the drawing room, over tea, telling her what little I knew. It was another wild Highland tale with which she could regale her friends upon her return to civilization, and I was reluctant to speak of it. I made my escape as soon as decently possible, saying there were preparations to be ordered for the funeral.

Elspeth had gone at once to Morag's croft to wait for Mrs. Hay, and I was spared her views of the matter as I dressed for dinner. She had merely clucked her tongue at the news, but I was not misled into thinking that that was all there was to say. In her own good time, she would express her opinion. We were both aware of how much rested on Morag's word.

145

I wore the gray wool against the unseasonable chill and felt no urge to compete with Fiona tonight. Morag's place in my life had been indefinable but real, and I could not play the peacock as she lay dead. As I came down the staircase, one of the maids, curtsying hastily, told me that Donald, the groom who had accompanied the Major and Mr. MacEwen to Morag's croft, was waiting to speak with me in the office. I thanked her and went to meet him.

He had been waiting for some time, and got to his feet clumsily as I opened the door. "Mistress," he said formally.

"Good evening, Donald," I replied. "You found Mrs. Hay?"

"Aye. She and th' smith's mither went oot to th' croft." He was turning his bonnet in his hands as if ill at ease.

"Good. Thank you."

"Aye." He shifted his weight. It was rare for him to come into the house, much less to seek me there, but I knew Angus was elsewhere and the man had had no choice but to report to me. "Mistress?" he said after a pause, as if he had made up his mind about something. The weather-reddened face was earnest.

"Yes, Donald?" I asked calmly, trying to help him speak what was on his tongue. "What is wrong?"

"I'd hae spoken to th' steward, Mistress, but he's no here," he began.

"And you were quite right to come to me," I said. "What is it?"

He took a huge breath and launched into what was on his mind. "I canna be certain, Mistress, but ta my way o' thinking, a' wasna well at th' auld croft. I didna' make o'er much of it at first, shocked by th' auld woman's death, and a'. But—when I rode ta th' village I remembered, and went back wi' Mrs. Hay ta hae anither look. Mistress, she would no hae built her fire sae hie, no even fra' the damp."

I was puzzled. "She was sparing of fuel, yes. All of us are," I replied. "What does it signify?" Coal was hard to come by and peat burned on the hearths of most of the crofts. Very little sufficed to keep these frugal people warm and cook their meals, particularly in the summer months. But the old felt the cold more, and if she had been ill, Morag might certainly have built her fire higher than was her wont.

But Donald was not convinced. His long face was dour as he searched for a way to explain what he had felt. " 'Twas no th' way she would do, Mistress," he maintained. "I canna mind a fire sae hie. I went aboot th' croft ta see. Her dress was muddy, but there wasna ony on th' cloak hangin' on th' wee peg by her bed. In th' garden, I found a place where th' plants were trampled and hastily set ta rights."

His words were calmly, quietly spoken, but I felt the chill of fear creep along the nerves of my spine. "And?" I asked, afraid to put my thoughts into his mind.

"I canna but think, Mistress, that th' auld woman was helpt ta her end." He added quickly, "Mind, I havna telt you that she was—only that I'm thinking it might be sae."

I knew then that the fear that had driven me by the old tower was born of such thoughts of my own. It was too horrible to comprehend. I could only sit speechless and stare at the hapless groom.

"Are you telling me that her death was not accidental?" I asked. He had served me well for years and I trusted his word. "Donald—is this true?"

"Aye, Mistress," he said gloomily. "I'd not hae telt ye if Angus were here. And th' Major—he hasna known me for long, Mistress."

"No, you did precisely the right thing, Donald," I said quickly. "I am very glad you have not spoken of it to anyone else." I was thinking rapidly, now, trying to piece together the evidence he had put before me. "Someone came upon her in the garden," I said, reconstructing what must have happened, "and before the rain, for she had not worn her cloak. Something occurred, we have no way of knowing what it was, and Morag injured her head. She was helped back to the croft and while she sat in the chair, the fire was built up—too high—by whomever was with her. And she died."

He nodded in agreement as he followed me. He had not said as much, but it was clear that he was wondering why the person with Morag had not seen fit to go for help—why the old woman had been left alone.

"I saw her heid, Mistress. She'd no hae gone sae far wi' sich a blaw. Th' Major telt us that she fell by th' door, and true, there was bluid there, though washt awa' by th' rain th' now. And she might hae crawlt sae far, but no fra' th' place I saw." He paused. "I would na hae ye think I was bletherin', Mistress, for I saw what I saw."

"Yes, I'm sure you did, Donald." I needed time to think and work out the many possibilities that raced through my mind. "For the present I would prefer to say nothing. Not even to Angus. Do you understand?"

"No ta Angus th' steward, Mistress?" he asked uncertainly.

"To no one! You see, if we are wrong, it would cause no end of trouble. And—and if you are right—someone has not yet come forward to explain what caused Morag's death. Perhaps they had nothing to do with it, but are afraid to speak out—I don't want to frighten them by shouting murder where there is none. Do you understand, Donald?"

"Murder!" he repeated softly. "Aye, it could ha' been. Verra weil, Mistress, I'll no speak until ye hae telt me."

I thanked him and watched him leave the office, feeling strongly that if my suspicions were correct, his silence might well be the saving of his own life. And then, summoning what poise I possessed, I went into the drawing room where my guests were already waiting for my arrival and the signal that dinner would be served.

Dinner was a dreary affair. Even in the best of circumstances, Mr. MacEwen would not have found Fiona Douglas a compatible dinner companion, and she in turn thought the solicitor exceedingly boring, though her good

148

breeding prevented her from showing this openly. Instead she concentrated her attention on the Major, who occasionally responded vaguely as if his mind were elsewhere. I had had no opportunity of speaking with the solicitor in private and consequently I felt ill at ease and not inclined to chatter. Besides, the old woman's death weighed down my spirits—she had been one of my people and in a sense I held myself responsible for what—possibly—had happened to her.

Who could have harmed her? Certainly not the crofters or villagers who knew her, and hers was not a croft that even a vagabond would choose to rob. The furnishings were plain and her life was simple to the point of Spartan, by her own choice. What had happened must either be an accident, in spite of any evidence to the contrary—or —connected in some way with my own affairs. There was no denying that her death affected me drastically—and Duncan Lindsay as well, for with Morag silenced, he might easily triumph.

And so the meal dragged by and I could not have said with any certainty what had been set before me.

Angus was waiting for me in the corridor as Fiona and I left the dining room. I excused myself to her and followed him into the office, afraid that Donald had broken his word. He had not taken the time to wash or change his clothes, and he wasted no time on formalities.

"Is it true then, what they are saying?" he asked bluntly.

"Yes, Morag is dead, poor woman," I said, waiting to see how much he knew. "Elspeth and Mrs. Hay have gone to the croft. She'll be buried on the hillside there, as she asked. It is fitting."

"Aye," he said heavily. "How did she die? I've heard nought but bits and pieces." He was watching me under black, frowning brows.

"They wouldn't let me see her. Ask Elspeth. Mr. Mac-Ewen said she had fallen against the door of the croft, but she managed to crawl before the fire and rest in her chair." I longed to tell him that someone had not wanted her to speak to Mr. MacEwen—and that it was I who had sent the solicitor to her, pleased to have scored against the Major. But intuition held me silent. Instead, I went on: "She was dead when they got there, Angus. She couldn't speak to Mr. MacEwen, not one word about who I really am! And she *knew* I was no changeling—Morag was the last link with my childhood! I could weep for her—and for myself!"

"I'd not take it hard, Mistress, for there was nought you could do to prevent her dying," he replied, quite gently for Angus. "As for your own affairs, time enough for worrying about them when the solicitor has had his say." He was drawing circles on the blotter with the tip of one finger, absentmindedly frowning down at the imaginary pattern he was creating. "Elspeth is at the croft, you say?"

I nodded.

"And the old dog?"

"Oddly enough, he came to me by the old tower, Angus. That is how I first sensed something was wrong and started for the croft."

He appeared to be surprised. "But he *never* left her," he said, "not since he was brought to the croft by his master."

"I'd forgotten him until now—would you send someone to fetch him from the tower and find a dry place in the stables for him to sleep? And some food, perhaps," I added hopefully.

I was relieved as he nodded slowly. "Aye, Mistress, it would not be a bad thought at that. I'll go myself."

I went back to the drawing room feeling that I had at last accomplished something useful out of the wreckage of the day. By taking on the responsibility for the dog, I could in some measure repay my enormous debt to Morag.

The gentlemen had not lingered over their brandy. I had hoped that Fiona would have taken herself off to bed in my absence so that I might have the opportunity to speak to Mr. MacEwen privately, but she remained in the drawing room and was in no hurry to be gone. It was Mr.

150

MacEwen, exhausted from his strenuous day, who first excused himself, saying he would talk to me on the morrow. The Major followed as soon as the solicitor was up the stairs and out of sight. At the door, he turned to me and formally offered his condolences. "I'm sorry. Truly sorry."

I nodded, uncertain how to respond, for he seemed to be sincere. He stood there, tall and attractive with the scarred side of his face hidden in the shadows, his eyes holding mine. Then I remembered that the Major had been out in the hills somewhere and could not be found to greet Mr. MacEwen on his arrival. Had he been near the croft and afraid to speak out? Or had he gone there deliberately to seek out Morag and at any cost drag from her the knowledge she had withheld from him before. He did not look like a murderer. But how *did* a murderer look?

After an instant he was gone. Only then did Fiona send for Graham to help her to her room, and I was left alone with the cluttered tea tray and the dying fire. It was then that I remembered Morag's words as she had spoken to me about her wish to be buried on the hills. I had taken it as metaphorical speech. "My time is nigh at an end," she had said. "Death waits for me outside, but I am old and have no regrets."

Had she meant that her death would be coming soon or had she quite literally warned me that death even then was waiting at her door? While I was inside, Fiona Douglas, Bruce Cameron, Angus, and the Major had stood without. *Had* she been pointing to one of them as her potential murderer? The thought was preposterous! And yet she had been right in her predictions more times than I cared to admit. Was I so blinded by the training and sophistication of my position in life that I could not accept the unexplainable? Or was it simply that the only one of the four to have cause to kill the old woman was the man I was fighting desperately not to fall in love with?

9

I woke in the night crying from the shock of Morag's death and the trying uncertainty in which I stood. If Elspeth had been in her bed, I'd have sent for her and in her clucking, bustling concern taken some comfort, but she was still up in the glen and I had no desire to disturb one of the maids. For an hour I tossed uncomfortably and then rose to smooth the rumpled sheets. Slipping my feet into shoes, I walked to the windows and drew aside the heavy curtains. Though the sea's angry wrath could be heard and felt in the darkness below, I could see nothing. The sky was heavily overcast and the distant humps of Mull had vanished altogether. I was reminded once again of Bruce Cameron, wandering somewhere over there, and wished he would come again soon. If nothing else, he could speak to Mr. MacEwen for me, and that had now become doubly important.

The solicitor might listen to his story and see that my objections to Duncan Lindsay were not the finicky whims of a spoiled child—and that any doubts the man had about *my* background were motivated solely by his own greed and desperate need to pay his debts. Surely then, he would investigate the Major's past instead!

While I stared out into the blackness, my mind wandered to Morag again. She had said there would be sorrow in the mist for me, to beware. Was I seeing it now, rolling in silently from the sea, spreading about the cliffs and the castle walls like wisps of veil? Or was this only a storm-dark night. In answer to my question, the wind threw a spattering of rain against the pane, and I let the curtains drop back into place. Whatever I might find when I awoke tomorrow, it was not of this night that I must beware.

A faint sound from the corridor caught my ears. I made my way quietly to my door, avoiding the furnishings and the edge of the carpet with the practice of childhood. With extreme care, I twisted the knob and cautiously opened my door the merest crack.

The corridor was in blackness, but my accustomed eyes caught something filmy white moving carefully along the far wall as if feeling its way in the direction of Fiona's room. I knew even without her slight limp that it was she, wrapped in the silken dressing gown Elspeth had found so shocking. As I stood there, watching in the stillness, I could not judge whether she had come from the direction of the stairs—or from Duncan Lindsay's room.

In spite of my restless night, I was up quite early the next morning and after breakfast went down to the stables to see how the old dog fared. The rain was still coming down, though from the color of the sky in the west there was some chance of clearing later on. I picked my way through the puddles and found Donald currying the fat pony that pulled Cook's market cart. He looked up and touched his bonnet as I came in.

"Morning, Mistress. Ye'll be cooming about th' dog," he said.

"Yes, how is he?" I asked, dropping the hood from my face and trying to brush the dampness-curling tendrils of hair out of my way.

"Angus brought him in last nicht, late it was. He telt

me he hae th' de'il's ain time wi' th' beast."

"Yes, I can imagine." I followed him to the stall where the dog lay stretched on his side in the straw, snoring lightly. There was a dish of milk with bread sops and a pannikin of water to one side. "Does he eat at all?"

Donald shook his head. "Mourning, likely enough. Ah weil, he's an auld one, d'ye see, and used to *her* ways."

"Take care of him for me, if you will. I'd not like anything to happen to him," I said, and tiptoed back to the wide doors.

"Aye, Mistress," he promised as I adjusted my hood to step back into the rain.

I'd have liked to walk, but instead went back to the castle to wait.

Mr. MacEwen sent for me after his breakfast, and I found him alone in the library. He set a chair for me and then pursed his lips as he sought a way to begin.

I sat with my hands folded in my lap to still their tremors. I would not have his sharp eyes detecting my fears and drawing conclusions.

"Miss Lindsay, you are placed in a most grave situation."

"Yes, I am aware that Major Lindsay's accusations appear to be well-founded," I replied calmly, meeting his light blue eyes. "But you must take into account the fact that he stands to gain substantially if I am proven to be Mrs. Fraser's daughter."

"Quite so. We have therefore the possibility of a drawn-out suit, which in the end will waste the estate, whatever the outcome. Neither of you will be permitted to live here or to draw upon the financial resources. Major Lindsay, I believe, has an income of his own, but you will be unable to support yourself."

It was not a pleasant prospect, and I began to see why the Major had not dropped the possibility of marriage altogether. If he needed money as soon as possible, a lawsuit was not promising in his eyes. I decided to attack at once.

154

"Mr. MacEwen, have you explored Major Lindsay's background?"

His eyebrows raised. "Most certainly."

"Did you know, for example, that he is deeply in debt and is willing to use *any* means of resolving his difficulties? I have never shown an inclination to favor his suit, and he has of necessity fallen back on the ruse of doubting my right to any portion of the estate. Before you are able to cast doubt on my position, I suggest that you find out *why* Major Lindsay wishes me to be Catriona Fraser!"

"Miss Lindsay! Are you implying that your cousin is planning to use his share of this inheritance to settle his debts?" he asked in astonishment.

"Exactly that!" I replied triumphantly.

"Wherever did you come upon such a foolish notion! We have explored his past as your father instructed and we have been in touch with the Major's man of business in London. I can assure you that his affairs are in excellent order! While he may not be so wealthy as you, he is quite comfortably situated and in a sound financial position."

I was shaken, but persevered. "Is it likely that he would admit to you that he was in debt when the will so clearly stipulates that he must be upstanding? You have the word of his man of business—but London gossip says quite the contrary!"

"Miss Lindsay, you are most ill-informed," he responded, "and as your solicitor, I suggest that you make no reference to this—this *gossip* in the Major's hearing, or he will be well within his rights to hold you for slander."

The sincerity in his voice convinced me he himself believed what he said.

"Will you at least make inquiries—other than his man of business?" I persisted.

"There is absolutely no necessity for it," he replied, and then with a sigh, "however, if you insist—"

"I do," I said firmly. Otherwise, he would never accept my word.

He bowed. "May I ask the source of your information?"

"I was told by a friend. I wish that he could be here in my place, perhaps you would listen to him. Unfortunately, he is presently on Mull."

"I see. I shall do as you ask, but let me offer a word of advice, Miss Lindsay. Duncan Lindsay has lived up to your father's expectation in every way. I cannot imagine why you have taken him in such dislike, nor why you should take the word of a friend over mine in the matter of his way of life. But you would do well to remember that your cousin is in every way suitable and that you yourself may be at fault. You are accustomed to freedom of choice and decision far beyond that of most young ladies, and you may well be—shall we say?—headstrong in this matter and unwilling to hold a detached viewpoint, especially since your governess failed to accustom you to your eventual duty." He leaned forward earnestly, his hands upon the desk. "Think what you are about, Miss Lindsay! You have prejudged this man and refuse to see any good in him."

Angry at his defense of the Major, I snapped, "While he is trying to prove that I am *not* Moira Lindsay? Unfair, Mr. MacEwen!"

"Whatever he is trying to prove, he has indicated his willingness to marry you, whoever you may be," he replied.

I got to my feet. "How generous! He strips me of my place in life, my father's money, my own home, even my good name—and then salves his conscience by offering marriage to the waif. No, I thank you!"

"Is it truly that way, my dear? Or are you hurt and striking out? Only yesterday he willingly agreed to abide by the old woman's testimony, in the face of your assurances that she would speak in your behalf."

I almost shouted out that he could have done so—knowing that Morag was already dead—but I caught my unwary tongue in time. I managed to swallow my fury and answer him more calmly. "I shall have to give it some thought," I replied, hating the words.

"Precisely! I am glad to see that your usual good judgment triumphs over your temper. As for your true identity, I must make what inquiries I can and discover what grounds there may be for a suit. Too bad that you did not take the precaution of getting the woman's testimony in writing, but of course you could not have foreseen this eventuality. I will give you my considered opinion as soon as possible, and in the meanwhile, try to see the Major as the man he really is."

I agreed politely and walked to the door, then remembered a question that had come to mind in the course of our interview. "Mr. MacEwen—if neither the Major nor I qualify for my father's estate, what becomes of it?"

He frowned as he looked toward me. "In that case, your father has provided a residual legatee. If neither you nor the Major survives or for other reasons is not able to inherit, the estate goes to his illegitimate son, Angus Moray."

Stunned, I could merely nod and make my way out of the door.

Elspeth had returned from the glen and told me that the funeral for Morag would be in the afternoon. Word had spread, as it always does, and those who knew her had made their farewells, coming to stand in her doorway and silently stare at the plain coffin that rested in the center of the small room.

I arranged for myself and my guests, as well as the servants, to attend the service and hoped that the rain would be gone by that time.

The Major met me in the hall as I came in from the stables, and asked if he could speak with me.

"I am terribly busy—could it wait?" I asked.

"Yes, certainly—but I suspect you simply have no wish to talk with me," he replied, half-smiling.

"That isn't true," I lied. "There is much to do—"

"—the funeral and your guests, yes, I know." He reached out and took my hand, leading me toward the library. "This won't take long."

With one of the maids dusting the steps above, I had no wish to make a scene and perforce followed him. The dim light of day struggled to penetrate the half-twilight, for the candles had been put out and rain blew against the windowpanes. I was glad that he could not see my face fully.

I refused the chair he placed for me and stood half-turned toward the door.

"I have spoken to MacEwen, as you have, no doubt. We have gotten ourselves into an awkward position, have we not?" When I remained silent, he went on easily, "Be that as it may, I want to discuss another subject." He turned to the empty hearth and with his back to me stared down at the ashes. "Morag is dead. And there were three attempts to kill me. Have you considered that someone may wish to see both of us out of the way?"

"If you are suggesting that Angus is a murderer," I replied coldly, "I won't stand here and listen. You—or I—may be guilty, but I don't believe he even knows that he stands to inherit."

"Oh, he does," the Major replied grimly. "Ever since we were boys and played on the tower, he has known." He turned to face me. "Why are you so certain that he is innocent and I am guilty?"

"Because," I said truthfully, "I have known him all my life. He hasn't made himself a public figure with his gambling and his attentions to other men's wives." Whatever the laws of slander, there were no witnesses now and no direct accusations. I would see for myself what he had to say.

To my surprise, he laughed. "Are you saying—yes, of course you are! Who told you?"

"It won't do to blame someone else," I said caustically.

"As you say. Was it Fiona? Or Cameron? Or Angus himself?" he mused.

"You have forgotten Elspeth," I added, determined not to betray my source. "Don't underestimate her!"

"I won't. She doesn't trust me, I suppose because of Mrs. Fraser."

"It has nothing to do with Fraser. Morag warned us you were coming and foretold that you were twisted with wanting, deceitful, bringing death in your wake. For all her Presbyterian upbringing, Elspeth has faith in the Sight."

"You have mentioned this before. What exactly did Morag say?"

I told him, recreating that misty morning for him. He listened intently, then shook his head as I finished.

"She had never liked me—but there was no other reason for her words. Unless she referred to my military service, of course." He was clearly puzzled, but I paid no heed.

"Are you planning to carry the question of my identity to the courts? Mr. MacEwen says we will beggar the estate if we do."

"I have told you that I will marry you," he replied quietly, "whichever way the court or anyone else may decide the issue. Moira, aside from Mrs. Fraser's letter, when I walked in that first day, I had a mental image of the girl I would find. You were nothing at all like her. In the next several days, I discovered that no one here had known you as a child, and that your own memory of your father was at fault. When I saw Catriona Fraser's grave in the churchyard, I could explain the unexplainable. Tell me—if you indeed *were* Catriona Fraser, would you wish to go on living a lie? Or would you rather have the matter set straight, whatever the cost to you?"

I had never seen the question from that angle. Slowly, I replied, "I would not live a lie—I couldn't face myself."

"Exactly. I don't blame you for hating me—I was thrust upon you unexpectedly and shortly thereafter brought you face to face with a most unpleasant fact. Believe me, I took no joy in telling you—but I would not write to MacEwen behind your back. If you were the innocent party to such a deception you still had every right to prepare your own defense." He paused thoughtfully. "I nearly left it too late. The next attempt to kill me might have been successful."

"You left it very late," I said harshly, to cover my feelings. "Morag is dead."

"Yes. And with her died your last witness. Tell me, now that it no longer matters—what did she say to you in the croft that day?"

"She told me that I was my mother's daughter—Moira Lindsay—and that someone outside her door would be the death of her, only I didn't understand properly, and did nothing to save her life—or my future. And that, Duncan Lindsay, is one more reason why I shall never trust you!"

He had frozen at my words, his eyes riveted to my face. I ran from the room before he could speak or stop me, unwilling to hear his denials, afraid to read his guilt in his face. So blinded was I by my haste, I didn't see Bruce Cameron standing in the hall. He caught my arms to steady me as we nearly collided, and I turned my head away so that he could not see my tears.

"Moira—Miss Lindsay! What is the matter?" he asked, deep concern in his voice.

"Let me go!" I demanded, my words muffled and unsteady. Jerking out of his grip, I almost fled to the stairs, leaving him aghast and staring after me.

In my room, I rang for Elspeth, but the maid who answered told me that Elspeth had gone once more to the croft in the glen. I wanted to ask her the nature of the injury that had forced Duncan Lindsay to wear a sling for the first days after his arrival. Surely as she had undressed him while he lay deathly ill from the poisoning, she had seen for herself what had caused the wound. If it were indeed a gunshot, as Bruce Cameron had suggested, I would confront the Major and Mr. MacEwen with irrefutable evidence. The solicitor was adamant in his belief that the Major was no fortune-hunter. He might feel differently when his faith in the Major's character was shaken at last.

I now regretted my hasty treatment of Bruce Cameron and wished to make amends. He had gotten a poor welcome from me and I had lost the opportunity to talk to him about his knowledge of Duncan Lindsay's past. But when I returned downstairs, I was told that Bruce Cameron had gone, after speaking briefly with Fiona Douglas. Disappointed, I knew there was no time to catch up with him before the funeral services.

We rode to the glen in solemn procession, Angus, the Major, Mr. MacEwen, and Fiona, attended by her devoted groom, spread out along the narrow track, each absorbed in his or her own thoughts. I found mine poor company, thinking as I did of the old woman who lay dead, possibly because of me. The rain had gone, and in its place the misting drizzle frosted my horse's ears and mane with tiny flecks of water. The heather had lost its bright glow with the blossoms that had fallen, leaving the green and brown landscape almost as drab as the sky. The way seemed long, though I knew it was my imagination that made it so.

The straggling groups of tenants and villagers were waiting when we arrived, and the Reverend Mr. Hay stood before the door. His black robes flapped about his tall, thin frame, giving him a fleeting resemblance to a crow. He greeted us and stood aside to permit me to enter the croft alone. The women seated there rose and left me, for as the laird's daughter and heir, I was chief mourner.

I stood in the dimness staring down at the rough wood of the coffin, my mind suddenly clear and at peace. Morag had spoken of death as an old friend long expected and perhaps overdue. She would have held no bitterness in her heart for me, for mine was not the greed that had made the deed possible. All that I could do for her now was to be certain that she *had* died at the hands of someone who wished to silence her, and then bring her killer to justice. The debt of her death must be paid.

I reached out to touch the wood, half in promise, half in expiation, then turned to find Angus at my side, his dark eyes unreadable as they roamed the peat-darkened interior. With an effort, he brought his attention back to me, and together we walked out into the wet.

Reverend Mr. Hay led the way up the hillside to where the newly turned earth marked the grave. We formed a half-circle about him, my guests and I to the right and the tenants and villagers to the left. Morag's coffin was borne from the croft, followed by Angus, his pipes beneath his arm.

The service was brief and simple, the familiar words of farewell reminding me of Fraser's death a year before. As I stood there, my eyes swept the faces about me. Who among Morag's mourners was a murderer? It wasn't likely to be the tenants or shepherds, not with their awe of Morag's gifts. The villagers? Smith or shopkeeper, old or young, each man and woman had lived together for so many years in the isolation of the House of Storms that a knowledge of one another was taken for granted. No, there was no murderer among them, whatever other human traits might lurk there.

I turned my attention to the five people ranged beside me. Mr. MacEwen was certainly guiltless. Elspeth had strong feelings about sin and would not kill a fellow human being at the risk of her own soul. Yet she might have done for me what she would never have done for herself. I must remember her fierce attachment and hold it at a distance to judge it impartially. Yes, she might break a Commandment for my sake and count even her soul well lost. But why would she have touched Morag, knowing that Morag was my one witness! Then I remembered with painful clarity that until Mr. MacEwen arrived, I had told no one that Morag would speak for me. Indeed, Elspeth and Fiona's dour groom had overheard me taunting Duncan Lindsay that the old woman had prophesied my wandering far from the House of Storms. In my ignorance, I had given Elspeth every reason to assume that Morag would speak against me! With sadness, I acknowledged that she must be left in the column of the possibly guilty.

My eyes passed on to Fiona. Her lovely face, framed by her shining hair, stared over the hills toward the sea, masking her boredom. Though she could walk more easily than she presently cared to admit, even I realized that she could not have come to the croft alone and on foot. If she had had any reason to silence Morag, someone would have had to act for her, and I knew so little about her groom that I could not make a guess at the limits of his loyalty. Would he have killed Morag at Fiona's command? I sought his straight, expressionless figure among the servants and wondered. Nothing in his face or eyes betrayed his thoughts as he watched the Reverend Hay. The man could not be counted a killer simply because his manner lacked charm. The question was, why should Fiona wish to be rid of Morag?

I could find no answer to that, and passed on. Bruce Cameron stood to one side of Fiona, his eyes in frowning concentration on the coffin as it was lowered into the earth. He too had no reason to dislike Morag, and I would have said that he could not kill anyone, so sunny and warm was his disposition. And he had been on Mull until this morning, which made it impossible for him to be involved. I placed him in the doubtful category with Fiona, and turned my thoughts to the Major.

The Major. I must keep an open mind and look at each person with as much detachment as possible. It was easy —and somehow painful—to think he might be guilty. He had had the opportunity and everything to gain. Why had he been late for his meeting with Mr. MacEwen? Experience in the Crimea had taught him to kill, and he might easily have been ignorant of the fact that fires were small and sparingly used in this part of the world. He had, too, the marred face so often associated with villainy. But I must recognize that it was to my advantage to see him blamed, and be wary of judging him unfairly. There were those unexplained threats to his life—if they were his own doing and an attempt to cast doubts on others, I would be well on the way to proving that he had killed Morag, too. But if someone else had been behind them, the Major might be as much a victim as I.

Yet who would wish to harm the Major? Only Elspeth for my sake—and Angus, for mine—or his own.

As the prayer ended, I opened my eyes and looked across the open grave toward the steward. My friend, my servant, my half-brother—and the residual legatee of my father's estate. He hated the Major and would have been happy to see an end to him. Yes, I could easily picture Angus in a flaming temper murdering the Major. As for Morag, he had shown her quiet respect through the years and I could not imagine him harming her now. Yet he too stood to gain enormously by her death. If Morag had lived to support my claim, he would merely have retained his place as steward. But if she died before proving that I was indeed Moira, and the Major could be blamed for her death, Angus inherited the whole of the estate. He might have accepted the risk to himself for such a reward. And where had he been that day? Reluctantly, I weighed the evidence. Angus was no skulker, he was no killer—yet the House of Storms was a very great prize for a man of illegitimate birth, whose future was uncertain at best. Who was immune to such temptation?

The gardener handed me a bouquet of flowers and I strewed them upon Morag's coffin, hearing with only half my mind their faint thud as they struck the wood. Angus must in honesty be classed with the possibly guilty. And he had been without the door that day as Morag spoke of death waiting for her outside. All of them had been—except Graham and Elspeth.

I stood for an instant looking down into her grave and then raised my eyes to the great stone just beyond. A'

Chloich Thuill—the Pierced Stone—it was called, for the great cleft in its surface. A rough, craggy rock that some said came from the Ancient Ones who had built the rings of Standing Stones scattered about Scotland, though Fraser held that only wind and water had eroded the split. Nevertheless it was a most fitting monument for Morag.

A hand cupped my elbow, and the Major led me down the hill once more as Angus settled his pipes beneath his arm and filled the bag.

There was the explosive sound of the filled pipes and then across the stillness the music poured out in the melody of lament. Angus played well, with great feeling and a sense of rhythm that matched his skill. The hills echoed the "Flowers of the Forest" as I turned to look back at his tall figure pacing slowly the length of the grave, the Lindsay kilt richly bright against the black of mourning and the great gray stone.

Bruce Cameron took advantage of an opportunity to speak to me as we rode home, asking quietly for a moment of my time when we had returned to the castle. I agreed, glad of the chance to apologize for my abrupt behavior earlier that morning. Then Mr. MacEwen was on my left, complaining of the constant rain in western Scotland, and the moment was lost.

It was not until half an hour after our return that I was able to join Cameron in the library where he had so patiently waited. As I closed the door behind me, I launched into my apology.

He laughed and cut across my words. "No, no! It serves me right for coming unannounced into a very trying time for your household." And then he sobered. "I was truly sorry to hear about the old woman. I wondered about the advisability of her living alone out there in the glen, aged as she was. But I suppose she preferred that to any more comfortable spot."

"Yes, I believe she would have refused even the suggestion of moving." Changing the subject, I added, "I hope you had a good stay on Mull?"

"Yes, delightful! It's a beautiful place, you know, and I could have spent weeks there. Iona was even more striking than I had expected. And I saw MacBeth's grave —at least the guide assured me that it was his!"

We laughed together, and then he said hesitantly, "I have had time to think, also, which is one of the reasons I went away." He toyed with the fobs of his watch chain and tried to find the words he wanted. "Miss Lindsay, I haven't a quarter of your wealth and have little to recommend me, but I must say what is in my heart. At first I thought of leaving and trying to put you out of my mind, but that is the coward's way and not to my liking at all." He looked up suddenly, his dark eyes on mine. "I have come to love you in these short weeks, and though your Mr. MacEwen will say I have no right to do so, I ask you to marry me."

Taken off guard, I could only whisper, "Marry you?"

He gestured forlornly. "Yes, I know it sounds presumptuous, but I love you most dearly, Moira, and love makes a man equal to anything. Could you love me in return? Ever?"

Touched, I smiled and then sat down abruptly in the nearest chair. "May I consider your offer?" I asked, and then to soften the disappointment in his face, I added, "You see, I must be honest and say I don't know what is in my heart. Will you give me a few days?"

He came forward to take my hand in his. "Gladly. I am only very grateful you haven't flatly refused me! I may still hope, and that is more than I deserve!"

"I won't keep you waiting for long," I promised, smiling still, but reminding myself that first I must sort out my own affairs, determine what my true feelings were toward Bruce Cameron and Duncan Lindsay. "Will you dine with us tonight? We aren't a very gay house party, I fear, but perhaps you will find it amusing to watch Fiona and Mr. MacEwen ignore each other."

He frowned. "My presence won't be an embarrassment to you?"

"Good heavens, no. Besides—I find it difficult to cope on my own."

He was smiling again. "Then I shall be happy to accept."

We set a time and he left for the MacDonalds' croft. As I reached the tops of the steps on my way to change I met Fiona, on her groom's arm, coming toward me. Waiting for her to hobble nearer, I resolved to make my first attempt at sending her on her way, at the same time wondering what reaction I might arouse in her.

"I've only to change, before tea," I began, and then, before losing my courage completely, added quickly, "Have you considered returning to Edinburgh with Mr. MacEwen? I am sure he would be delighted to escort you there."

Her delicate brows rose. "Would he? I rather think he dislikes me." She shrugged. "It doesn't matter. Whatever you wish."

I was not prepared for such easy agreement. "I'll speak to him, then," I replied and hurried on my way to my room.

Elspeth was waiting, my dress laid out across the bed. "You'll be wanting your bath?" she asked.

"Before dinner, I think," I said, busy with the hooks on my riding habit.

She clucked her tongue. "I'll be glad enough when the house is empty again and we know what we are about. Did you speak to that Douglas woman?"

"Yes," my voice muffled as the habit came over my head. "Just now."

"And?"

I looked at Elspeth. "She agreed," I said simply. "Just like that."

Her lips set firmly, she shook her head.

"But I thought you'd be pleased!"

"Saying is one thing, doing another. I'll believe she is

167

gone when I see the back of her going out the gates."

"Elspeth, what do you think of Bruce Cameron?" I asked as she began to brush my hair.

"A nice enough gentleman, and mannerly. But not for you."

Surprised, I said quickly, "Why not?"

"I don't know," she replied thoughtfully. "I daresay you'd find him easy enough until he was crossed. Beyond that, I can't say. But it's these quiet ones that have the deepest ways."

"You don't like the Major, either, and I'd say he is exactly the opposite of Bruce Cameron."

"True enough, I don't like the man. But for all that, he would be the better match."

I turned to face her. "That's a change-about!"

"No, Mistress, and none of your putting words into my mouth! I know his faults, and well do you, but he says what he thinks and not wrapped up in fine linen either. And he comes from a better family. But greed is his downfall, there's no gainsaying that." She stepped back to let me pin my hair into place. "Take my word for it, Miss Moira, and bide a while before choosing a husband! There are enough men who will come fluttering for your fortune —wait till there's one who comes for *you*!"

I opened my mouth to speak, and then was struck by what she had said. "Wait until one comes for you." There was the crux of my problem, the possible cause of Morag's death. What would happen if the Major and all the rest thought I was *not* Moira Lindsay after all? Which side of their characters would come to light then? So long as the Lindsay inheritance was mine, even remotely, I stood in the way of some people and protected the position of others. What would happen if the circumstances were suddenly reversed? Would the killer feel safe and thereby betray himself?

It was an interesting idea to speculate upon. But how could I hope to put it into practice without losing my right to inherit after my mission had been accomplished?

Anyway, it was well worth considering from every angle before I dropped the idea completely.

"Stop gaping like a codfish," Elspeth said irritably. "What is the matter?"

Pulling myself together, I cast about for something to say and remembered the Major's wound.

"Could you tell me something? It may be important, Elspeth. When you helped Angus undress Duncan Lindsay the night he was poisoned, did you think to look at his arm? The one he had worn in a sling?"

She smiled grimly. "Aye, I did."

"Well? What was the matter with it?" I asked impatiently.

" 'Twas badly bruised."

"That's all?" I demanded blankly. "Only *bruised*?"

"Aye."

"He couldn't have been shot?"

"In the name of heaven, no! And what made you think of that?"

"No matter. I had thought—from gossip—that he had been shot by someone, that's all." I felt curiously deflated.

She snorted. "Shot indeed! 'Twas badly bruised, no more. From falling off his horse."

"Falling—are you certain of that?" I asked, suspecting she was teasing me. I had seen the Major ride for myself.

"Aye. He told me so himself, when I asked. Said he was a girt fool to try a stone wall on a new mount, and took a spill. He didn't want his fine reputation as a cavalry major spoiled when he came to meet his future wife, and kept silent. Now stop that laughing, do, and pin your hair!"

10

Between tea and dinner, I managed to think over the idea that Elspeth had inadvertently given me. The problem was, how to protect my future claim to my inheritance while temporarily abdicating it. I wished to solve the question of Morag's death, but there would be other ways to do so without jeopardizing my future.

At first I considered going directly to Mr. MacEwen and explaining the situation to him. But he was a man of limited imagination for all his skill and training in the law. Besides, he already thought of me as flighty for refusing the Major's fine offer. Would he listen to me at all or go directly to the authorities at Oban, possibly stirring up a mare's nest rather than solving the murder? I could not say with complete certainty that Morag *had* been murdered.

How to protect myself then?

In the end, I sat down at my desk and wrote a letter to Mr. MacEwen, setting forth my intentions and what I hoped to gain through them. After several false starts and blotted efforts, I managed to produce a satisfactory document. To protect my legal position as Moira Lindsay, I was explaining why, in public, I was prepared to deny my heritage and claim to be my governess's child. It was for the purpose of discovering what, if any, part my identity had played in the death of Morag that I was attempting to mislead everyone. Then I gave the evidence as set forth by Donald, the groom who had first noticed the oversized fire and then had had the sense to search further before bringing his suspicions to me. (This time I would be wise enough to go to the stables and have Donald sign a brief statement giving his testimony, to be included with this letter of mine.) And lastly I confirmed that Morag was prepared to support my claim to be Moira Lindsay, for which reason she may have died. If I could prove this one fact, I would settle the matter of my identity beyond any shadow of doubt.

And then, because I was ignorant of the workings of the law, I gave myself a time limit of one month from this date to work out a solution. If I had not succeeded by that time, I was not likely to do so ever and there would be fewer problems with the authorities if I did not delay them for too long.

Rereading my efforts, I was pleased with what I had done. I had stated my ideas clearly and had been very careful to make no false accusations. That, as Mr. Mac-Ewen had reminded me, would be grounds for slander, and I had no wish to cloud the issue if I discovered that Morag had died of natural causes after all!

Slipping out to the stables, I persuaded Donald to sign the statement I had prepared for him, and then, back in my room, put the two documents into a large envelope. I closed the flap with wax and pressed my father's seal ring into the warm red thickness. Then I addressed the envelope to Mr. MacEwen, and beneath his name wrote my instructions that it was not to be opened under any circumstances until one month from the present date.

I took the envelope to his door while he was dressing for dinner, slid it partially beneath the heavy wood paneling, and then tapped lightly. Within several seconds the envelope disappeared from my sight, and I knew that he

171

had taken it up. Hurrying back to my own room, I changed quickly into a rose silk and set about arranging my unruly hair.

Even with all my haste, I was the last to enter the drawing room. The Major had acted as host in my absence, and sherry had been served. Bruce Cameron rose as I came through the door and smiled warmly at me.

"Good evening," I said, hoping my pink cheeks didn't betray my flurry of activity in the last few hours. "Thank you, Major Lindsay, for attending to my guests."

"Will you take sherry?" he asked, his clear gray eyes sweeping my face.

I accepted the glass he held out to me and managed to carry on my share of the conversation while mentally waiting until an appropriate moment arrived for unleashing my surprise.

I had decided on my way down the stairs that I would make my announcement tonight before I lost my nerve or Mr. MacEwen pried the truth out of me. Judging from his face, however, as I had entered the room, he found nothing odd or unusual about the letter he had received, and greeted me with his usual courtesy.

Dinner was served shortly after my arrival, and as we sat in the formal dining room I stared down the table at my guests. What would be their reaction to my words? Surprise? Relief? Concern? There was no way of knowing, of course, but I found myself speculating all the same.

Bruce Cameron would be relieved, if it was true that he felt my wealth to stand between us, or disappointed if he was a fortune-hunter as Duncan Lindsay had suggested.

Fiona Douglas had no interest in my affairs, but would she be pleased to find the Major suddenly in sole possession of the whole estate? I had no doubts that she was attracted to the man, but where money was concerned emotions mattered little in many marriages. She would see this night's announcement as it affected him, not me.

Mr. MacEwen would be surprised, surely, since I had

maintained so strongly that I was Moira. If he were not to be suspicious as well, I must make my statement as reasonable as possible, declining perhaps to beggar the estate in a suit. Yes, that would strike him as ultimately reasonable.

And Elspeth, who was busy serving us? Likely enough she would forget herself to call me to order for such foolishness. There would be fiery words when she came to my room at bedtime.

Angus was not present, but he would hear soon enough. What would he do? I knew his reaction would be violent if he was innocent of any wrongdoing. But if he was guilty? My main concern was that he might in some way attack the Major. It was a risk I must take, and with his admitted experience in defending himself, I thought he would manage.

At the foot of the table sat the Major, his eyes suddenly meeting mine as I looked his way. Would he be glad to have me out of his way at long last or suspicious about the sudden change of face? That too would depend on what lay in his heart. Most of all, I dreaded to see him exultant, but perhaps Mr. MacEwen would take note of it and draw his own conclusions at last.

Had Bruce Cameron been wrong about the gossip concerning the Major? I felt a sudden qualm. What if I had misjudged the Major entirely, as Mr. MacEwen had suggested! In that case, I was taking a terrible chance in playing out my game rather than turning to him for assistance. Yet how could I be certain that I was not taking a murderer into my confidence as I poured out my story? No, far better to play the game as I had begun and then watch the reactions. After all, if ever it began to get out-of-hand, all I had to do was explain myself and call a halt in the proceedings. Or so—in my innocence —I told myself.

There was a natural pause in the conversation as several threads of talk came to a conclusion at once. I had been rather silent for some time, leaving Bruce Cameron to carry my share of the party's flow, and I knew that the moment had come when I would receive maximum attention. With a deep breath I got to my feet.

"If I may change the subject to more personal matters," I began, and felt every eye turn toward me, "I have an announcement to make."

There was a sudden stir to my right and I knew that Bruce Cameron expected me to announce our engagement. I felt a surge of remorse for so cruelly disappointing him, but there was no other course for me now.

"For some time—since his arrival in fact—Major Lindsay has expressed his concern that I am not Moira Lindsay at all. I had hoped to prove that I am, with the help of Old Morag. With her death, my proof is lost forever. Mr. MacEwen has explained to me that a suit to determine who is indeed the heir to these lands and my father's wealth would waste the estate enormously, and even then might not prove conclusive. I love my home and my land very dearly. I don't wish to see them squandered on my account, even with the knowledge that they are rightfully mine. So—here, publicly, I am declining to contest the Major's allegations and am foregoing my claim to my father's estate. I now consider myself to be Catriona Fraser, and in return ask only that I be given a month's time to make plans for my future before I am forced to leave the House of Storms."

There was a tumult in the formal dining room as I finished and sat down rather quickly.

Bruce Cameron, beside me, had upset his wineglass, spilling the dark red liquid across the white damask cloth to encircle the base of the tall silver candlestick. Mr. MacEwen, speechless for once in his life, was staring at me. Fiona, after one swift look at me, had turned to smile triumphantly at Duncan Lindsay. Elspeth, somewhere behind me, had dropped a dish. But my attention was on Duncan Lindsay. Down the long polished row of candlesticks, his face seemed to be framed in a shimmering distant light that confused me until I realized that my eyes were full of tears.

There was a fleeting, puzzled expression that changed to consternation as I watched. But no gloating pleasure, no shame, not even relief, merely consternation. And then he was on his feet and about to speak.

But it was Mr. MacEwen who was able to make himself heard first. "Do you know what you have said?" he demanded. "Are you prepared to face the life you are choosing?"

"Anna Fraser was a governess and a very good one. Why can't I be the same?" I asked, keeping my voice steady. "I should think you know of many families who need a good governess. Or perhaps a nurse for young children?"

Fiona laughed softly. "Are you asking him to recommend you?"

Bruce Cameron glared angrily at her. "Stop it!" he shouted and then turned to me. "Don't be a fool, Moira, for God's sake! Don't let them frighten and bully you into giving up your birthright! Hold on and you will win—"

"She needn't win anything," Elspeth said, coming to stand by the table. "She doesn't need to prove she is herself, and be worrying herself over nothing until she doesn't half-know what she is saying! It is your fault she is confused, and I'll not have any more of it—"

"I think," said the Major, "she knows very well what she is about. The question I ask myself is—why?"

I had sense enough to hold my tongue and sat there almost breathlessly as the noisy exchange went on. Bruce Cameron was hotly defending me while Mr. MacEwen pointed out all the serious consequences of my actions. Fiona, smiling, watched first one and then another, occasionally making a remark calculated to fan the flames. Elspeth, with fine disregard for her future employer, was taking advantage of the opportunity to read the Major's

175

character, her long-pent resentment laced with biblical overtones. The Major, his face set and his mouth grim, finally gave up trying to speak to me above the uproar and started down the room.

Breaking off her diatribe, Elspeth said abruptly, "There's one who will make you hear reason! And you, Mistress, as well!" With long purposeful strides she covered the length of the room and went out the door to the main hall.

Duncan Lindsay towered over me and my throat ached with the strain of looking up into his face.

"Well? Explain yourself!"

"I have nothing more to explain, Major Lindsay," I replied as coolly as I could. "Everything has been said."

"Then I'll hear no more nonsense about governesses and nursery maids. You'll marry me and have an end to it!"

Stung, I resented his cold assumption that I must accept his charity. "I won't!" I said, rising to face him. "I'll marry Mr. Cameron first!"

He was suddenly so angry that I moved back instinctively, forgetting my chair and nearly falling as I collided with it. He caught my shoulders to steady me, and then swept by his own fury, ended by shaking me violently. "You won't!" he snapped. "I won't have it!"

Then, so roughly that I had to catch the chair back to prevent myself from falling, he was spun away from me and sent crashing against the paneled wall with a force that jarred the room.

I had not seen Angus come in, but he stood by the table now, breathing hard and beside himself with anger. "What have you done?" he demanded of me. "Have you lost your senses?"

"I have refused to bleed the estate to prove my case," I said, my voice shaking and losing some of its assurance.

"Nonsense! You are a Lindsay and know it! Tell yon Edinburgh lawyer you were playing a silly woman's trick and didn't mean a word of it."

His voice filled the silence that had fallen, the roughness of it penetrating the thudding of my heart in my ears.

"No," I said stubbornly, and shut my mouth quickly until I could control the trembling in my voice and limbs.

"Let her alone," the Major said from behind me. "I suspect she knows what she is about, in her own foolish way."

"Aye," Angus said, turning on him, "you'd like that well enough!"

"Don't force my hand, or I'll forget where we are," the Major said between his teeth. "I told you, leave it!" His fists were tightly clenched.

"I think dinner is ruined, anyway," I put in, forcing myself to speak normally. "If we must discuss the subject, let's go elsewhere."

Unexpectedly, Mr. MacEwen spoke up. "I quite agree. Miss—Lindsay, if I may offer my arm?" He stepped in to do just that, and I allowed him to lead me away from the two angry men. "I suppose," he said resignedly, "that it is too much to expect anyone to discuss the matter calmly."

With Bruce Cameron's help, Fiona rose and followed us, while the Major and Angus, without a single word between them, came after. We walked to the drawing room, and it was Elspeth who closed the door as we entered, and stood there with her back to it.

Mr. MacEwen went to stand before the fire, his face frowning as he balanced himself on the balls of his feet and rocked from heel to toe. It must have been his most formidable stance as he faced clients and broke the worst, I thought in fleeting amusement. Clearly, he was ready to bring the force of his profession to bear on my future.

We argued for nearly two hours. In the end, by the single expedient of refusing to be drawn into contention and persevering with my single purpose, I carried the day. But it was a painful victory and long before it was won I had begun to worry about the wisdom of my whole plan. I hadn't anticipated the strong force of emotions I had unleashed, nor the lack of ready acceptance of my scheme.

Only Fiona was openly on my side, and that only because she was delighted to think of Duncan Lindsay as heir to the whole of the House of Storms. A glorious new world had opened before her and she had no intention of letting it slip through her grasp. Her pleased little smile annoyed me.

Mr. MacEwen held to the impersonal workings of the law and the irrevocable step I was contemplating. I was glad to think that I had had the foresight to prepare the letter explaining my purpose, otherwise I should never have been able to continue the masquerade. It was a bleak picture he painted for my eyes, and I knew doubts again. Only the thought of Morag dying for my sake kept me from blurting out the whole story.

Angus and Elspeth, furious with me, with the Major, and with Mr. MacEwen, tried to persuade me to change my stand and alternately threatened the Major if he accepted my withdrawal, until Mr. MacEwen had to remind them that they were liable to the law.

"Aye, and what good is the law?" Elspeth snapped. "Tell me that? It has caused nought but trouble this night!"

Bruce Cameron, deep concern in his eyes, tried to reason with me, pointing out the long-term problems with my decision and asking me not to be so hasty.

The Major, standing across the room from me, had little to say, though he rarely took his eyes from my face. No more was said about marrying him and I tried to tell myself that I was relieved. Why had he been so adamant in the dining room? He now had everything he could wish for—lands, the castle, more than sufficient money to keep both and live well. Why had he wished to take on the burden of a penniless, nameless wife? Was it his conscience that had spoken, refusing to rest easy when he had forced me out of my rightful inheritance? It must be that—or a deep-seated fear that I knew more than I had admitted. If he had indeed killed Morag, the simplest way to silence my suspicions forever would be to make me his wife, for then I could never testify against him.

Finally, the session came to an end, and I was called upon to put forth the final effort of seeing my guests settled for the night—or, in Bruce Cameron's case, sped upon his way.

Angus, brushing past me and out of the room, glared angrily and said he would speak to me later. I was spared giving him an answer as Cameron came forward to take my hand.

"I'll not disturb you tomorrow," he said quietly. "You'll have enough to contend with, God knows. Sleep on it, Moira, and be sure! All your life long you may regret this decision!"

I shook my head as we walked out into the hall. "No, I won't change my mind, I know what I have done."

"Rest well! We'll speak of this another time," he replied, as if he hadn't heard my words. "Good night!" And he was gone into the darkness where the groom waited with the horses beyond the gate.

I closed the heavy door and turned to see Fiona in the hall by the stairs. She was leaning on Elspeth's arm and her smile was blindingly beautiful. "Do you know?" she said softly to me, "I don't believe I shall care to leave with the solicitor after all."

It was on my tongue to tell her she had no choice, and then I remembered that the house—supposedly—was no longer mine to order as I saw fit. "As you like," I said, trying to keep my voice as light as hers.

But I noticed with satisfaction that Elspeth was less than gentle as she helped Fiona Douglas up to her room.

Mr. MacEwen, standing in the drawing-room door, said as I came to him, "I shall give you three days to reconsider."

I smiled. "Thank you—but that won't be necessary. I know my own mind."

He sighed heavily. "Do you? Well, it is too late to argue

179

the matter all over again. I don't think I shall sleep as it is. Good night."

"Good night." I watched him start upward, knowing full well as I stood there in the hall that the Major was waiting for me in the drawing room. It was cowardly of me to refuse to give him the satisfaction of having the last word as everyone else had done, but I seriously considered slipping away instead. My head ached and what little food I had swallowed during dinner seemed to be lodged in my throat.

"Don't go," said his voice behind me, and I turned, flushing, for fear he had read my thoughts.

He waited while I came toward him and passed into the drawing room, then closed the door upon us.

"We seem always to rub each other the wrong way," he began, walking past me to lean his shoulder against the mantel in his characteristic way. "I don't know why it must be so," he added thoughtfully. "Perhaps it is the common heritage of the Lindsay temper and stubbornness. Angus has both in full measure, God knows, and from all I have heard, our common grandfather was the worst of the lot."

"We haven't got a common grandfather any longer," I said warily, unwilling to be trapped into an admission of anything. "I am Catriona Fraser."

"Are you, my dear?" he asked, smiling, and once again the smile touched and warmed the gray eyes, bringing them to life. The scar, so startling against his tanned face, lost its importance. "I admire your courage. And in spite of your shrewish ways and touchy temper, I have come to love you, strange as it may sound. Like calling to like, possibly."

I felt myself grow cold all over and then the warm blood rushing to my face in a telltale blush. "I don't enjoy being made game of, Major," I said harshly.

"I am not taunting you, my dear," he said softly. "But I am asking you again, in my own rough way, if you will consider marrying me."

It was my second proposal in a matter of hours. Suddenly I had a wild desire to tell him the whole, to drop my weary burden and worries at his feet and leave him to cope with everything. My throat was so tight with tears that I couldn't have answered if my life had depended upon it. And then I told myself I was tired and no longer able to think clearly, that this sudden weakness would pass and leave me stronger if I could only endure a little longer. But the days ahead seemed terribly bleak. Oddly, the thought that flickered most clearly in my mind was that I was glad that I was not truly Catriona Fraser. Much as I had loved my governess, I did not want to be her daughter—only myself, as I had always been until now.

In the lengthening silence, the Major smiled again, this time rather ruefully. "Flattering, aren't you? But I'll give you no peace until you have said yes."

I edged toward the door. "I don't understand why."

"I have told you," he said simply. "For my sins, I love you." And I could almost believe him.

As my hand touched the knob, he said, "You play a dangerous game, Moira. Do you know that?"

I nodded, silent.

"Be careful, my dear. I wouldn't wish to see anything happen to you. Good night—sleep well."

"Good night," I whispered, and nearly ran from the room.

Elspeth was waiting to see me to bed, and as I changed my clothes she demanded to know what had gotten into me this day.

"Please—I'm so very tired," I begged. "I don't want to talk about it again."

"Aye, like as not!" she said coldly. "But grand gestures won't help you find a position as governess half so fine as that of your own home."

"No, perhaps not. But I'll try."

"And when you change your mind it will be too late,

181

mark my words! Catriona Fraser indeed! I've half a mind to go to that MacEwen myself and tell him that you are no such thing, and swear to it anywhere he likes!"

"Would you perjure yourself for me?" I asked, roused to interest.

"Perjury indeed!" she said harshly. "God's truth! Didn't I know yon Anna Fraser for many long years? She'd have spoken out if you were her own, as a mother will, and she never did that. Not even on her deathbed. Would she have left you to learn such a thing from *him*? 'Twas Catriona's death that made her daft over you, poor woman. If it is twisting that the truth needs to make it stick, that's not perjury to my way of thinking!"

She finished putting away my clothes in grim silence and spoke again only to wish me a good night as she blew out the candles and left the room.

So exhausted that I could scarcely lie still, I stared into the darkness of the high ceiling and listened to the sea's voice beneath my windows. But in my mind's eye I was haunted by a pair of warmly smiling gray eyes and a soft deep voice that spoke of love.

I awoke late to find the house stirring about me, but when I came down to breakfast there was no one else in the small dining room. I ate a hasty meal and hurried out to the summer garden and the path leading to the sea cliffs. I sat there on the smooth turf watching the water change in color with the sky and fling itself in white froth high above the rocks toward the tiny patches of wild-flowers nestling in the crevices. The familiar scene soothed me as I tried to recapture my dreams of the night, but they were lost in the morning sunshine. All I could remember was the fear that pervaded them, but not what had caused it. With a sigh, I gave up the attempt and began to toss pebbles into the sea below.

Perhaps it was the half-remembered effect of the dream or simply my overwrought nerves, but I suddenly became aware of the sounds behind me and whirled around.

I could see no one amongst the flowers and shrubs, but I could have sworn that someone had moved along the path toward me, his steps muffled by the pounding of the sea. I searched carefully, even getting to my feet to see more clearly, but I was alone. Nothing stirred, not so much as the smallest leaf.

Uneasy, I stood there for a time, expecting to see one of the gardeners pottering about and minding his own affairs. And then I recalled the Major's words the night he had been struck on the head—"I might have been rolled over the edge of the cliff and into the sea with no one the wiser." Had I, in sitting here this morning, presented an inviting target to someone? Or had my mind played tricks with me?

There was no way to tell, but by now the peace and serenity of the gardens was lost to me. It was impossible to sit down once more and turn my thoughts inward because each nerve was on guard. The Major had suggested that I ought to be careful. Was it a warning? Or had he meant that I must choose between marrying him and an accident of some sort?

Shaking myself out of such morbid thoughts, I turned and walked back the way I had come—leisurely, to convince myself that there was nothing to fear except my own active imagination. But my throat felt dry as I rounded the castle's corner and saw the gates open and welcoming before me.

Fiona Douglas and Duncan Lindsay spent the afternoon riding. Elspeth told me afterward that Fiona had quite shamelessly suggested the idea, claiming her ankle had begun to feel quite well enough to make the attempt worthwhile. Since they were gone for several hours, I had sufficient leisure to wish I had accompanied them.

Mr. MacEwen had ordered the carriage and driven into the village to take lunch with Mr. and Mrs. Hay. I suspect his reasons had more to do with me than with Mrs. Hay's cooking. Here was an excellent opportunity to question them at his leisure without arousing curiosity or unpleasant speculation. Since he was determined to hold to his three-day period of waiting for me to change my mind, nothing had been said to the tenants or servants concerning our private affairs or possible changes of ownership. Still, I knew that few things were secret in so isolated a corner of the world and had no doubts that the least stable lad had already heard the first whispers.

Bruce Cameron had kept his word and didn't come to the castle at all. I was torn between relief and disappointment.

In spite of my efforts to avoid him, Angus found me after luncheon. I followed him reluctantly to the small office, steeling myself for his views of my behavior last night at dinner. Knowing Angus, they would be forthright and of uncertain temper, but I was determined to stand my ground.

He began before the door had shut completely. "So you are going to become a governess, are you?" he asked mockingly as he stood before me. "While yon Major lords it in your place."

"Yes," I replied, meeting his glance. "So I have said."

"Aye," he grunted. "And not two weeks ago, you were in a panic that just this would happen."

He was uncomfortably close to the truth. "I have learned to deal with my fears," I said, hoping I did not sound as lame to him as I did to myself. "I'm not a child, Angus."

He laughed harshly. "I have walked with you over nearly the whole of the property, Mistress. I have fetched you dripping out of the loch and lied to Mrs. Fraser about the tears in your dress from climbing the rocks or the old tower. I have caught lambs for you to pet and frightened away the cattle—a hundred things, Mistress. And you tell me now that you give up your lands without a single regret, without a sorrow in your heart. I don't believe you."

I swallowed hard. "It is not for you to judge me," I said haughtily, trying for the right note. I was never a successful liar.

"As you say." There was a pause, and it appeared for the moment that he was satisfied. "What about the old dog? Do you intend for it to remain in the stables?"

"Yes. Why not? There is no one at the croft to care for him."

"The groom—Donald—has grown attached to him, I think. He tells me nothing about the death of the old woman," he added, catching me completely off my guard.

"Why should he?" I asked, walking to the window to look out blindly.

"Donald is usually a gossip," he said. "But not about this matter."

"I rather think he was shocked by her death. Morag seemed so permanent, indestructible."

"It could be that," he replied thoughtfully. "But I'm not satisfied about her dying—and you aren't, either."

I turned quickly to face him. "What do you mean?"

"Have you given up the House of Storms because you are afraid you also may die?"

For an instant I could not speak at all, could only shake my head in weak protest.

"I wondered last night if you were daft, but now I wonder if you are afraid?"

"Of what?" I asked, surprised at my voice and the steadiness it had contrived on its own. "Murder? Don't be silly!"

"It is not I who am silly, and I think you should tell me what has caused you to worry." His face was dark and unreadable. Once again I was struck with amazement that he could be my half-brother, for I understood him very little. Dark forces moved in Angus, perhaps from his dead mother, perhaps because of the stain on his birth. Even now I couldn't be certain whether he asked for my sake —or for his own.

So far, the only reaction I had stirred in anyone was suspicion about my own motives. "There is nothing to tell," I replied and closed my lips firmly.

He was suddenly angry. "Why do you refuse to trust me?"

"It isn't a question of trust. I can't make up what I don't know," I said resolutely. "I never saw Morag dead."

"Do you suppose that I have had a part in her death? Yes, I can see it in your face. What sort of monster do you think I am!" He paced the room like some caged beast, filling it with his fury. "Duncan Lindsay put that doubt in your head, didn't he? Damn the man!"

"He has said nothing to me, Angus. If you want to know about Morag, ask him—or Mr. MacEwen. They found her, after all."

But he paid no heed. "After that day in the heather, when we fought, I learned a grudging respect for the Major. No man who handles himself that well could be the coward I'd thought him. But if he takes the House of Storms in this way, I'll see he finds no peace, damn his bloody soul!"

"Angus, why do you insist that Morag was not killed by her fall?" I asked.

But the dark eyes that came back to my face were betraying nothing, only his temper. "I wasn't here. How do I know?" he demanded roughly. "But—it was *timely*, was it not? Take care with your suspicions, or you may find yourself dead as well! If I killed Morag, why should I not murder you as easily!"

He bolted from the room with the violence that had so often frightened the maids and held the tenants in line. This time he nearly collided with Fiona in the corridor, brushing past her without the least word of apology.

She stood there looking after him, her eyes smiling whimsically. "A very attractive man, your steward. A pity he is quite so rough-hewn." She turned back to me. "You refused Duncan's hand in marriage last night. Remember that. Now it is my turn to try my luck. I don't think," she added, her head tilted to one side as she considered me, "that you should take the offer seriously. After all, you had placed him in quite an awkward situation, hadn't you? Withdrawing from all this—" she gestured about her expressively "—for the simple life of a governess, and in his favor. A gentleman's chivalric urge, nothing more."

"I shall take care not to let it go to my head," I replied curtly. "If you want Duncan Lindsay, by all means try your chances. I shan't stand in your way."

Her lovely green eyes were suddenly cold and unrelenting. "See that you don't. It would be—most unwise." Without another word she walked unhurriedly away from me and out the door, never looking back or making any attempt to cover the fact that she was only slightly limping.

I walked down to the loch and sat there in the late sun, feeling its warmth against my skin but not in my heart. Would Fiona be successful with the Major? I couldn't possibly guess, but I had looked often enough in my own mirror to have no doubts that she was far lovelier than I could ever hope to be. Now that he would own the House of Storms—or so she thought—she would make every effort to capture his interest. And he had not shown himself to be completely oblivious to her charms; few men could ignore Fiona.

It was a depressing thought in a thoroughly depressing day. For all my fine plans, I had gotten nothing for my pains but lectures, threats, and impudence. Perhaps it was all my imagination that Morag had died because of what she knew. I wished heartily that it might be so. But already the Major and the steward had warned me that my guesses were dangerous to me, and so, therefore, they must be. But which man had my safety uppermost in his mind—and which my death?

11

Two days later Mr. MacEwen left for Edinburgh and Fiona Douglas did not accompany him.

He had used his time trying to discuss my decision with me, to no avail, and finally spent two hours closeted with the Major. The result of that conversation was his announcement to me that he must return to his office but that he would be happy to come back to the House of Storms when I summoned him for further instructions. His manner was decidedly cool, leaving me in no doubt of his feelings, and to be honest, I was happy to see him go. No one would accept my decision as settled so long as the solicitor remained here arguing with me.

I stood at the gate watching his carriage roll along the rutted road toward the village and wondering under what circumstances I might see him again. No use pretending, I was concerned for myself and for my future. The letter he carried with him was my only surety and even that was based on my inadequate knowledge of Scots law.

The next few days were disappointing. Bruce Cameron gave me no peace about my decision, deeply concerned as he was for my future prospects and the way of life I had forced upon myself for seemingly no reason. Indeed, I began to think that his constant defense of me might inadvertently upset my carefully laid plans, and so I finally asked him to give me time to consider my situation in private. He agreed with such a warm smile of relief and reawakened hope that I felt guilty for misleading him.

Fiona ignored me beyond the merest civilities, concentrating her energies on devising little stratagems to keep the Major near her. I would have found her sudden interest in sheep ludicrous under other circumstances for she couldn't tell a Dorset from a Cheviot in broad daylight, but her laughing, charming display of ignorance resulted in the Major's willing offer to instruct her. To his credit, Duncan Lindsay never badgered me about my withdrawal in his favor, but I made every effort to avoid private conversation with him until I felt more certain of myself.

Angus was angry with me, suspicious of my reasons for behaving as I had and unwilling to accept my refusal to attend to estate affairs. Our once-comfortable relationship was now an uneasy truce. Elspeth, tight-lipped and grim, said little—her actions spoke well enough of her feelings.

And no one behaved in any way that might lend color to my belief that Morag was murdered, much less betrayed unassailable guilt. I was beginning to wonder if my whole scheme had not failed miserably. I could foresee a bitter and much deserved tongue-lashing when Mr. MacEwen returned, ending in my utter humiliation. He would tell me that I should have presented my case to the proper authorities, and he would be right. Yet I had felt so strongly that this was the better way—how could I have been so completely wrong? My sleep was tormented by that question, echoing to the throb of the waves beneath my windows.

I had taken flowers from the garden to Morag's grave, kneeling there for a time thinking of the old woman and her prophecies. As the eagle screamed in the silence overhead, I gently smoothed the mounded earth and wished for a sign, a guiding hand out of this morass of suspicion and fear and hatred that had begun with my birthday. To

Morag alone I could have turned in safety and certainty. But Morag was dead—I must find my own way, however hard it might be, and pay my debt to her before my own inner peace could be achieved.

I rose to my feet, whispered a little prayer for her, and turned away. Duncan Lindsay was climbing the hillside from the burn, and I stopped short in surprise. Swallowing the rising panic in my throat, I forced myself to move calmly past the neat, empty croft to meet him.

"Were you looking for me?" I asked as he came near.

"No." He smiled. "I am glad to find you all the same. Will you walk with me, Moira—I'm sorry, you prefer Catriona. Will you walk with me?"

"I have much to do indoors today, Major Lindsay. I have been away too long already," I said evasively. "Perhaps another time?"

He smiled, more ruefully this time. "I am sure the servants can manage without you this one morning." He put his hand under my elbow and we started across the heather-clad hills. "Where is young Cameron? I haven't seen him lately."

"No. He has said he wishes to give me time to reconsider my decision about the estate. But he is coming to tea today. One of the MacDonald lads brought a note before I left." It was a subject I wished to drop.

"And is he still determined to marry you?" he asked, persisting.

"I—don't know. He has the right to withdraw his offer. After all, circumstances have changed since it was made."

"So they have. But I haven't changed, my dear. I still want very much to make you my wife." It was quietly spoken.

"I don't understand why. I'm penniless now. Or are you buying your conscience?" I asked coldly, for all that my heart was thudding against my ribs in stress.

"Like Petruchio's Kate, you'd see me hanged on Sunday first. I can't say that I blame you."

We walked on in silence, cresting the hill and angling

down toward the glen beyond *A'Bheinn Bheag*, The Little Peak. Finally as we crossed the burn that trickled beside the rough grazing, he spoke again.

"Do you know, I was glad of Mrs. Fraser's letter to me. It not only explained why I was exiled from the House of Storms over the years—it also meant I no longer faced an unwanted marriage. After all, I knew your father's wishes and had had many years to come to a grudging acceptance of them. Not, mind you, that I particularly cared for the idea of a bride thrust upon me for the sake of inheritance, but I had learned to love this land in the brief summer I was here. It meant more to me than you did, and I was quite prepared to trade my freedom for the House of Storms. There was no way of knowing what sort of person you might have become—Mrs. Fraser's letters were never lengthy and informative." He stretched out his hand to help me across a bare ridge of rock that jutted into the track, washed out by the constant rain as were so many of the formations that ran like ribs just beneath the soil. "She wrote of your progress in your studies, your bouts of childhood illness, your accomplishments in needlework and music and horsemanship, but never anything about the *girl* who one day must be my wife. Coldly formal recitals, as if she wished to discourage any interest on my part or perhaps feared I might inquire too closely if she allowed the smallest opening for curiosity."

"You hadn't impressed her with your character and trustworthiness when you were here the first time. She said as much in her last letter," I interjected in Fraser's defense.

"No, I clearly hadn't. Still, the unexpected revelation that you were a changeling, coming on the heels of that disaster at Balaclava and the painful, dreary recovery from my wounds, suddenly opened a new world for me. Can you understand that, my dear?"

Oddly enough, I could. The words he had left unsaid were there as well—the rebellious pride that must accept my father's imperious interference in his life, the chafing knowledge that an unwanted bride was the price of inheritance, the humiliating snubs that marked each refusal to permit contact with me—to a man of the Major's caliber, these constant reminders of his dependence must have cut deeply into his spirit.

He took a deep breath, as if throwing off the burden of memory. "And so, I welcomed that letter, and said nothing to MacEwen or anyone else. Instead, I waited patiently for the year of grace to end while I recovered my health. And then I came unannounced to Edinburgh and suggested to MacEwen that I accompany him and greet my bride on her birthday, all the while exulting in my secret knowledge and eager to unmask the impostor." He made a wry gesture. "In spite of myself, in spite of my plans, I soon found that you had crept into my heart and made a place for yourself there, and now I don't give a tinker's curse whether you are Moira or Catriona or a determined little devil who won't even look at me when I speak to her—I want you very much, you *and* this land. Selfish of me, I suppose—greedy, you'll tell me. But with all my heart I want both. Do you think you could stop feuding with me long enough to see me as a man and not as the wicked cousin? I suspect—hope—you care for me more than you have admitted even to yourself, which may explain your refusal to listen to anything I have to say." He was smiling quizzically as he turned toward me.

"Please don't press me, Major," I said with some difficulty. "It isn't fair." I kept my eyes on the cattle in the distance ahead of us.

"It isn't fair for you to go on with this independent stubbornness of yours, either. Tell me one straightforward reason why you can't love me, and I'll swear never to speak of the subject to you again!"

I was silent, trying to sort out my thoughts. He had asked me to be honest, and I owed him that much. But where to begin?

After a time he laughed wryly. "I have charged into certain death with fewer qualms than I feel now, waiting for a slip of a girl to speak her mind. Is it so difficult?"

Taking a deep breath, I said, "I have been told you are a gambler and that you have a taste for other men's wives."

"I have gambled, certainly—I doubt that there's an officer in the Hussars who hasn't—but never beyond my means and never for anything more than the passing pleasure of the evening. As for my tastes in women, God knows I'm not a monk, but seduction has never held any charms for me. You'll have to take my word for this, of course. I have no way of proving myself."

"Did you really fall off your horse?"

"Who the devil—? Elspeth, of course! Yes, God help me, I did. Very lowering to a crack cavalry officer's self-esteem, but not a blemish on my character, I hope!"

I laughed in spite of myself. "No."

He looked down at me. "Does my scarred face frighten you?"

"No," I said, surprised. "Why should it?"

"I thought perhaps your questions were polite ways of avoiding the real issue."

"No," I said again, and then with perhaps foolhardy courage, I added quickly, "Would you have harmed Morag to prevent her speaking the truth to Mr. Mac-Ewen?"

"Ah! I thought that might be worrying you. What makes you wonder about that? The fire?"

"The fire?" I asked, a shade too hurriedly for innocence.

"Someone had built the fire high, so that the time of her death might be in doubt. Who told you? Elspeth—or the groom?" His eyes were searching my face closely.

"I saw the smoke from the chimney," I lied, hoping he wouldn't know that that was impossible.

"No. But it doesn't matter who told you. Stay out of this one, my dear, I mean that. It isn't safe to inquire too closely. Leave this to me." Suddenly his voice changed. "Stay where you are," he said quietly. "Don't move."

Looking out of the corner of my eye to our right, I

saw the bull, head down, watching us warily. He was not ten yards away. In our involvement with our own thoughts and words we had approached the herd more closely than the bull liked.

These great shaggy Highland beasts, like something left forgotten by primeval eras, were quiet, rather placid animals on the whole. But this bull, jarred perhaps by our intent voices or unhappy with the way we had walked straight into his domain, or just feeling irritable this morning on general principles, was taking exception to our presence. The long, gracefully swept horns were pointing in our direction and the tips were backed by the weight of the head and the heavy shoulders.

"Give him time and he'll lose interest," the Major said softly. "But if he should charge, get out of here and leave me to deal with him. Do you understand?"

"He could kill you!" I whispered fiercely.

"Hush." Suddenly his eyes smiled down into mine. "If that heathen beast removes the two of us, it will be Angus who lords it at the House of Storms. A lowering thought."

"And it will be Angus who charms Fiona," I added before I had thought. It was unkindly spoken, and I regretted the words as soon as I had uttered them, but far from being angered, the Major, I found, was shaking with silent laughter. "God save the man," he said under his breath, and before I could know what he was about, his arms came around me and I was gathered into them like a wayward child.

But it was no child's kiss that he gave me. Unprepared as I was, I felt myself swept along on the fierce tide of emotion that raced between us, caught up in feelings that I had never experienced before. The resentment and bitterness and suspicion melted away as my wary pride accepted the truth, that I had come to care for this man very deeply. How odd, I wondered in some undazed corner of my mind, that our first mutual dislike for each other had changed into this deep, responsive attraction that I had tried desperately to deny.

"I love you, my dear, you know that now," he said against my hair, "and if you are honest with yourself at last, you will know that you love me, as well."

"Yes," the word barely whispered. But he did not ask me to repeat it and I was grateful. I needed time to think. Morag had warned me about this man, and yet here in his arms I could not believe that he was not to be trusted. Would I feel the same, an hour from now, shut up in my room and away from the sound of his voice in my ear? Or had the green girl succumbed to practiced charm?

I stepped back at arms' length to look up into his eyes. In spite of that disfiguring scar, the strength and character of the man were there in his face to be read if only I knew how. Suddenly I wished that Fraser were here, with her quiet good sense and serenity in the face of every problem. And yet—she had sent the boy Duncan away because he had lamed Angus, finding excuse after excuse for refusing him permission to return to the House of Storms. Confused, I shook my head and was about to move away, but his grip on my shoulders reminded me that the bull was still watching us with wary interest.

"We began badly, I grant you, my dear, but there was good reason on both sides," he said, sensing my uncertainties as clearly as if he had read my mind. "Put that behind you, if you can, and let me try to make amends. Pride is a harsh taskmaster, but if you will look into your heart, we'll find our way yet! I promise you!"

The cold light in his eyes had warmed to the clear gray of sun glinting on wintry ice, striking deep into its heart to reflect hidden lights. My wavering defenses were near collapse, *wanting* to believe his persuasive voice, but a distant part of my mind reminded me coldly that Morag had been murdered—possibly by this very man. He seemed deeply in earnest, I could feel the tenderness in his words and his arms, see it in his eyes, and all my being strained to respond.

But that distant corner of my mind remembered Morag's words—that he hid his greed behind a mask. When

Duncan Lindsay had all my inheritance and could have Fiona as well at the crook of a finger, why would he want me instead, unless for love? Why, indeed? And could I trust to the evidence of my own senses, which tried to tell me that this man was all I wanted him to be—or would they betray me in their own hunger to believe? Could I trust him—*dare* I trust him? And that distant part of my mind said, reasonably, Test him and find out—accept his proposal and see what happens before this month is out! Yes—!

Shocked, and yet strangely glad at the same time, I managed to smile. "I'm willing to try," I said, haltingly, and he caught me close once more, heedless of the snorting bull and the curious cows watching us.

"It hasn't been easy to be patient," he said, laughing, "but God knows it has been well worth the effort made!"

"Not if we are gored by that silly bull!" I reminded him, uncomfortably guilty over my duplicity. "Duncan, we can't stand here all day, waiting for him to lose interest in us. Those horns are deadly!"

He sobered instantly and turned to look at the lowered head. "He'd have charged at once if he thought we were in his way. If we retreat, a step at a time, he ought to be willing enough to see the last of us." Taking my arm, he shifted backward one full step, and then halted. The bull tossed his head restlessly, as if an insect annoyed him, but made no move in our direction. Duncan took another step, and another, stopping abruptly as the animal shifted its weight ominously. Behind it, two of the cows, leaving the herd and staring our way, edged closer as if to see better. Cows have always given me the impression of being shortsighted, and these, overcome by their curious natures, apparently wanted to have a closer look at the intruders.

For the first time I felt really frightened. If the cows came toward us and gave the bull reason to believe that his charges were in any danger, he might lose his head entirely and take action.

Speaking quietly, Duncan said, "Keep moving slowly away, a step at a time. I'll stay here and hold his attention."

"No," I said sharply. "For all his bulk, he *can* charge, and you haven't a hope against his horns. Let's wait until he tires of the game."

"Do as I say and don't waste time," Duncan ordered curtly, and I felt the authority of a man used to command. "I can deal with him on my own, but I can't look out for you as well. Clear out and give me space in which to move if I have to."

His order made sense, but I left him reluctantly, slipping back while careful to keep him between me and the herd. As I did so, he began slowly, very slowly, to unbutton and remove his coat, his movements masking mine. The two cows had stopped just short of the bull, uncertain now but still interested, and the rest of the herd had drifted closer to their more adventurous sisters. I stopped at a safe distance, unwilling to go farther than necessity required.

"All clear," I called softly.

Without turning to look, he began to drag his coat in a slow circle at the full extent of his arm, waiting until the bull's eyes followed its nearly hypnotic motion before inching away as I had done. The strange and steady sweep of the coat, never faltering in its prescribed circles, fascinated the herd. The cows had strung out into a line just behind the bull but made no effort to come any closer, their attention centered on the curious movement of the unfamiliar object. Even the bull appeared to be mesmerized, his shaggy head lifting and flicking away the tawny hair in order to see more clearly. And all the while Duncan Lindsay was adding to the growing distance between the herd and himself.

As he came up with me, I breathed again and stretched out my hand to take his. The coat described one last circle and then was still as we walked off at an angle, but the animals had lost interest in us now, and several were returning to their grazing, though the bull remained where he was until we were out of sight.

"Whatever made you think of using your coat in such a way?" I asked as we paused for him to put it on again.

"I've seen the Spanish matadors do it in the bullring. It gives the beast a target if he decides to charge, and allows the man time to dodge away while his cape is being ripped to shreds. In theory. I had no way of knowing if these prehistoric creatures think the same way as their Spanish cousins—at least they appear to be more placid than the black bulls!" There was an undercurrent of excitement in his voice, the daring that had made him a good officer. He laughed suddenly. "I shall tell our grandchildren someday that you accepted my proposal of marriage in the face of an angry bull and then calmly walked away from him."

I smiled at the note of pride in his voice, but my thoughts had taken a different turn. If Duncan Lindsay had wished to be rid of me, he could have managed my death quite neatly on the hillside just now. There would have been risk for him as well, but he was experienced in judging the danger in terms of the gain. Surely while the bull spent his fury on me the Major could have managed his own escape. No one had even known he was with me. Yet he had sent me to safety first. Had I misjudged him after all—or was I no threat to him now that I had accepted his proposal of marriage?

His hand reached out once more and I felt the warm pressure of his fingers as they closed over mine. The sky seemed suddenly very blue, the air clearer than ever before, the sunlight dancing over the distant sea, and I knew that whatever might come, for this moment at least, I was completely happy.

Fiona Douglas was standing in the hall as we entered. Her eyes went from one to the other of us and an eyebrow lifted quizzically, but she made no comment. I hastily

198

excused myself and went upstairs to change for luncheon. My mood was too uncertain to chance her capricious tongue.

Elspeth, still displeased with me for renouncing my inheritance, was waiting for me in my room. There was no way to coax her out of her grim silence. Surprisingly enough, as she was pouring water into the basin for me, she spoke. "You were walking with the Major?"

"Yes," I answered, burying my blush in the skirts I was lifting over my head. "Yes, we walked."

"Aye. And what does the Major have to say of your foolishness?"

"He asked me again to marry him," I replied, not looking up at her.

There was neither an answer nor a second question, and I couldn't judge whether she was pleased or not in the lengthening silence.

Fiona was unusually charming over luncheon, but I was preoccupied with my own thoughts. I had decided that Bruce Cameron should be told first of my decision to marry the Major—I owed him that courtesy—but somehow the words with which to break the news eluded me, even as I tried to compose the briefest announcement.

As if he understood my difficulty, Duncan took up the burden of entertaining Fiona, who paid little heed to my distraction. As they laughed and talked across from me, I wondered again that he should have chosen me when she was so clearly his for the asking.

Tea, and the arrival of Bruce Cameron, came all too swiftly, and I still had not decided how to tell him. It chanced that Fiona and the Major were already downstairs when Cameron was announced, and so I had no opportunity to speak with him privately. Postponement both relieved and unsettled me.

He stood beside me as I handed him his cup and smiled in the frank, boyish way he had. "I've been along the shore this morning, watching the seabirds. Mr. MacDonald considers it a witless pastime, I'm quite sure, but their grace and swiftness appeal to me."

"Mr. MacDonald is interested in nothing that hasn't got four legs and fleece," I said, laughing. "Pay no heed to him!"

His eyes were on Fiona and Duncan, speaking together in low voices at the other end of the room. She was at her most persuasive, and I lost Cameron's next words as I wondered what they were discussing. Pretending to have been absorbed with pouring my own cup, I said, "I'm sorry?"

"I merely commented that he was a fine actor. One moment he says he cares for you and the next you'd think Fiona was the light of his life. I don't know what the man's thinking half the time, and I doubt if she knows, either." The smile was gone, a frown in its place.

"She was asked to leave with Mr. MacEwen," I said quietly, "but for some reason she was able to persuade the Major to allow her to remain for a little longer." I, too, had had difficulty in deciding what the Major's interest in Fiona really was. Out on the hillside I had found it easier to believe in his love for me than here. Or was he simply allowing me an opportunity to speak privately with Bruce Cameron without arousing Fiona's curiosity? "I'd like to talk with you before you go. Will you walk in the summer garden with me after tea?"

I glanced up at him in time to catch the swift flare of hope in his eyes. "Yes," he said, striving to hold the eagerness out of his voice, and I felt like blurting out the truth here and now. It was unkind to raise his hopes falsely, even for so short a time. But before I could add a word to prepare Bruce for the news, Duncan came across to the tea table to pick up the dish of buttered scones and carry them to Fiona. The moment was lost.

And then Fiona Douglas was suggesting a ride and picnic toward the north coast for the next day, confident that no one would refuse such a simple and pleasant outing. It was with great pleasure that I told her that I must attend a christening tomorrow afternoon.

She pouted prettily. "Must you? Surely you wouldn't be missed in the press of friends and family!"

"The child will be named for me," I said. "It would be awkward if I didn't appear."

"Will she be Moira—or Catriona?" she asked, smiling archly.

"She will be given both names, as it happens," I replied. "One at least will be correct, and both are pretty enough." I was angry inside though I managed to return her smile.

It was a relief to walk into the gardens with Bruce Cameron after tea. Duncan had gone to meet Angus at one of the farms and Fiona was left to amuse herself. The air was cool, but I drew my shawl tighter because of the shiver I felt as I recalled the last time I had walked here. Who had followed me to the summer garden that day?

Cameron offered his arm, and we took the main path toward the sea. "You wanted to speak with me," he said as we passed behind the screen of lupines. "I can only hope that what you bring is good news for me!"

I took a deep breath to steady my voice. I would not for the world hurt him, and yet there was no other way. "It has not been an easy decision to make," I began. "I have agreed to marry Major Lindsay."

His arm tensed beneath my hand and he swung around to face me, disbelief followed by understandable anger in his eyes. "You can't be serious, Moira! Not after what he has done to you! The man has stolen your name, your home, your heritage without the slightest scruple—how can you *possibly* choose to marry him?"

"He says it doesn't matter to him whether I am Moira —or Catriona," I replied defensively.

"Of course it doesn't! He has everything now, can't you see? And just to be safe, he will marry you as well, in case the governess' poor daughter proves to be the heiress after all. And yet he spends his time listening to Fiona Douglas and ignoring you completely!"

Torn by my own fears, I cried, "He loves me!"

"Fiona would argue that fact with you! Ask her and see!"

I broke from his hold and hurried ahead on the path, my fragile composure shattering about me. But he came after me, and stopped me where the path turned toward the castle wall.

"Moira, Moira, listen to me! Marry me and together we'll force him to return what he has taken from you. You have given in completely to that man—won't you for once take *my* advice and let me help you find yourself?" His hands caught my shoulders and shook me angrily. "Are you afraid of being penniless and having to make your own way in this world? Is that why you have agreed to marry him? Moira, I haven't got a tenth of what he has, and I can't give you the House of Storms, at least not at first, but if you marry me you'll be spared a life of poverty and service without selling yourself to that fiend. And we'll fight this case through every court in Scotland, and take it to the Crown if need be! But for God's sake, tell me you won't marry him!"

"Please," I whispered, turning my face away from the light of battle in his eyes, "please don't make this harder for me! You are a fine man, deserving every happiness, and it hurts me to hurt you, but I can't pretend what I don't feel! Can't you see? I'm in love with Duncan Lindsay! God help me, I don't know why, but I am, and I hope he loves *me*, not my money nor my father's property nor anything else!" The words tumbled out, and I realized how much, how very much, I wished they were completely true.

His hands fell from my shoulders and he stepped back, stunned. "You *love* him?" he asked, as if he had not believed his ears. "In spite of what he is and what he has done to you?"

I nodded, unable to speak.

His face was white beneath his tan and he turned away abruptly as if he needed time and privacy to compose himself. I stared out to sea, emotionally empty and unable to find words to comfort him. I had expected him to take my answer better. Instead, he was deeply disturbed by my choice and somehow unwilling to accept my decision as final. Perhaps I had gone about this too baldly, but it had seemed kinder than the formal phrases of rejection that left hope lingering painfully.

He said quite softly, "How has Fiona taken the news?"

"I haven't told her—or anyone else. I felt you should be the first—" I was unprepared for the irrelevant question.

"Yes. I see. Thank you." He turned back to me, having gotten his feelings in hand once more, and his face was nearly calm. "I'm sorry, my dear, for pouring out my anger on you! It was just that—but I won't add to my sins by saying more. Am I forgiven?" His voice was contrite.

Wordlessly, I held out my hand and, smiling tremulously, nodded.

He took my hand in his and said gravely, "May I speak to you as a friend, one with your welfare at heart?"

"Yes, by all means," I replied, dreading what might come.

But he said simply, "I would ask you to give your heart a day or two to consider your choice—marriage is forever, after all. Be *sure*, Moira, that's all I ask. And if you feel in your heart that this *is* right for you, then I shall be the first to wish you happy!"

Relieved, for this was a small matter he had asked of me, I said, "I shall consider it. But I know the answer will be the same."

His face was tired and set in lines of worry in spite of my assurance. I wished that I might tell him that my marriage to Duncan Lindsay was by no means certain. It was wrong to deceive him so, and yet I felt that I had to.

"If you could understand the price you will have to pay—" he began, and then broke off. "No, I'll say no more to you today." Rousing himself with an effort, he took my arm again and turned back the way we had come. "You must tell Lindsay for me that he is a fortunate man!"

"Thank you. I shall."

"I must leave here shortly—my holiday should have been up a fortnight ago, yet while I had hope— But I shall return for the wedding, if I may!"

"Of course! We shall be happy to have you come." *Would* there be a wedding for Duncan and me?

We walked to the steps in silence and then as he turned to go, Bruce Cameron said, "I'll call tomorrow afternoon, if you have no objection?"

I knew that he was hoping to hear that I had changed my mind, but there was no polite way to discourage him. Standing by the door, I watched him walk disconsolately down the drive, pausing to speak with his usual courtesy to Fiona's groom who had crossed from the stables. With a sigh I went inside and tried to shut the lonely figure from my thoughts.

I made an opportunity to tell Elspeth about my forthcoming marriage while she helped me to change for dinner. To my surprise her only comment was a brisk, "So I know."

"You know?" I repeated.

"Aye. I've not lived with you these many years, Mistress, without learning to read your face. Now, will you be wearing your hair up or with the curls in the back?"

"Well, I have not become engaged before," I replied tartly. I had been braced for an adverse reaction and was disappointed to have none at all. Perhaps I was seeking reassurance for myself. "How could you possibly tell?"

"Give over, Miss Moira, do!" She began to dress my hair with the curls to the back, and from the look on her face I knew she had no intention of satisfying my curiosity.

"Do you approve the match?" I asked, toying with the crystal scent bottle before me.

" 'Tis not for me to speak of it if you have made up your own mind."

"You didn't like him from the beginning. Neither did I,"

I said thoughtfully. "We struck sparks that first day."
Looking up, I was in time to catch the fleeting glance she gave my reflection.

"He was ready enough to cast you out and is now willing to wed you. I'd be wondering myself if the man knew his own mind best," she said to the curl she was brushing around her fingers. "But marrying him makes more sense than tossing away your inheritance as if it were chaff before the wind! At least you know now that he isn't wedding your fortune only."

And that was all that Elspeth would say on the subject. Not one word of direct censure nor yet of congratulations, almost leaving the impression that she preferred to wait and see what time brought. The only grain of consolation that I could take from her words was that the Major was no longer fortune-hunting—unless, as Bruce Cameron had suggested, he was covering the remote possibility that I was indeed Moira, after all. I had one chilling thought as I rose to go down to dinner—had Mr. MacEwen opened my letter before he left instead of waiting the full month? And if he had, would he have told the Major what it contained?

Going down the steps to the drawing room, I felt little of the happiness and excitement of a woman in love and about to marry the man of her choice. And I was no closer to Morag's murderer than I had been before I began this dangerous game, so far as I could tell, unless today's encounter with the cattle could be considered evidence in the Major's favor.

Angus stood at the foot of the stairs, waiting for me. I felt my heart sink as I saw his face, black and set and far from friendly. Lifting my chin, I came to meet him and managed a smile.

"He told me," Angus said abruptly.

"And you have come to wish me happiness," I said with heavy irony.

"I've done nothing of the sort, as you well know. Are you daft, Mistress? Or will you have Lindsay at any price?"

There was scarcely controlled fury behind the words he flung at me.

I gasped wordlessly, then found my tongue as my own Lindsay temper rose to match his. "Speak plainly, Angus. What price have I paid?"

"It was foolish enough to toss the estate away, but to accept him *now* is tantamount to your death warrant!"

He turned to go but I caught his arm. "And who will be my executioner? Can you tell me that as well?" I demanded.

"I, for one," he said savagely. "I tried to warn the Major, but he wouldn't listen—he's half-daft himself with success and says he can look to his own! You ought to have trusted me, Mistress—for all I'm your father's bastard, I've served you well these many years. Now it's too late. The harm is done, and you must live with the trouble you've brought upon yourself by your own blindness!"

"And you might have trusted me as well," I snapped. "You might have weighed those twenty-one years you have known me and realized I am no fool!" I turned away, but this time it was Angus who halted me, his eyes suddenly alert.

"I thought that night—but then you accepted his offer of marriage—*how much do you know?*"

"About what?" I asked, all at once chilled by a sobering realization of what he had been saying to me. Was it his confession, pouring out in an angry flood, heedless in his blind rage? I didn't want to believe it. "What ought I to know, Angus?"

Before he could answer, the drawing-room door swung open behind us. Angus swore softly. As Fiona stepped into the hall, he released my arm and strode briskly away toward the estate office without another word to me. There was no opportunity to go after him, and I was not certain that I wished to until I had myself in hand once more.

Fiona was dressed with her usual care and elegance but her expression was set in cold, angry lines. Ignoring her interruption of my quarrel with Angus, she said, "I thought

I heard voices. Duncan hasn't come down yet—there is time for us to talk."

Walking toward her with a calmness I was far from feeling, I said, "I have little to say to you."

She laughed. "No, of course not. Victorious, aren't you? And puffed up with conceit." She waited until I had entered the room and then firmly closed the door.

There was a fire on the hearth and a tray of decanters and glasses set upon one of the tables. One glass was still half-full of sherry. Clearly, Fiona had not waited upon ceremony or perhaps had fortified herself for our interview.

Crossing to where I stood, she went on in the same hard voice, "Do you really believe that Duncan Lindsay wishes to marry you? How completely naive you are— inexperienced, provincial, and simpleminded as well! You silly fool!" There was biting disappointment in her tone.

"Sour grapes, Fiona?" I asked lightly, trying desperately to hold on to my swiftly raveling temper.

For an instant I thought she would strike me. The words had gone home with far more success than I had dared hope. And then to my utter surprise, she smiled quite naturally and answered, "Of course. What else?"

She watched my reaction with grim satisfaction and then went on. "I don't intend to let you have him, you know. Pure chivalry on his part—the poor child who has lost everything and must creep out into the cruel world and earn her living as her mother had done. Yes, he feels every sympathy for you—it was wise of you to decline your inheritance, my dear, the wisest move I have seen you make. If he had had to force you out of it, he would have happily abandoned you to a most deserving fate. But this noble gesture—well, you can see for yourself how well it succeeded. But do you really wish to marry a man who pities you? Has your pride sunk so low? If it has, I'm not about to sit idly by and let you ruin his life!"

Struggling with the stress and anger tearing at my heart, I said as calmly as I could, "In your own blindness, you have not noticed one thing, Fiona. Duncan Lindsay, for reasons I can't pretend to understand, has fallen in love with me! Salve your own pride by calling it pity or anything else you like, but the fact remains—in spite of all your beauty and charm and experience, he has chosen me, even without the estate! Try to take him from me, I can't stop you. Use every weapon at your command. In the end, you'll know the truth for yourself." I prayed desperately that I spoke the truth, as I reached a shaking hand toward the decanter.

When the drawing-room door opened to admit Duncan Lindsay, I was in the act of pouring a glass of sherry for myself. Whatever reply Fiona would have made was lost, and with an effort of will she turned her back on me and swept across the room to greet the Major.

It was impossible to say what was served for dinner that night. I neither saw nor tasted anything on my plate and swallowed every mouthful with the same painful effort that a meal of wool would have required. Somehow I kept up my part of the conversation brightly enough, the brittle smile on my lips threatening to fall and shatter at any moment. Duncan was quiet and solicitous, but I read other meanings into every kindness and courtesy. Fiona outdid herself in a spectacle of wit and charm that I might have enjoyed under other circumstances. As it was, every word grated on my raw sensibilities—why had he chosen *me*? As soon as the interminable meal was over, I pleaded a headache and excused myself, leaving Fiona to cajole Duncan into a walk through the gardens. I forbade myself to look back from the top of the stairs to see if she had succeeded.

As I lay in bed, listening to the night sounds and the sea's dull boom against the cliff, I thought how little I had gained with my charade. Fiona, Angus, even Bruce Cameron, were angry with me, and Elspeth was merely satisfied to see me regain my lost fortune, even at the price of Duncan Lindsay as a husband. I didn't know why Duncan wanted to marry me, and I was growing desperately afraid that Angus was the killer I sought. Twice he had told me that my life was in danger—but would my own brother harm me? And why? On what ought to have been the happiest night of my life, I lay tossing miserably in my bed, working myself into a headache, indeed, while my betrothed walked in the summer garden with a woman who had sworn to take him from me.

In the end, I rose to bathe my face, staring at the unhappy bride-to-be framed in the mirror. And then, resolutely, I vowed to continue with my masquerade until my debt to Old Morag was paid—even if I lost my life.

12

The morning dawned fair, but by nine o'clock clouds had rolled in from the sea. It was not a day for an expedition, after all, but Elspeth told me that Fiona had breakfasted early and ridden out with only her groom for company.

Duncan had waited for me in the breakfast room and rose to pour my tea as I came in. He glanced at my face and smiled. "Second thoughts in the night?" he asked gently.

"No," I said evasively, unable to confess the truth, "no, my headache prevented me from sleeping properly." Then, with a hastily summoned smile, I added, "It has gone away, thank goodness."

He set my cup beside my plate. "I haven't changed *my* mind, either," he said, and dropped a kiss on the top of my head. "Angus will be pacing the floor waiting for me, I must go with him to speak with the shepherds. Don't mind his ill humor—it will pass."

My eyes flew to his face. Had Angus told Duncan of our encounter? Surely not! Seemingly unperturbed, he was smiling down at me. "He can swallow my coming here as your husband," he went on, "but he has no liking for me as lord and master in my own right. I can't say that I blame him, actually, he hasn't forgotten his fall. And he has been a damned fine steward, from all that I can see."

He was turning to go, but I caught his hand. "Duncan—will you tell me how that accident occurred?" I asked.

Frowning, he said, "You would do better to ask Angus."

"I wish you would tell me what happened on the tower ruins. Was it your fault? It must have been the accident that turned Fraser against you—I know now that it was because of Angus' bad leg that she saw to it that he went to school and later worked under MacLeod, the steward."

His eyes strayed to the windows and the shadowed castle wall beyond. "We were quarreling as boys will. Lindsay had promised the estate to me and strictly forbade an army career. Angus, who knew he had no hope of inheriting, was nevertheless envious—his father showed him scant courtesy and would not allow him about the house, for he had no desire to be reminded of past indiscretions. It was Mrs. Fraser who recognized Angus' abilities and saved him from remaining in the stables as groom, but that was later, of course, and unexpected. For all that he was born in a city, Angus felt a deep and silent love for the estate, and tried desperately not to show it. So as we climbed that day, Angus was resentful of my future and threatening to run away and join the army. I wanted to be a soldier as my father had been, but instead, perforce, had to wait for a brat in the nursery to grow up and decide if she would have me. Taunts led to a quarrel. He was older and began showing off, I refused to have any part of it and let go of his hand. He missed his hold, then—and fell. It was my fault, and I'd just said angrily that I hoped he would break his neck, but in spite of that, I would not have had it happen." He fell silent, and turned to look at me.

"Thank you," I said quietly. "I'm glad you told me."

"It isn't a pleasant memory to have upon one's conscience, God knows," he said heavily. "The blame is mine and I accept it. Lindsay called it a boy's prank, but I knew better." He touched my hand lightly and added, "Have a rest this morning. You'll feel better." Then he was gone.

I finished my breakfast thoughtfully, seeing again the two small figures on the tower, each trying to hurt the other to ease the pain they carried inside. Had my father known the seeds of dissent he had sown? Or had he cared only to suit himself? I couldn't begin to guess.

As I walked from the castle to the village for the christening service, there was a dampness in the air and a chill that promised nasty weather before night. I hoped that it would hold off until I was at home once more for I had not bothered to order the carriage to come for me.

The christening went well, though the chill in the church urged us not to linger there when the warmth and cheer of the MacRae house beckoned us. The small cottage was ablaze with light, and a kettle whistled on the hob as we entered the small, whitewashed parlor. The furniture had been removed to provide greater space, and a table pushed against one wall. From its size, I suspected that it had come from the kitchen, but the long, immaculately white cloth fell to the floor, hiding its more ordinary purpose. Chairs were ranged about the hearth for the old and infirm, but everyone else was too busy talking with friends to bide long in one place. Social life was so limited here that any excuse served for getting together and having a party. The child was laid in her bed by a fond grandmother and other women hurried to bring out the tea and whisky and specially prepared cakes. I had sent flowers from the garden at the House of Storms, and these were arranged in a bowl in the center of the rapidly filling table. Laughter brightened the tiny room.

As Mistress, I was expected to lead the toast to the child's good health and future happiness. When the cup of whisky was placed in my hands I would merely pretend to drink of it. In my place, my father would have drained the contents, but I was a woman and must not touch strong spirits. I proposed the toast in the time-honored fashion, barely let the whisky touch my lips, and smiled to myself. This was MacRae's first child and he had sent to

Oban for fine malt whisky with which to wet her head, though it was well-known that on a hidden braeside, Mac-Rae distilled his own spirits. He and his father before him had undoubtedly provided the liquid refreshment at every party within twenty miles. Once the toast had been drunk in proper style, MacRae's Own would be the offered beverage.

I slipped back into the crowd after my duty was done, willing to watch the pleasure and conversation flow around me until I might reasonably take my leave. There were no strangers here, and in the fashion of the Highlands, every degree of relationship had been explored and established long since. The clan system might have been wiped out at Culloden Moor, but not the intense interest in blood ties that existed in these people. Even though half the murders in Scottish history had probably been committed by a family member, kinship was considered the most certain safeguard between people. Genealogy outranked anything but the price of wool and the quality of the whisky as favored topic of conversation.

Finishing the honey cakes that were on my plate, I stood near the hearth listening to an old man begin one of the traditional tales in the style that had been handed down for centuries. "In the days before time was, and in the sunshine of morning neither late nor soon, a young man came to the door of a croft, and he tired with the walking. . . ." The story of the canny Scot outwitting the crafty dwellers in the strange house unfolded in predictable style, but the old man's listeners leaned forward eagerly as if the tale were new and unheard before. I found myself caught up in the spell, and soon lost track of time.

The cottage door opened and the smith's son stepped in, smiling shyly at Dugald MacRae's sister as she hurried to meet him. I saw the scattered drops of moisture on his coat and asked if it had begun to rain.

"Aye, a little as I came along, but there's a sea mist coming in as well," he replied.

"A mist?" I repeated quickly, suddenly alarmed.

"Aye, a thick ain."

I turned quickly to make my excuses to Mairi MacRae.

"Will you have Dugald to walk a part of the way with you, Mistress?" she asked courteously, but I would not hear of taking him from his guests.

"I know my way well," I replied, and thanking her, stepped out into fine drizzle. I shivered, drawing my cloak closer about my shoulders, though it was more from buried fear than the chill in the air. A mist.

Already the pale daylight was darkening into night as the westering sun was blotted out by the fog bank. Hurrying in the direction of the castle, I made my way through the village and on its outskirts chose the shortcut across the low hills that led toward the sea cliffs. The mist lay ahead, a soft rolling blanket whose fringes had already woven about the huddled cottages and wreathed the church tower, deadening the sound and yet making twice as loud in my ears each pebble that rolled away beneath my feet. I seemed all alone in the empty vastness of the world, alone and cut off from all sanctuary.

Hesitating, I debated turning back the way I had come and begging Mrs. Hay the loan of her groom and a horse to carry me safely to the castle, then scoffed at my own fears. For twenty-one years I had lived on these acres above the sea and never before had I known silly terrors as I walked my lands. Day or night, early or late, I had gone about my affairs secure in the knowledge that my people wished me well and would do me no hurt. There was no reason to suspect that harm would come to me now just because Morag had warned me of the mists.

Squaring my shoulders, I walked forward again, trying to laugh at myself but knowing well that every muscle and nerve in my body was taut with the effort of listening and watching.

Even so, I started violently when a voice called my name not ten yards to my left. Turning toward the muffled sound, my heart beating heavily, I was relieved to see

Bruce Cameron waving and hurrying toward me over the uneven ground.

"I was on my way back to the MacDonald croft," he was saying. "Remembering that you were in the village this afternoon, I thought you might be glad of company on the way home. Or—will they be sending someone in to meet you?"

I shook my head. "No. I left no orders. You mustn't linger for my sake—I know my way in the mist and you don't—even now you'll never find the MacDonalds' unless you hurry."

He laughed. "I'll borrow one of your horses and a groom if need be."

I didn't urge him further, secretly glad of his presence. He joined me and together we turned toward the thickening mists. Already threading fingers explored the ground before us, and though I could still see for some distance behind us, all that lay ahead was lost in the silent gray folds. Bruce Cameron was talking comfortably beside me, his solid presence a bulwark against my fears.

Eventually he broached the subject of my inheritance. "*Do* you feel that you have done the right thing?" he asked anxiously. "I worry about that—and about your marriage to Lindsay. Forgive me for being blunt, but—I cannot think he really loves you. I believe he feels guilt, nothing more. After all, he has taken from you your name, your home, your fortune and left you with a life of drudgery at best. God knows, any man ought to feel ashamed! I love you too much, Moira. I can't stand by and watch your life ruined by blindness." There was a pleading note in his voice, echoing hollowly as the mist closed about us. "He has persuaded you to renounce everything—even your happiness—do you think he'll stay by your side here in Argyllshire once you are married? *You* will be left here in loneliness and heartache, while he and the Fionas of this world enjoy *your* money! Can't you open your eyes and *see*?"

I shook my head and then spoke aloud, for it was becoming difficult to judge gestures and expressions now. "My eyes *are* open, Mr. Cameron. I was wrong about the Major and so were you. I love him—and I sincerely believe that he loves me. There is no more to be said." I had spoken abruptly, perhaps, but it was unfair to him to continue so painful a subject. All the firmness I could muster went into my last words.

"So be it," he answered, so softly that I had to strain to hear him. The disappointment in his voice saddened me, and I hoped that one day he might find such happiness as he deserved. Then he added, "Be careful—won't you? I'll not try to convince you against your will, but I can't live with my conscience if I don't warn you. *Be careful!*"

Suddenly I felt uneasy, the same strange sensation I had had in the summer garden above the cliffs—a shivering trickle along my spine as if someone unseen stood behind me. I looked quickly across toward Bruce Cameron and started to speak, but his solid form was reassurance enough. I lectured myself for giving way to superstitious nonsense as we walked silently along the nearly invisible track, and yet was relieved as I took each step nearer the safety of the castle.

All at once Cameron stopped. "I say—are you certain of your direction? I'd swear I heard the sea on the wrong side."

I stopped to listen. The sound of the waves hitting the rocks came faintly from my left, as it should. After a time I said, "It's the mist—it plays tricks with sound. We are on the track cutting just above the road. A shortcut I have taken all my life. The castle is perhaps half a mile farther on."

"I could have sworn—wait here, I'll check over on this side."

"You'll lose yourself!" I cried quickly, but he was already disappearing into the shrouded gray darkness to his left. Half-angry, half-impatient, I stood where I was and listened. There were scattered sounds here and there. The sea. A bird murmuring in the distance. A branch of heather creaking beneath the weight of rain. A pebble rolling as if disturbed by a foot. "Mr. Cameron?" I called. "I'm here. Can you see me?"

There was no answer. I turned swiftly to look behind me, but there was no one in sight. Undecided, I debated what to do. Should I wait until he found his way back to me or go on alone and send the grooms out with torches to search for him? How foolish to walk away like that, I thought in exasperation. He ought to have known that he would lose himself! I felt panic again, a white-hot wave of fear that took my breath away. What if something had happened to Bruce Cameron—what if he *had* heard more than the sea—what if he had come to meet me because he really *was* afraid for me—?

The questions spun wildly through my mind, followed by the final unreasonable doubt. What if *he* had killed Morag and now lay in wait for me? Impossible! I told myself, but all the same I now hurried along the track, picking my way carefully over the rough ground, driven by an urgent need to reach home and safety. I could no longer stand still and *wait* for whatever lay watching me, stalking me somewhere in the mist. If I could reach the castle in time—

In spite of my efforts to be quiet, the sound of my passage echoed loudly in my ears, a crashing stumbling progress that advertised my panic as well as my presence. Stopping to check my bearings and to catch my breath, for the heavy beating of my heart made every lungful of air painful to draw, I felt again that odd sensation of something lurking in wait. My ears strained with listening but heard nothing more than my own breathing. I was too frightened to call out again and yet the fear of being alone with something nameless was almost too much to bear. The castle was not too far away now, surely. Someone would be there to lead a search for Bruce Cameron. I dared not chance wandering about on my own.

Hurrying, I caught my skirts in the heather by the track, tangling the soft wool in the wet branches as I passed. In my haste to pull them free, I overbalanced and fell head-long into the slippery grass, throwing up an arm to protect my face from the stiff prongs of the shrub. Too late I heard the rush of footsteps behind me. Smothered in the damp folds of my cloak, flat on my face and jarred by my fall, I tried desperately to move, but my assailant was already upon me before I could even attempt to defend myself. Something hard struck my head, pain searing through me before I could cry out. Light seemed to flare in the gray mist as the darkness came down.

When I opened my eyes, there was nothing to see. Frightened and confused, I flung out a hand to orient my-self. It met cold, wet stone, and then I realized that the strange opaque emptiness was mist and evening shadow. I must have been unconscious for some time. But where was I? Certainly not at the castle. And the damp stone beneath me was not the braeside between the village and the House of Storms. The smell of the sea was strong, and I could hear water lapping gently somewhere below. The ancient peel tower?

I lifted my head in an effort to sit up, but the wave of nausea and pain threatened to pull me back into black-ness, so I lay still, moving my hands as far as they would go, then my feet. Stone all about me. And—yes, a beam of wood by my left leg. The fallen roof of the old tower's third floor. I felt a little better, knowing where I was.

Rolling over on my side, I began to lift my shoulders, keeping my head as level as possible. It was not until my third attempt that I could sit upright without being over-whelmed with dizziness, and even then my head felt rather strange.

Thinking was a physical effort. Straining my eyes, I stared about me and then up above, but the gray walls and gray mist seemed to blend so completely that I couldn't say with any certainty where one began and the other ended.

After a time I got carefully to my feet, dreading to faint again and fall on the stone floor, but my head had cleared a little and I managed to stand. Moving slowly, with my hands outstretched before me and my feet slipping carefully along the debris-cluttered floor, I tried to define the dimensions of my prison. I soon found that the only door was locked from the outside. After several minutes I knew for a certainty that this was the upper floor of the old tower—which meant that someone had deliberately brought me here. My last memory was of falling on the heather, then hearing someone come to stand over me as consciousness ended. Whoever had struck me over the head must also have carried me to the tower.

I shivered and drew my cloak more closely about me. Why should I be *here*? Bewildered, I shook my head, forgetting, and felt the surge of dizziness return. For several minutes I leaned against the wall and put everything out of my mind except the will to remain upright.

As my strength gradually returned, I made another circuit of my prison and then a third, but I knew that there was no way out. Stone walls with a single door across the stairs, and that secured from without, no windows, stone floor that I knew for a certainty to be several feet thick, and above me the half-fallen roof of the tower, one heavy beam lying diagonally across the tower room and another sprawling over the stone steps cut upward into the wall's thickness, leading nowhere.

Drizzling rain began to fall and, miserably cold, I sought shelter under the edge of the collapsed roof. Even my feet in my sturdy walking shoes ached as the wet soles pressed against the floor. Huddled beneath the damp folds of my cloak, I tried to concentrate on logic in place of my misery and my fears. *Why?*

Surely as night came on, Elspeth would worry and send

for Angus or Duncan Lindsay. And they in turn would go to the village and find that I had left hours before. What then? Would they search for me along the road and the track over the hill, and, not finding me, decide that I had stopped to wait out the weather in one of the village houses? It wouldn't matter—whatever direction they took from the village there was not a single track that led to the tower. It was possible that no one would even consider searching here, so far out of the way. There were cliffs beyond the castle—

They would believe I had lost my way in the mists and somehow stumbled off the cliffs into the sea. It would be days, even weeks, before my body washed ashore on some narrow strand of beach or tangled in a fisherman's net. I could not have found my way to the tower without stumbling into the burn that fed the loch, in itself a landmark to point me safely home. After all, with the door of the tower padlocked still and the ladder safely in place below, who was likely to think of searching for me here? I might scream until my voice failed—chances were that no one would hear me, or if they did, would mistake my faint cries for the mewing of the gulls constantly skimming the waters of the loch and wheeling above the sea. And the person who had brought me here would see to it that the search never came too close, indeed, might volunteer to look here himself and report no sign of my presence.

Who had done this? Who was my enemy? My throat felt dry, and I swallowed with difficulty. Had someone struck Morag on the head in just the same way, coming upon her in the garden of her croft as she gathered her herbs? And as she lay at her murderer's feet, was she also lifted up and carried away, this time to be placed in her chair before the fire, as if she had dragged herself there after falling and striking her head by the door? I could picture him building the fire high enough to last until he had had an opportunity to divert suspicion from himself, hurrying away to establish his presence elsewhere.

But I had been younger, stronger, than Morag. Such a

blow killed her, yet merely stunned me; perhaps it had been partially deflected by my hood and the heavy coils of hair beneath it. And so I had been locked away here to live or die as God saw fit. Perhaps it was simple enough to creep up and strike down an unwary victim, but something else again to finish the task when the person lay senseless and helpless at one's feet.

Who was it? Bruce Cameron had been with me, only to disappear shortly before I had been attacked. Was he also a victim of my assailant? Was he even now lying dead along the track from the village, or thrown over the cliffs to the sea—or had he slipped away to strike me down from behind! Besides, he had been on Mull when Morag was killed. And how had he come by the key to the tower padlock? As far as I knew, it was either on the ring at Angus' belt or in the drawer of the steward's desk. No, it couldn't have been Bruce Cameron.

Angus. Cameron had nothing to gain by killing me, but Angus stood to inherit the whole of my father's estate if I was dead and Duncan Lindsay could somehow be implicated in murder. He had the key, and according to Duncan, he had attempted murder three times before Morag was killed. He, too, knew that I was in the village and that I might choose to take the track over the hill, hurrying homeward before the weather broke. And yet—somehow, I could not accept Angus as my assailant. Hot-tempered, angry with me though he was, I could not believe he would harm me, not even for the House of Storms. Throughout my childhood he had been my guardian and protector, teaching me to love my lands as he himself did. Not Angus!

Duncan? But I would have staked my life on his love for me—or had I indeed done so and lost! Why had he not left me to face the angry bull and been done with it? There was no reasonable explanation for sparing me then and striking me down today. Besides, he believed he already possessed the estate, unless, as I had feared earlier, Mr. MacEwen had broken his trust and prematurely revealed the contents of my letter. Duncan had every reason and every opportunity to kill Morag, but there was no need to do away with me, not now.

Who then? Elspeth? Nonsense! There was nothing to be gained by harming me, unless she had hoped to frighten me into believing Duncan had attacked me. In that case, surely she would have left me on the track and not brought me here. Elspeth might conceivably kill Morag to protect me, but she would never touch me. Fiona might well wish to see me dead, might even have managed to kill Morag to prevent me from inheriting the House of Storms and marrying Duncan. But even with a fully healed ankle she could not have carried me so far.

Morag had been killed, most likely because she knew the truth about my birth and could establish my identity once and forever. Before that, three attempts had been made against Duncan. Now my life was at hazard. Why? The House of Storms, *Tigh-nan-Sian*, was the only common factor. Duncan had threatened to expose me as an impostor, a changeling. Morag had held the key to my identity. And was I to die because I had renounced my claim, or because I had agreed to marry Duncan Lindsay? Angus was the only person who stood to gain from all three deaths. I had to face that. No matter how I twisted the facts, I couldn't escape the answer: Angus. And Morag's prophecy might well apply to him. He could easily have come to the village to meet me, only to find me in Bruce Cameron's company. He had managed to separate us, and I in my panic refused to wait for Cameron to return and foolishly walked into the trap of Angus' making. It must be so. Surely Bruce Cameron would not harm me—he wanted to marry me!

It must be Angus, though every fiber of my being rebelled at the idea. I had known him all my life! I couldn't believe—

As if he had been conjured up by my unhappy thoughts, I heard his voice bellowing my name. It echoed across the loch, muffled and distant in the mist, reverberating hollowly against the walls of stone. I froze and tried to listen. Just my name—nothing more, repeated at intervals as if he walked along the verge of the loch itself. My coldness vanished in a wave of indecision.

If I answered—and he heard me—would he rescue me? Or come in to finish what he had begun? If others were with him, surely he must pretend to save me now. Yet try as I would, I could not hear any voice but his. He was my half-brother! Surely I had nothing to fear from him! Yet, because he was illegitimate he had no hope of inheriting the estate—so long as Duncan and I lived.

My father—his father—had never let him forget that he was unwanted. Lindsay, happily married to my mother, had not wished to be reminded of his past, and would have left his son to the workhouse in Edinburgh. Angus, with his stiff-necked Lindsay pride, was sent to the stables only because my mother took pity upon him. He was steward now only because Fraser had recognized his ability and allowed him to develop it. If anyone had a right to hate, it was Angus.

Frightened and uncertain, I listened to that deep voice calling out over and over again, but could not find the courage to answer him. Let him think me unconscious still, or dead.

In the narrow confines of this tower, I couldn't escape from him, and even in the mist-shrouded darkness I could not hope to elude him. So long as I remained conscious and unharmed physically I might yet survive, and if I had wronged Angus by doubting him, it was a risk I must accept.

Reluctantly I held my tongue and listened to the voice come closer and then slowly fade away.

The silence afterward was worse than ever. I shivered uncontrollably and sank down again into a huddled heap for warmth and what comfort I could muster. Now I must consider what to do, how best to protect myself. How long before I began to suffer from this exposure to rain and cold, lack of food and dry clothes, losing ability to think and act? In the next day or so, someone would surely come to the loch—one of the shepherds, or a crofter, or even a lad, escaping his mother's watchful eye, to fish for an hour or so. I had only to wait. But how would I know, enclosed in these windowless walls, when someone was out there?

In spite of myself, I remembered my great grandmother, locked away here long ago because she was mad. As a child I had heard the stories about her, for she had died raving in this very room on a stormy winter's night. How long until, like her, I too raved in a madness of fear and thirst—?

With an effort, I caught my racing imagination and forced my mind away from such thoughts. In time I would be found, for every tenant, crofter, and villager would be searching for me by morning. Other men would surely come this way, not all of them would concentrate along the cliffs above the sea!

I felt depression settling on my spirits, and my aching head added to my misery. There was no way out of my predicament—I should have called out to Angus and risked everything on the one small chance of rescue!

I have no way of knowing how much time passed, for I slipped in and out of consciousness as my aching head and numbed body made themselves felt. Confused dreams tortured my rest and jarred me back to wakefulness, only to drift away again before I could make sense of them. Faces and people, unfriendly and terrifying, threaded their way between reality and nightmare in feverish, inexplicable activity.

Cramped and shivering with cold, I woke with a start to the sound of my name being called. The echo of sound seemed at first to be in my own mind, as often happens in dreams, and I had no desire to move from where I was to listen for more tricks of my own imagination. But the shout came again, and I lifted my head to hear more clearly, trying to shake off the lethargy that engulfed me.

The third time the shout was nearer, and I recognized Duncan Lindsay's voice.

Almost weeping, I scrambled to my feet and then fell headlong as the sudden movement caused a stab of pain in my head and aching protests from my stiff limbs. The shock of a puddle of cold water beneath my face revived me and I stood again, this time more gingerly. Moving carefully, I found the walls and then the door. He was nearer, and as my own name faded away in echo, I called out with all my might.

A shattered croak came from my throat. I tried again, desperate to be heard before he went out of hearing. Finally my aching throat managed a cry that was unlike my own voice but nonetheless clear enough to reverberate in the tower room and carry down to the water.

A shout answered almost at once, and I began to hammer on the heavy, iron-bound door. My fists made muffled thuds and I cast about frantically for a stone to pound on the wood. This made considerably more noise and spared my voice. I brushed away the hot tears of relief as Duncan spoke again, this time quite clearly, as if he stood on the tumbled rocks at the tower's foot.

"Are you alone?" he asked.

"Yes, yes," I replied. "Do you have the key?" I dreaded being left alone even long enough for him to return for it.

"No. But I have my pistol. One way or another I'll reach the ladder."

There was a silence and then the ear-splitting report as he fired at the padlock on the door below where the ladder was kept. It must have yielded to this treatment, for I heard Duncan pound it twice with a stone before I heard the sound of the door creaking open. Again there was silence, longer this time.

Then Duncan called, "It isn't here—I can't find the ladder."

Suddenly frightened, I cried, "It must be! Search carefully—you'll find it!"

"It isn't here. Moira, it could be on the main level. Where are you?"

"On the next floor—the old solar. There is a door to the stairs, but it is locked, from the other side. Please be careful—"

"Hold on!" he yelled. There was a shot and then another as he fired at the heavy padlock on the door to the first floor. Standing quietly, I strained my ears to follow his movements. What use to break the lock when without the ladder fifteen or more feet of stone stretched vertically between him and the door above? He had no choice but to return to the castle now—

I caught the sound of small stones or bits of rock skittering to the ground and realized suddenly that he must be trying to climb the face of the tower as he and Angus had done as boys. What if he fell? The rain-slick blocks of stone with moss and wildflowers eating away the mortar in the crevices would be nearly impossible to grip anyway, and the lightweight boy was now a tall, fully grown man!

My heart was in my throat and I stood tensely gripping my hands together to still the uncontrollable shivers that wracked me. I dared not call out for fear of distracting him at the wrong moment, but every fiber of my being tried to cry out to him to go back before it was too late. Time seemed to creep and yet to fly. How long had he been climbing now? A few seconds—or ten minutes. I could picture him, spread-eagled on the stone face, trying to choose his footholds and purchase for his hands as the mist swirled about him in the darkness. Each movement must be felt out and carefully tested, his fingers, reading what his eyes could not see, traveling over the rough-hewn rocks with the sensitivity of a blind man. One mistake and he would plummet to the rocks below to be horribly injured if not killed outright.

A shower of small pebbles and mortar seemed to thunder in the stillness, and I waited, horrified, for the crashing fall but there was none. Somehow he had managed to

226

cling to the wall in spite of whatever had created that small landslide. I pressed myself against the cold wet walls, trying desperately to hear and in some way share his daring effort, cursing the three feet of stone that prevented me from seeing and even possibly helping him climb.

And then after endless minutes of uncertainty that tore at my nerves, I heard the spinning clang of the padlock as it was unclasped and dropped free. The heavy door creaked as it was eased open with great care. I felt weak with relief.

There followed a prolonged silence, and then the faraway breathless voice calling, "So far, so good. Yes, the ladder is here, I feel it by the stairs." Footsteps rang across the floor below and, two at a time, came up the steep, curving stairs. My ordeal was nearly over and tears of relief mixed with joy spilled down my cheeks. Outside the door now, Duncan said, "Another padlock. Cover your ears and stand clear."

I quickly did as I was told.

The explosion of sound in the confines of the stone stairwell cut into the thickness of the tower wall filled the air, deafening and expanding until it buffeted my body and shattered my aching head. Instinct told me that he had fired twice, but I could not differentiate the sounds. As the echoes rolled through the tower and reverberated over the loch and the hills, I became aware of something else—something too indistinct for my battered ears to hear clearly at first. A muffled clattering, a heavy thudding.

I stood there uncertainly, my dazed mind sorting out the noises. Two men were fighting outside the door! With a cry of alarm I raced across the floor and pulled wildly at the handle. Although the broken padlock was gone, the hasp held. Jerking with all my strength, I tried again and again. Finally the hasp gave, as if the metal had been cracked by the shots. Summoning all my reserves, I pulled once more, the handle biting deep into the flesh of my chilled fingers.

The heavy door swung open so suddenly that I lost my balance and fell, jarring every bone in my back. But there was no time to waste on self-pity. Unknowingly, I had lured Duncan to the very place where Morag's murderer lay in wait, now, when I had been so certain that the nightmare had ended and safety was within my grasp at last.

13

With the door open, the sounds of the struggle became clear. Duncan Lindsay shouted to me to keep out of the way as I scrambled up and hurried to the steps, but there was little I could do. The two men filled the black stairwell with their flailing limbs and bodies, scarcely able to see each other and yet locked in deadly combat. I couldn't possibly tell them apart, and any well-meaning attempt to help might have done more harm than good.

Whoever had brought me here must have been hiding on the first floor, unseen by the Major as he had entered the dark room. He had merely waited until the gunshot masked the sound of his movements and then attacked Duncan from behind.

The tumbling figures rolled down the steps and burst into the open beyond. I followed them, feeling my way down the curve of the wall, frightened by the savage battle going on in the darkness, poised to help or to flee as the need came. Something under the sole of my shoe grated harshly on the stone and fell heavily just ahead. I thought at first that it was the shattered padlock, then bent swiftly to feel with trembling fingers for—yes, the pistol that Duncan had dropped or that had been knocked from his hand. I dared not fire now but if Duncan failed to win—

I refused to think of it and huddled unseen just out of range of the wild struggle going on in the cluttered room at the foot of the stairs. It would be unbearable to have his death on my hands! I had brought him here—was that what the murderer had hoped would happen?

Someone struck the ladder, grunting hoarsely as it shifted under his weight. Something brushed by my skirts and I stepped back so quickly that my shoulder struck the wall behind me, nearly causing me to drop the pistol.

Then without warning, one of the figures rose heavily to his feet and aimed a kick at the second man, who rolled away just in time to avoid the savage thrust. The first figure backed away to regain his balance and then stumbled blindly over the ladder. The other man was on him almost at once and they crashed against the far wall.

Somehow in the struggle they misjudged the open doorway. There was a shout as I cried out in warning, and then a man stood outlined clearly against the paler darkness of the mist beyond. He flung out an arm to catch himself, poised there for an instant framed by the rectangle of stone, and then, as his opponent reached out to him, he plunged, screaming, out of sight.

I thought surely that the second man, overbalanced and half out of the doorway himself, would follow. There was seemingly no way that he could help himself; but then he managed to catch the door's edge and, with enormous effort, throw himself back to safety.

The echoing cry was cut short by silence below, leaving only the sound of heavy breathing not twenty feet from me. It had all happened so swiftly that I had been unable to move. Now I clutched the pistol to me, uncertain whether friend or foe had survived and ready to dash back up the stairs the way I had come, before I too found myself falling through that rectangle of misty darkness. All the while something inside me was crying out for Duncan.

And then to my unspeakable relief, Duncan Lindsay said hoarsely, "I couldn't reach him. I'm sorry."

With a cry I stumbled forward to kneel by him as he

got to one knee. His arms, warm and comforting and *alive*, came about me, and I rested my head against the hard muscle of his shoulder.

"My love," he murmured gently, "my dearest love." And I felt his lips brush my hair.

All that I had suffered—the blow on the head, the cold and fear—all these melted away as I clung to him. What matter whether I was Moira or Catriona? So long as I had his love, what more could I ever need?

After a time, he said, "You are shaking with cold! I must get you home."

"Who was he?" I asked, dreading the answer. Duncan helped me to my feet.

"You don't know?"

"Angus?" I asked unsteadily.

"Good God, no. Bruce Cameron, unless I miss my guess."

"Bruce Cameron?" I cried, startled. "But *why?*"

We were interrupted by the orange glow of torches and the shouts of several men. I could see them coming across the hill toward the loch, the bright flames flickering across the water.

"I must move the ladder," Duncan said. "Stand—there, that's it. I can't risk striking you in the darkness." He began to manhandle the heavy ladder to the door and shift it into position for lowering.

I could hear Angus clearly now, his voice nearly hoarse with shouting. Duncan replied, and the group of men turned quickly toward the tower. As they came nearer, Duncan called again.

"He's there below—on the rocks. Can you see him?"

The torches bobbled crazily as the men broke into a run. And then there was silence for long seconds before Angus called, "Dead, damn him! And Moira?"

It was the first time that I had heard him use my Christian name. I felt deeply ashamed of my suspicions of him as I caught the anxiety in his tone.

"Safe, thank God. But wet and cold. Here—I'll lower the ladder. Watch for it."

The ladder went rattling over the edge as Duncan braced himself carefully against a ringbolt in the floor, guiding it down to the eager hands reaching up for it. When it was steadied into place, he came back to me. "Can you manage? Or I'll carry you, if you prefer."

I shook my head. "No. I'll go alone."

"Hold on tightly. I'll be just below you and can climb back the instant you need me," he said, guiding me across the floor to the door. I found my footing on the first rung, and aided by the torch light, stepped out to grasp the ladder. Once I was securely settled, he moved past me and together we began the slow descent. As we neared the bottom, Duncan swung off to the left, his body blotting out the horrible scene on the rocks.

Angus lifted me down, helping me over the rough ground away from the ladder—and Bruce Cameron's body. "It isn't pleasant," he said harshly, "but it was merciful. I'd have killed him with my bare hands, else."

Duncan and two men, whom I now recognized as Donald, my own groom, and Graham, Fiona's, came after us. "We must take her back as quickly as possible," Duncan was saying to them, "but someone ought to stay with the body."

"I will," Graham said unexpectedly. "Leave me a torch."

Duncan nodded and walked back with him while we three continued on our way.

"Can you walk?" Angus asked, watching me carefully.

"I believe so. It's just that my feet are numb with the cold," I replied, trying to ignore the ache in my cramped knees.

"Then walking will improve the circulation," he said, his hand under my elbow.

Duncan caught up with us and took my other arm. My feet stumbled at first, then began to work as the blood flowed into them. The pain was excruciating, but I was so grateful to be safe that I could have endured any discomfort. We moved at a slow but steady pace, and after we had crested the hill beyond the loch, Donald was sent ahead to warn the household of our coming. By that time I was too tired to ask the questions that raced through my mind. As it was, Duncan carried me the last hundred yards.

We swept through the open doors of the House of Storms and Duncan asked the stunned maid, "Where is Elspeth?"

"Still at the auld croft, sir. Waiting for word."

"Send one of the lads to fetch her. But first bring something hot—soup, tea, whatever—to the drawing room." Then over his shoulder to Angus, he added, "Find the whisky."

Angus nodded and we went into the drawing room where a fire burned brightly on the hearth. I could have wept at such a welcome sight. Duncan set me on my feet and turned a chair to face the warmth. "Sit down," he said, loosening my hood and lifting away the wet, cold cloak. Then, kneeling beside me, he began to chafe my hands. Angus came in with a whisky decanter and glasses. Without waiting upon ceremony he poured three generous measures and passed them out.

"I dare not!" I said, refusing mine. "Not on an empty stomach."

"Drink it and never mind," he ordered, tossing off his. "You need the warmth."

"Drink it," Duncan echoed, and I began to sip the heavy golden liquid, almost at once feeling the fiery glow of it seep through my body. My hands and feet began to ache in earnest as the blood slowly coursed back into them, and tears came unbidden into my eyes.

"Do you feel able to talk? Can you tell us what happened?" Duncan asked.

"Yes, but I know so little—" I began and went on to recapitulate the events of the evening from the time I had stepped out of the MacRae cottage into the advancing mist. "I didn't know who struck me," I ended. "I never saw him."

"Show me the wound," Duncan said, and swore softly

as I lifted my hair from the painful lump behind my ear. My gently exploring fingers could feel the crust of blood over the broken skin and the dimensions of the bruising even though it was hidden from my sight.

The door opened and the maid came in, bearing a tray of tea and soup. "With Cook's compliments, Mistress," she said shyly. "I've sent Donald to fetch Elspeth and brought you a blanket as well. Can I help you, Mistress?"

"Not now," Angus told her and sent her away. He brought me the bowl and I drank it eagerly—a rich mutton and barley broth that filled my empty body and whirling head with nourishment.

Pushing away the empty tray, I turned to Duncan, who had sat beside me quietly while I ate. "Why—tell me *why* Bruce Cameron wished to kill *me*."

He looked at me for a moment and then said slowly, "I don't know that he did. Perhaps he hoped to frighten you into marrying him in place of me. It's the only explanation for locking you into the tower, surely."

"He had begged me to reconsider my decision—he said we'd fight the question of my identity through the courts, if I would accept his proposal. So he was a fortune-hunter, after all!"

"He was more than a fortune-hunter. He was a murderer," Duncan replied grimly. "Cameron was prepared to kill for what he wanted."

"Morag?" I asked, bewildered. "How could he have—he was on Mull!"

"He tried to make everyone *believe* that he was there." Duncan glanced up at the steward's impassive face. "I thought at first that Angus was behind the attempts on my life—it made sense. Instead, it was Cameron who lured me out into the dark summer garden and the cliff's edge. He didn't know then that Angus and I were at odds, and possibly expected my death to be taken as an accident. Fortunately, I was used to defending myself in tight places. Somehow he found a way to tamper with the luncheon after we visited Morag—I suppose the herbs in her garden gave him the idea, if not the means itself. He must have recognized some of them and knew which would heal—and which might kill. He fired at me also, though we can't find where he had hidden the pistol—the MacDonalds swear that they never saw a gun in his belongings. I was certain then that it was Angus, who had gone out to destroy the ewe." Duncan stopped and took a deep breath as if throwing off a burden. "But after we fought that day, I began to doubt. Angus—knowing himself to be innocent—thought I was lying about the attempts on my life until I was angry enough to face him there on the hillside. When our tempers had cooled sufficiently to think, each of us suspected Cameron. Angus followed him to Mull—no, you didn't know that, of course —we couldn't prove a thing, after all!" he added as I started to speak.

"You should have warned me!" I cried.

"I tried to earlier," he said ruefully. "You thought the pot was calling the kettle black."

And so I had. Certain that Duncan was wrong about everything, wanting to hate him, I had refused to listen.

"You see, ever since we had discussed fell climbing in Cumberland, I'd been wary of him. He knew damned little about the Lake District, and I'd spent several summers there with school friends. Still, fortune-hunting doesn't mean that a man is a killer, God knows. But Angus lost him on Mull and came back to find that Morag was dead."

"It was my fault," I said quietly. "I let it be thought she was a witness against me. That silly tale about the man with red hair—Bruce Cameron believed me, didn't he?"

"You thought I had killed her," Angus said, leaning his shoulders against the mantel. "Why?"

"Because—because if I was disinherited and Duncan blamed for her death, the House of Storms would come to you," I whispered, deeply conscious of wronging him. "I thought it must be Duncan—or you."

"She was my grandmother," he said bitterly. "Do you suppose I'd have harmed her even for *Tigh-nan-Sian?*"

"Grandmother!" I echoed, and saw the surprise in Duncan's eyes as well.

"Aye. It was she who came to tell my father that my mother had died, leaving me with no home but hers. He would have no part of me, though he knew well enough that I was his. It was the Mistress—your mother—who forced him to give me a place here. Morag took the empty croft in the glen to see that I prospered, but forbade me to tell anyone that she was my grandmother."

"So—" I said swiftly, "so that was what my mother had done for Morag! She spoke of it at the croft, and I didn't understand what she meant—"

"Aye, it was that. Your father was used to having his way, but the Mistress stood firm against him. In the end he relented—for peace with her, not for me."

So much lay at my father's door—the bitterness that rode Angus like devils, the rivalry between the two thwarted boys, the consuming anger that had blinded me to any good in Duncan—even *his* unbearably tender pride which rebelled at the necessity of marrying the heiress chosen for him. All the outgrowth of my father's overweening arrogance and his determination to have his way as it pleased him. Had he ever cared for anyone save my mother? I couldn't believe he had, not deeply enough to put another before himself.

"I ought to have suspected Bruce Cameron—he lied about you, Duncan—but I could see no advantage for him in harming me, and I thought his lies were simply jealousy." I pulled the blanket closer about me. "He saw you as a dangerous rival, and Morag as a witness against me, but I don't suppose we'll ever know exactly why he struck me down or left me in the tower. Unless he hoped to lure you there and make me believe that you were to blame, that he had killed you while rescuing me," I said thoughtfully.

"It could be true," Angus replied, refilling my glass. He smiled across the decanter at me, oddly at home here in the drawing room, though incongruously large amongst the delicate furnishings. "If so, he reckoned without yon female."

"*Fiona?*" I asked in dismay.

Duncan gave me a half-apologetic glance. "You hadn't returned when I came in. Fiona tried valiantly to make me believe that you'd run away with Cameron—he'd come here in the afternoon, hoping to find you, and told her that you had changed your mind about marrying him. I went to the village at once and questioned Mrs. MacRae and she said you had left long since."

Angus chuckled softly and Duncan flushed. "He set out like a madman, horse and pistol, on the road inland."

"Yes," Duncan admitted. "I was in a rage of jealousy. I couldn't believe you'd go willingly, and yet—Fiona was very convincing. By chance I met a carter who had come down that way and he had seen nothing at all save a flock of sheep. I turned back to find that Angus had been searching on his own."

"As soon as the mist came in," Angus said. "When there was no sign of you, I went to the tower. Remembering that the old sheep dog—Morag's dog—had been found by the tower, I thought he might have trailed her murderer so far, and that it was a likely enough place to hide. But both times the outer door was locked and I had the only key."

In spite of the warmth and brightness about me, I felt suddenly chilled. "I lent him the key once! He must have copied it! I never dreamed— But do you mean to say that Cameron was hidden in the tower, having come back secretly from Mull? He was there, that day, as I sat below the walls?" It was a horrible thought.

"Very likely," Duncan said quietly, reaching out to touch my hand.

"Were you conscious when I called?" Angus asked gravely.

"Yes," I admitted, owing him honesty. "I was afraid. I

was locked in—and to my knowledge, you had the only key. I was afraid you were merely pretending to search, and that if I answered you might come to finish what you had begun." I stretched out my hand. "I couldn't believe, in my heart, that you were guilty, but I dared not take the risk! Can you understand and forgive me, Angus?"

He took my hand in his great one. "There was reason enough for your suspicion, God knows," he admitted roughly. "I can't blame you for that." There was a glint of the old friendliness in his eyes as he added, "You'll not be so hardheaded with me in future." He turned to Duncan. "Even with a copy of the key, how did the man manage to lock himself in?"

"He didn't, of course. But from below, the lock *appeared* to be intact. By the time I reached it, it was damaged by the shots I had fired at it—"

My thoughts wandered away from them. It was still impossible to think of Bruce Cameron as a cold-blooded killer. Yet—he had been utterly shocked to learn that Morag was *my* witness. I would need time to absorb the truth, to see him as he had been and not as he had pretended to be. Because of the violence in their natures, I could have accepted guilt in Duncan and Angus more readily than in mild-mannered Bruce Cameron! Morag had said I must not be deceived by the mask that evil wore. But how little one understands about the man beneath the façade, the heart behind the graceful words, how hard to *judge*— Even though she disliked Duncan because of Angus, Morag had been scrupulously fair—I was the one who had misunderstood. But I had found her killer, and while it was too late to help me settle the question of my identity, I was satisfied—

The door opened suddenly and Fiona in a dressing gown of palest blue, her hair cascading down her back, came swiftly into the room. Her eyes flew to my face. "Then it's true—you have found her!"

"As you see," Duncan replied, rising.

"And Cameron?"

"He is dead." To soften the words, he added, "There was no elopement. He tried to kill me at the old tower; we fought, and he fell to his death on the rocks."

She fumbled for a chair and sat down suddenly, her face paper white. "My God," she said softly. "My good God!"

"He had carried me there after trying to kill me," I told her, understanding the disbelief she must be feeling. "Perhaps—" I broke off, my voice winding down at the look in her eyes.

"I found her in time," Duncan was saying, his hand resting briefly on my shoulder. "She never intended to leave with him whatever Cameron may have told you."

Fiona looked up, fighting for control. "I was certain he spoke the truth—you could see that he was mad about her—"

Duncan nodded. "I understand." He gave her a moment to collect herself and then added, "Elspeth hasn't returned from the croft and Moira is exhausted. She ought to be in her bed. Will you take her to her room, Fiona?"

Angus came forward to lay a hand on my forehead. "She's feverish," he said. "No doubt she'll be ill after this."

Indeed, my throat was aching abominably and I shivered under the coolness of his touch. I looked up. "I'm terribly sorry I failed to trust you after all these years."

"Go to bed. We'll talk tomorrow." He smiled. "We had all come to suspect our shadows, and I was not beyond doubt. The House of Storms is prize enough to tempt any man."

Duncan helped me to my feet. "I'll carry you upstairs," he said, and swung me into his arms.

The corridor seemed cold after the fire's warmth and Duncan's arms tightened as I shivered involuntarily. "You are safe, now," he said. "It will do you good to sleep as long as you can tomorrow. I'll send Elspeth to you when she comes."

"No," Fiona said behind us. "I shall sit with her until

239

she sleeps. Let the woman rest tonight—Moira will have need of her tomorrow."

We went up the stairs in silence, but at my door Duncan set me on my feet and then bent to kiss me. I responded, my lips warming to his, and wished that time could stand still for a little while as he soothed away my fears and misery. It was such a wonderful thing to love—and be loved in return.

Lifting his head and smiling down at me, he said softly, "Morag was right. It matters nothing to me whether you are Moira or Catriona. You are—yourself. That is enough for me and always shall be. Whatever is mine is yours, and most of all, my heart!"

"I love you," I said shyly. "I think I have loved you since you came, but in my pride I refused to believe it."

Fiona opened the door to my room and Duncan stepped back. "Sleep well!" he said gently and touched my cheek with his finger.

She closed the door firmly and led me across to the fire. "There is hot water. Take off those wet clothes and I'll help you bathe."

I shook my head. "I'm too tired, Fiona. Tomorrow. I'll just wash my face and hands."

She went to the bed as I washed and turned back the covers. "There is a hot brick ready for your feet. Moira—did Bruce Cameron say nothing to you about—his intentions?"

"No, nothing," I said, rinsing my face and reaching for the towel. "He tried to persuade me to reconsider rejecting my inheritance and to marry him, rather than Duncan. I refused." I laughed bitterly. "There's the joke, Fiona. Mr. MacEwen has a letter stating that my actions were based on a plan to ferret out Morag's killer by pretending to be Catriona for a month. And it worked."

She had stopped stock-still, a pillow in her hands. "MacEwen has the letter now?" she asked sharply, her eyes on my face.

"Oh, yes. I gave it to him before making that dramatic announcement at the dinner table. At least—I hope the letter is valid in Scots law. At any rate, Duncan doesn't care and neither do I, oddly enough."

She was frowning, the pillow forgotten as her mind took in what I was saying. And then she tossed it on to the bed and came across to help me change. "Do you really believe Duncan loves you?"

"Yes," I replied simply. "I can't imagine why he should, but he does."

Fiona shrugged. "Perhaps. But all this while he has been making love to me."

I stopped short. "Nonsense!" I snapped after the briefest hesitation.

She smiled. "Is it? Look into the mirror, my child."

I glanced into the glass before I could prevent myself. The hazel eyes and tumbled hair of golden-brown set off a pale face, strain marked in every line. Pretty, perhaps, but no match for Fiona's brilliant coloring, the lovely face tilted now to catch the warm sparkle of candlelight deep in the green eyes.

She laughed softly. "He may indeed marry you—but only to protect his interest in the estate. When that is done, boredom will send him back to me. Are you prepared for that?"

"Nonsense," I said again, curtly this time. My throbbing head made the room seem to spin and her words were half-lost in the fatigue that swamped me. I fumbled with the buttons on my gown and managed to undo them. She picked up my night dress and turned to hold it before the fire while I removed my petticoats.

"So you will marry him and Mr. MacEwen will see to it that you retain a share in the estate," she murmured as she slipped the warmed gown over my head.

"So it would appear," I replied. "Perhaps you should plan to leave as soon as possible. It would be better—for both of us."

241

"Indeed," she said noncommittally, and waited while I got into bed. "We shall see." She tucked the covers close about me. "Warm enough?"

"Yes. At last," I sighed.

Fiona bent to snuff out the candles. "I'll sit here while you sleep. If you need anything just call."

I murmured drowsily, "I'm sorry we can't be friends, Fiona. But—thank you!"

She laughed coldly. "For what?" she asked and turned away to take a chair by the hearth.

I snuggled into the bed's warmth, my bruised head cushioned on the pillows and my sore throat carefully protected by the high neck of my gown. Mine were practical clothes and much more comfortable when one felt miserable than the shimmering silky things that Fiona wore. My thoughts drifted feverishly. Poor Bruce Cameron lying broken on the rocks. In spite of what he had done I could feel sorrow for him. He had seemed so gentle and kind, so bright and full of life, yet he was ready to kill for what he wanted. What had warped his spirit in such a way? Greed? Whatever the reason, he had paid dearly for it. How easily it might have been Duncan lying there in his place! I could see his scarred face clearly, the smile touching his eyes, as he wished me good night.

I felt myself floating deliciously into the soft border of darkness that waited for me. My last recollection was of Fiona seated by the fire, staring into its heart with a frowning, unreadable face that shone as if tears glistened upon her cheeks.

I woke abruptly, struggling for breath. My lungs burned and my throat felt torn apart. The room was in blackness and a heavy weight across my body pinned me down. Pneumonia, I thought incoherently, I'm dying of pneumonia, but in the next instant I realized that a pillow was held over my face and I was being smothered.

Frightened out of my wits, I began to struggle wildly,

reducing the air in my lungs even further. The world burst into a kaleidoscope of colors and I was doubly afraid now as my senses began to slip away. In one last frantic effort I thrashed about on the bed, ripping at the binding bedclothes with my hands, kicking with my feet.

The weight on my chest shifted and for an instant the pillow over my face shifted fractionally, allowing precious, life-giving air to flow into my lungs. With the extra breath I found new strength, and as the pillow clamped down once more, I drew up my knees and lunged. The pillow fell away again and I threw myself off the bed, brushing my shoulder against the night table as I crashed to the floor. My assailant came down on top of me and I fought madly, my hands ripping at the sheer silk that fell over me. Fiona. Fiona Douglas was trying to kill me!

We rolled about the floor, Fiona striving to pin me down as I struggled to wrench free. Exhausted, feverish, I was no match for her, and my tortured lungs wouldn't permit a scream even if my raw throat could have formed one. Desperately I flailed out, hoping to touch some weapon I could use. My foot collided with the table by the bed and I gave it a vicious kick, sending it crashing against first the wall and then my ankle.

I gasped and rolled away, trying to reach the hearth and the poker that rested beside the glowing coals. Guessing my intent, Fiona caught my arm and drew me back, her strength ferocious. She forced the pillow once more over my face. Thrashing about, we overturned one of the chairs and then my source of air dwindled into nothing and my lungs sucked in vain at the soft crushing surface of the pillow. I tried to fight but found my limbs unable to carry out my commands. The darkness spun crazily, then burst into a shower of light as the tightness in my head and eyes became unbearable. I had almost ceased to struggle, when the door of the room burst open and voices filled my ears.

Fiona and the pillow were flung away. Cool fresh air

swept my face, but my lungs were not able to pull it in. I choked and gasped as Duncan lifted me and carried me across the room.

"Open the window!" he shouted, his voice ringing through my very skull. The curtains were torn aside and the window shoved open. Without hesitation, he thrust me half-way out into the blackness of the night.

The cold air striking my skin and the sensation of falling through space caused me to gasp and breath flowed into my body. Sobbing with pain and the joy of filling my lungs, I put out my hands and touched the icy dampness of the castle walls as the sea below seemed to fling itself toward me in great white plumes of spray. Lifting my head, I saw the midnight black of the sky pricked by stars and overhead a faint brightening as the first pale glow of false dawn tinged the eastern horizon. The mist had cleared, I thought wonderingly, and the day to come will be fair.

Assured that I was breathing normally again, Duncan pulled me back into the room and swung the window shut with his right hand as his left supported me. Fiona, crying incoherently, was fighting Angus' heavy grip on her arms. Her red hair was wild and tangled, her gown ripped from our struggle, but she had lost not one jot of her defiance.

"She deserved to die," she was repeating again and again. "She *deserved* to die!"

Angus shook her savagely. "Shut your mouth, woman!"

Duncan brought a blanket from the bed to wrap about me, then knelt in grim silence to make up the fire. As its warmth filled the room, I limped toward it and Fiona glared at me.

"Bruce died because of you!" she shouted. "Did you know that? He should have killed you on the hillside as we had planned, but he must have weakened at the last and thought there was a chance you'd still have him, especially after I had married Lindsay. The fool! The blind, silly, beloved *fool!*" Her voice broke on the last words and her lovely face twisted from anger to grief.

Duncan, his arm about me as he stood by my chair, ignored her outburst. "You'll be warm again shortly. Can you breathe properly?"

"Yes," I whispered, the effort of speaking torturing my throat.

"What shall I do with this hellcat?" Angus asked.

"Take her downstairs. We'll question her later."

"No!" I managed, lifting my hand to halt Angus. "I want to hear—"

"You ought to be in bed," Duncan insisted, worry sharpening his voice. "You'll take your death of cold—your hands are hot and dry from fever as it is!"

"She has the right," Angus said quietly.

Duncan turned as if to argue and then said in resignation, "That's true enough."

"I'll sleep more soundly afterward," I promised, my hands tightening gratefully in his.

He turned and closed the door, then gestured to chairs. Fiona sank heavily into the nearest as Angus released her, but he refused to sit; instead he stood by the hearth to one side of her, his *skean dhu*, the sharp little knife, glittering in his hand.

"I think you had better tell us the whole of it," Duncan was saying to her. "It will all come out in time anyway."

She lifted her head to stare defiantly at him. "Why not? There's no shame!" Her tear-wet face turned to me. "I might have been another of your father's bastards," she said abruptly. "Your half-sister—and his." She gestured toward the towering figure of Angus. "Indeed, my father treated me as if I were, and my mother paid her life long for Angus Lindsay's infatuation with her. She lived with my father's doubts and suspicions, because *your* father pursued her and gave her no peace. What if she was good and loved the older man she had married—she had a pretty face, and your father was not the sort of man to consider anyone but himself. What else was my father to think, here in this very house, when he found his wife in his host's arms? A younger man, dashing, handsome, attentive? My father was a plain man of plain ways, and he believed that his wife had betrayed him. He gave me his name, but not a thread of his love, his care for my upbringing, but not a word of tenderness, his protection for so long as he lived, but not a penny of his estate when he died." She laughed shortly at my expression. "Shocking, isn't it? How do you imagine *I* felt when my mother told me? All those years I had never known a father's love and couldn't begin to guess why! I was eleven, and he was dead, and there was no one to hate but your father. I cried for three days when she told me that Lindsay too was dead. I had planned to come here and make him suffer for what he had done to my mother and my father—and to me; but it was too late."

"Why did you come now?" Duncan asked to cut her short.

"Why do you suppose? Lindsay was out of my reach, but his daughter was not. Oh, yes, I knew all about you, my dear Moira," she added savagely. "For years I had gathered every crumb of information I could find about the Lindsays, waiting until you came of age. I've had nothing but the tiny income my mother left me, and a cloud over my name that kept prospective suitors at arm's length." Her lips quirked in a painful smile. "Except for Bruce. He never realized, you know, that I had chosen you out of malice and not for your inheritance alone. Bruce and I were to be married—once your fortune was secure. He was to meet you accidentally—and contrived to do just that. I was waiting in Edinburgh, but one evening, at a party, someone spoke of meeting you, Duncan, and I was astonished to learn that you had returned from the dead."

"Which brought you to warn Bruce and keep me occupied?"

She smiled quickly. "Of course. You were not an easy mark. You fought off the attack in the summer garden and survived the poisonous herbs we managed to slip into your luncheon. You had even hidden the miniature too well for me to find it. When Angus took out his pistol, Bruce tried again."

"Where did you find a weapon?" Angus asked.

She tilted her head to glance up at him. "You didn't know, did you? Graham carried it for me—and had to shoot our horse after I so carelessly ran him into a ditch. I was afraid someone might remember that, but you were all too tightly caught up in one another. We expected Angus to bear the blame, you see."

"So Bruce Cameron was on the hill that day hoping to meet me," I said slowly, remembering how readily I had accepted him. "Be not deceived," Morag had said—

"You were so gullible, my dear Moira—accepting Bruce, accepting me, eager to believe any tale." Fiona tossed the lovely red hair from her shoulders. "And then it occurred to me that there was another way—since there was doubt enough about your identity, I decided to let you taste the world of genteel poverty that had been my lot for so long. Bruce thought he had killed Morag to protect you, but *I* already knew she was your only witness. A more satisfying revenge, after all—you a lowly governess, while I was mistress of the House of Storms in your place."

"How did you learn so much about the Lindsays?" Duncan asked grimly.

Fiona laughed. "From Mrs. MacNeil, of course. She was willing enough to talk after Mrs. Fraser dismissed her. We moved to Inverness after my father's death, and found her there, housekeeper to a friend. My mother knew her at once, and I pried the story of the family from her." She glared at me suddenly. "Don't look hopeful, my dear. She's dead, and I'm prepared to swear in court that she was dismissed for refusing to countenance the switch in children!"

Angus moved swiftly, the knife resting against Fiona's soft white throat, the point pricking into the skin. "I'll see you dead first!"

"Angus, no!" I flung myself forward to stop him in time, but it was Duncan's voice that stayed his hand.

"You. won't have the opportunity, I'm afraid. Although Moira has renounced her claim, I'm not going to test it."

"Yes," Fiona said viciously, "that announcement was quite a shock, wasn't it? It caused the only quarrel Bruce and I had—whether he should marry you still and fight the case, or whether it would be best for me to marry the Major. I suppose he never really liked my new scheme—at the last, he bungled his attempt to kill Moira, yet there was no choice, none, once she had accepted your proposal in place of his. I was to spread the elopement story to turn you against Moira. He couldn't go through with it, and so he died—in vain." Her voice rose suddenly. "It was all a trick—if he *had* succeeded in forcing you to marry him he'd have been master here, because you played a filthy trick on all of us!"

"What are you saying, woman?" Angus demanded sharply.

"Ask her," Fiona cried angrily. "She tricked us, I tell you!"

In a halting voice I explained about the letter that the solicitor held for me. "It was the only way I could think of to find Morag's killer," I added unhappily. "Because Donald had told me of the fire, you see, and I *knew* she couldn't have been alone that day. She died because of me, Angus, and I had to do something!"

He smiled grimly. "You're a foolish child, Mistress, but a woman of courage for all that. And I cannot blame you for trusting so little. As Morag said, her time had come, and it was no doing of yours."

"I *owed* her, Angus," I said simply, and he nodded in understanding.

Duncan shifted at my side, and I turned to face him. "And you? You don't mind my deception?" I asked diffidently.

"No," he replied, and reached out to take my hand in his. "I have told you—it doesn't matter any longer

248

whether you are Moira or Catriona—so long as you are mine, I have all that I need." His eyes told me all I wanted to know. With a sigh, I felt the tension drain out of me.

It was then that Fiona made her move. Quick as thought, she rose from the chair, struck out at the hand that held the *skean dhu*, sending it in a flashing silver arc toward the bed, and before Angus could recover and reach for her, she was jerking open the door and racing down the passage.

Angus and Duncan nearly collided as they met at the door, and then both were out of the room. I followed, my bruised ankle threatening to buckle under me as I tried to keep pace. Fiona, fleet and sure, all trace of her limp miraculously gone, had already reached the stairs and was racing down them as the two men came after her. The sound of her laughter, wild and high, echoed through the stairwell and filled the passage behind me. Looking over her shoulder at her pursuers, she didn't see Elspeth enter the hall below and stand motionless at the foot of the stairs, her face grim and her arms dangling by her sides.

"Stop her!" Duncan shouted, and Angus added a curt explanation in Gaelic. They were halfway down, now, and I hobbled after them.

Elspeth moved and I saw the ancient brass-bound pistol held barrel down in the folds of her cloak. She must have taken it with her on her way to the croft, for there had been no time to snatch one from the many displayed upon the walls. With slow deliberation she raised the barrel to point it straight at Fiona, who merely laughed at Elspeth and ran on toward her and the door beyond.

Even I doubted that the old pistol was loaded and could not imagine that it had been fired in three generations. Fiona was at the last step, and still Elspeth held her aim without pressing the trigger. Angus was cursing angrily and Duncan shouted again. Ignoring him, Fiona brushed past Elspeth without a glance and flung wide the great front door, calling wildly for Graham.

The man moved swiftly out of the darkness and into the

square of light cast by the door, his face contorted with suffering. Fiona had nearly reached him when Elspeth fired at last.

The great crash rolled deafeningly into the stairwell and reverberated in the hall, the smell of gunpowder strong and sharp. Angus and Duncan checked at the foot of the steps as if blocked by an unseen hand.

Outside, in the square of light, Fiona spun slowly toward us, her face startled and breathless. I thought surely that Elspeth had missed her aim, for the wide green eyes swept us as arrogantly as ever. Then, quite gracefully —as she did everything—Fiona sank to the ground.

Only then did I see the leveled, smoking pistol in the trembling hands of her groom. Tears were rolling unchecked down his face, but his lips were set in a grim line. Elspeth had missed her aim—he had not.

It was Duncan who reached Fiona first, lifting her gently and cradling her in his arms. I was already flying down the last of the stairs, and Angus, his bad knee undoubtedly feeling the strain of running, was limping to stand over them. The groom had not moved and neither had Elspeth, the heavy pistol hanging limply at her side.

"Is she dead?" I asked fearfully as I came to kneel beside Duncan.

"Nearly," he replied quietly, gently brushing the heavy red strands of hair back from her white face.

The green eyes, vividly alive and bright with anger, turned toward me. "Just as well," she said huskily. "Better this way than to hang." She smiled then. "Mrs. MacNeil still lives at Laurel House beyond Inverness. Mrs. Fraser sacked her in a quarrel over Catriona's death, not yours. There's your proof, if you want it. Call it remorse—or a last twisted vengeance—whatever, I have the satisfaction of knowing that your identity is in my gift. In your happiness, you have no choice but remember me!"

"I am grateful," I said gently, though Angus moved sharply beside me. "Thank you, Fiona."

Her darkening eyes turned then to Duncan. "I'd have